For Dave,
and with special thanks to Juris for his brilliance,
and Alison and Bob for their generosity

MAY 26th

For SALLY,

Jan Merete Weiss

May You Burn

With love and
fondest wishes!

Jan M.

AUSTIN MACAULEY PUBLISHERS™
LONDON • CAMBRIDGE • NEW YORK • SHARJAH

A CIP catalogue record for this title is available from the British Library.

ISBN 978-1-78693-459-8 (Paperback)
ISBN 978-1-78693-460-4 (E-Book)
www.austinmacauley.com

First Published (2017)
Austin Macauley Publishers Ltd.™
25 Canada Square
Canary Wharf
London
E14 5LQ

Chapter 1

The sun glanced off the silver braid and scarlet trim of her uniform collar as Natalia Monte strode across the small plaza in front of the Gothic church of San Domenico Maggiore. It was the lunch hour. In dark corners, stone angels directed their trumpets skyward and pigeons had gathered on a saint's head, casing the area for humans who might be sharing their bread. The braver birds darted in and out of packs of students from the nearby university who stood about laughing and talking. Their voices rose and fell, joining the cooing in a happy mix. Fresh-cheeked, smooth-skinned; the youths tipped their faces toward the next fun thing. A Frisbee sailed out of the crowd.

Two Bangladeshi men dusted their display of Day-Glo hairbands, bracelets and sunglasses as Middle-eastern pop boomed from their radio. Seeing her uniform, one turned down the volume. Captain Monte slipped by them, stepping onto Via Librai. She crossed over to the even smaller plaza by the two-story, red and grey church of Sant'Angelo a Nilo. In warm weather Neapolitans and tourists sat there on a circular stone bench to eat ice cream and chat with friends. Today, a dog, teats hanging, scratched at fleas and lay back down next to where a couple of vagrants slept in their cardboard bedding. A strong odor of urine rose from the ground.

A thin man in an ill-fitting suit exited the chapel and stepped around them. 'SPUTNIK' was scrawled high on the wall in fat black letters taller than he. Neither the Vatican nor the City of Naples had yet allocated funds to remove it, since the small historic church building attracted few tourists.

A number of Natalia's elderly neighbors, who could no longer manage early worship services elsewhere, attended Father Montalba's special eleven o'clock mass Thursday mornings in the chapel and made their confessions just before. Montalba lived in the rectory out back and oversaw both the small Sant'Angelo and the much larger San Domenico Maggiore just down the way.

The odor of pee receded as Natalia pulled open the front door and the sweet aroma of lilies took over. The massive refectory table in the foyer was stacked with brochures. Next to them sat a mahogany donation box with a gleaming brass lid. An old man dozed in a rickety chair next to a hunched old woman knitting beneath a dark crucifix. Her withered fingers moved rapidly, the needles clicking.

"*Giorno,*" Natalia said.

The old woman barely looked up. "*Giorno, Signora.*"

Natalia made her way to the Donatello altar in the Brancaccio chapel, surveyed the gothic pews carved from dark walnut and the sepulcher which was sheltered by a white marble canopy, edged in gold. Echoing the motif, two chubby winged putti aimed their trumpets downward at the sculpture of the cardinal, laid out atop his sculpted tomb.

Captain Monte made the sign of the cross, kissed her fingertips, and slid into an empty pew. She bowed her head for a moment, mumbled a few words, then sat up and contemplated the robbery.

The wall was brighter where the painting had hung, preventing dust and dirt from accumulating behind it over

6

the many years. A person could have easily lifted it from its elevated place – but how did they get it? The pews closest were not secured in place. Easy enough for someone to drag one over to use it as a step stool. But that would have been noisy.

Off to the side was a small platform, perhaps used at the podium by shorter deacons or Gospel readers, or by a thief to reach the painting in its elevated place on the wall and carry it off.

The thief or thieves had chosen a small Segli canvas rather than the well-known and far more valuable Cavoretti *Madonna* displayed opposite; Likewise, the enormous ornate candlesticks made of gold and silver that flanked the main altar. Too heavy probably.

A swell of voices broke the quiet. Natalia took out her cell phone and took digital photos of the empty spot in which the Segli had hung, as well as the immediate surroundings. She glanced around the chapel. As she suspected, there were no cameras keeping an eye on things, no alarm system to speak of, nor any guards other than a few faithful retirees who also directed visitors. Up to date security systems and well-trained personnel were prohibitively expensive for churches and few had either. Thieves took full advantage, stealing more art and antiquities from churches than from museums, galleries and private collections combined. Thousands of pieces vanished each year. Some were recovered, some ransomed. A good many vanished and were never seen again.

Two couples pushed their way past. One pointed to something in her guidebook, and the others gathered around to consult. Natalia went back to the entryway.

"*Signora,*" Natalia Monte whispered to the woman at the information table.

"*Si?*"

The tiny woman shifted her knitting. More than likely she had never been more than a quarter mile from her neighborhood or her church and knitted enough yarn to reach Rome.

"*The Ascension*?" Natalia said, feigning a smile. "My mother's favorite." This, in case the woman wondered why a Carabiniere officer was inquiring after it. It was a silly fiction but the Church insisted on minimum information being made public about thefts.

"Ey!" she shouted at the old man seated across the way. "Where's the sign?" He awoke from his snooze, bewildered. She banged her needles on the table. "The sign, the sign! For the painting."

He pulled himself upright, slowly reached into the bookshelf for a piece of cardboard and brought it over.

"I told you. Put it on the table so people can see," she scolded, and grabbed it from him. "What's the matter with you - you forgot?"

He mumbled something and returned to his chair and his nap.

She held up the sign for Natalia to see.

'The Annunciation'

Has Been Removed For Cleaning

"When was it removed?" Natalia asked.

"It was there yesterday during Sunday Mass. When I came in this morning it was gone."

"Was anyone here when it was taken down?"

"We're not here after midday on Sundays. We don't come in Tuesdays or Thursdays. Fridays...?" She shrugged. "You're the first visitor to ask. Me, I say it's a blessing they took it down. It was filthy."

Natalia thanked her and dropped a few coins through the slot of the donation box. It wouldn't go far toward replacing the Segli but might contribute to a more comfortable chair for the old man to enjoy his snooze.

Natalia went outside and walked around to the priest's quarters and rang the rectory bell. On the street, a girl all in pink with a pink teddy bear rucksack putted along Librai on her motor scooter headed east toward the university. The priest's housekeeper answered the door, a dour woman in a navy skirt and matching sweater. She led the way down a long hall paneled in dark wood, passing several massive cabinets and tables. Except for their footsteps, it was silent. The thick stone walls muffled all sounds from the street.

The housekeeper asked her to wait and pointed to a massive leather chair, before disappearing through an ornate doorway. Natalia heard the clink of cutlery and muffled voices. A moment later the woman returned to escort Natalia into a formal dining room. The priest stood, dabbing his mouth with a linen napkin, as his housekeeper scurried to remove his plate and the carafe of white wine beside his glass. A crystal vase with peonies graced the oak table.

Not a bad life, Natalia thought, everything taken care of – housing and meals, laundry. His room kept tidy for him, his bed made. A charwoman would keep the refectory swept and clean and the floors regularly mopped and polished. Nuns didn't fare as well as the male clerics; they did their own housework and picking up, laundry and mending, and were expected to provide their order with a generous dowry before taking their vows and donning their wedding rings as brides of Christ. The priests got free educations and most were served hand and foot.

"Please, have a seat, Captain," the priest said, ushering her toward a straight back chair.

"Father?" The housekeeper hovered over him.

"That will be all, Signora," Father Montalba smiled.

"No coffee, Father?"

"I'll have some later." He turned to Natalia. "Unless you would like some refreshment?"

"No, thank you."

"The Monsignor is coming for dinner," his housekeeper reminded him. "I'm making a roast."

"Very good. I'll ring if we need anything."

"Yes, Father."

They waited until she was gone before speaking. Natalia imagined her picking at leftovers in the kitchen each day after the priest was fed.

"I have a few questions." Natalia flipped open a spiral notebook.

"Of course."

"The church is locked at night?"

"After seven, yes. There's an evening Mass twice a week, so we lock up an hour later on those nights, but not last night"

"Which was the night of the theft -- Sunday."

"Correct. Yesterday, Sunday. The caretaker's afternoon off. I locked the doors myself around five."

"Any sign of a break in?"

"No."

"Could someone have stayed behind after closing and hidden in the building? Or are the premises closely checked?"

"The caretaker usually makes an inspection. A deacon checked last evening. Not terribly thorough, I would imagine. You think someone might have hidden somewhere, removed the painting and waited for daylight?"

"Possibly, yes. Are worshippers ever admitted after hours? Individuals having a crisis of the soul?

10

"Rarely. We have such a small congregation. But certainly now and then."

"And on the night of the theft?"

"Actually, someone telephoned. He requested I heard his confession early the following morning. A supportive parishioner I couldn't refuse. He wanted to come in before going to his work. Around six a.m."

"And that parishioner's name and contact information?" Natalia said.

"That's not pertinent," the monsignor said.

She looked up from her notebook, pen poised. "How not?"

"He's been coming to confession for years." Father Montalba seemed annoyed at her persistence. "Once a month I get a call, always requesting the same time, the same day. First Monday, six a.m. He's a creature of habit, as are we all. And most generous."

"So – a regular visitor?"

The priest nodded.

"You unlocked the front doors of the church when he knocked?"

"No. Beforehand, around a quarter after five. Then I came back to the rectory for coffee and a bite."

"And you went into the church when? "A few minutes before six."

"So the church was open and unattended for perhaps forty minutes. When did your parishioner arrive?"

"He was there already, waiting in the confessional."

"Father, won't you please identify him? I'm not asking you to violate the confessional in putting the question to you."

"He is a private person. I don't feel at liberty to give you his name."

"Was anyone else in the church at any point?"

"Not that I was aware. Although anyone could have come in and gone out I suppose."

"What happened after you heard his confession?"

"I returned to my quarters. I start the day with meditation and prayer. My housekeeper arrived at her regular time, around seven. We chatted for a few minutes, then I left for the church offices across the street."

"Does she live nearby?" Natalia asked.

"In the Spanish Quarter. She's worked for me a dozen years."

"Are you certain this penitent left after you heard his confession?"

"I him leave. No one was in the chapel when I came out from the booth. I'd been in there with him for perhaps twenty minutes."

"Did you relock the doors then?"

"No, I don't usually bother. The caretaker and the Monday volunteers arrive a short while later, at seven. The doors would normally open to the public then. There seemed no point in relocking the front door. We are hardly a citadel."

"You say you first unlocked at a quarter after five, so someone could have come in even earlier, while you were still in your quarters," Natalia said, "at prayer."

"I'm afraid that's possible too. Yes."

"When did you learn the painting was missing?"

"Just before eight. The caretaker called my office across the street. I rushed back. The frame was empty, the painting gone. I can tell you, it was a shock. I got up on a chair and quickly took the frame down – brought it into my private quarters."

"May I see it?"

"Of course." Father Montalba went to retrieve it from his quarters.

12

Great, she thought, the only piece of evidence was already compromised, but she slipped on her gloves anyway when he returned. The frame looked original, a work of art in itself, made of thick wood intricately carved and layered in gold leaf. The thief had made a hasty job of it – a coarse cutout, corner to corner. She could see several fragments of the linen sticking from the empty frame like miniscule weeds. Certainly, the crudely cut edge would bring the price down for the thieves. But it was the simplest and quickest way to remove the canvas.

"We'll need to have the frame examined," Natalia said. "Please keep it in your custody until our forensics team gets here?"

"Of course."

"Has anyone else been in touch with you about the missing work," Natalia asked, "anyone at all?"

"No. No one other than the Vatican curator. The painting has been on permanent loan to us forever."

Natalia made a few more notes and closed her notebook. There were no witnesses to corroborate or challenge Father Montalba's story. It was doubtful if he had perpetrated the crime but it wasn't unheard of for priests to sell off an antiquity or piece of religious art. She thanked him and left. The housekeeper stood in the front hallway.

"Is there a problem?" the housekeeper asked in a challenging tone as Natalia opened the door.

"No problem," she said and stepped out onto the sidewalk.

Natalia couldn't imagine this woman had anything to do with the theft, but they'd need to run a check on her nonetheless. She had access at the very least, the deacon too. Natalia imagined she made next to nothing in salary. The women who filled these positions didn't consider them jobs as much as callings. Many were widows or had fantasized about becoming nuns. You never knew what was going on below the surface of anyone's life situation -- a husband laid off, an illness, a debt come due. Whatever was or was not going on in her world, the woman seemed overbearing but not particularly anxious.

Natalia wondered about the finances of the parish itself. Rome was notoriously stingy when it came to providing funds for the south, even showcase operations like Sant'Angelo. Had Montalba grown tired of budgets and managing the much larger three-nave church across the way? It boasted an ancient Roman market below its chapel. And several upper floors exhibited splendid religious art which also attracted tourists. His was a prestigious post, but it offered challenging work for little worldly gain. The priest no doubt worried about insufficient donations to make up for Rome's shortfall. Cutbacks might also have deprived the good Father of funds for personal luxuries: brandy, cigars and the like. Was he forced to accept inferior cuts of meat, coarse wines? As the churchman in charge of Sant'Angelo and San Domenico Maggiore, he might easily have felt entitled to a lifestyle more in keeping with such a position.

Then again, it was probably more likely that the painting had been removed during the night by a castaway in the church. Or else, it had been cut from its frame by someone making off with it while Father Montalba was tucking into his *cornetto* before his confessee arrived. Or sometime after six when the doors remained unlocked after the penitent and Father Montalba left. The streets would not have been very active; just street cleaners pushing their brooms, merchants opening their shops for the day, a vendor arriving to set up. Someone could have easily made off with a small rolled up canvas. Brazen and efficient.

Natalia strode along the passage back toward Via Librai. Towels and sheets fluttered from a line strung between the buildings. A child regarded her from a balcony clotted with plants. Legend had it that the artist Caravaggio had once lived and worked here, she remembered. Officially he'd resided with his relative, the Marchesa di Caravaggio in her *palazzo* in Chiaia, but had taken a simple room here, where he could paint and indulge in whatever amorous pursuits he desired. His room overlooked the garden of a church. Natalia imagined the artist waking to the swifts whose descendants now darted and twirled over the spare trees.

In his time Naples was the capital of the two Sicilies, one of the most important cities in Europe. And one of the most violent. Duels were commonplace. Citizens stepped over bodies daily. No one dared remove them – at risk of their own life. Smoke clotted the air from open fires. The city stank of human sewage, and garbage.

Yet there were compensations. The clop of horses sounded in the alleys. And the markets were verdant with flowers and goods. A musical city, always – singers practiced arias – their voices spilling into the streets below.

A slim young woman hurried past in a velvet beret, torn jeans, and a blue and white polka dot blouse topped with a sequined jacket. She might just as well have worn a sign that read *'artiste'* as she headed east along Librai toward the university, sketchbook tucked under her arm.

Two blocks farther, a heavyset man gutted a fish and threw a clump of bloody entrails into a bucket. A skeletal dog approached and the fishmonger tossed him a fish head. A slice of the Tyrrhenian Sea glittered between the buildings. Earlier that morning that fish had sliced through those same blue waters as a thief sliced through canvas.

A December wind gusted up from the harbor smelling of the sea. Natalia's nose started to run. Her father never left the house without a fresh cloth handkerchief tucked into his shirt pocket. She stopped to purchase a package of tissues from a gypsy hawking sundries. The woman wore a faded green blouse, on which only a few pearl buttons remained. She took Natalia's euro without making eye contact, dug into the pocket of a long rust-colored skirt and threw down a handful of breadcrumbs.

Natalia knew the superstition. For the past month, things had been relatively quiet in law enforcement. Did the gypsy know something that required Natalia to try and protect herself from a violent time ahead? If only that was all it took to keep away the evil eye.

Chapter 2

Natalia arrived at the Casanova regional station and signed in to begin her day. She spotted her nemesis, Marshal of the Carabinieri, Tomasso Cervino, waiting by the staircase door. Shit. He must have come in just before she had, maybe noticed her on the monitors and waited. Cervino was the in-house misogynist, jealous of her rank, resentful of her gender in the boys world of the '*Arma dei Carabinieri'*. Intent on bringing her down any way he could, he fomented trouble over her Neapolitan roots among the poorer and less than upstanding residents of the city's old districts. Strict regulations discouraged fraternization with the likes of her unsavory childhood friends, some of whom were alleged Camorra thieves and contrabandists, or worse. Marshal Cervino had begun to track her every movement and it worried her. Sometimes she feared it was just a matter of time before he succeeded.

He must have seen her arrive on the closed circuit monitors at the security desk in the small lobby, and he Cervino, worked his thumb and index finger over the thin grey bristles of his mustache as he held the stairwell door open for her and saluted. Military courtesy and disdain: quite the combination. She returned the salute and sprinted past him up the stairs. Natalia tried to recall the latest protocol regarding facial hair. Originally, it was strictly forbidden. In recent times, as far as she knew, only those of highest rank were permitted a mustache. The rules must have changed. She wondered if her colleague was experiencing a mid-life crisis. She'd swear she smelled cologne. Next thing he'd be pulling into the lot in a Maserati.

"What's wrong?" Angelina said, as Natalia burst into their small office and slammed the door behind her.

"Cervino. Why do I get the feeling the marshal is stalking me?"

"Because he is?"

"They grow smart girl corporals in Palermo," Natalia said.

A bouquet of tulips and narcissus peeked from a paper cup on her partner's desk.

"Pretty," Natalia said as she put her bag down.

"Luigi," Angelina answered. "I had to swear I wouldn't tell my boyfriend."

Natalia laughed. Parked on his chair outside the garage next door, or else at the Arab's at his regular table, Luigi must be pushing eighty. A handyman, robust when Natalia started at Casanova, he'd ridden to jobs as far away as Via Nardones. Frail now, missing teeth, his handshake remained strong as did his charm.

Natalia had her sleeve halfway out of her uniform jacket when Angelina held up her palms.

"Wait, wait. Don't get too comfortable. The Colonel wants to see you the moment you come in."

"He wants to see me alone?"

"Your lucky day."

"Great." Natalia shrugged her arm back in the sleeve and rummaged on her desk for a lipstick. "Any idea what our dear boss wants?"

"I wasn't made privy to that information."

Natalia snatched up a silver tube, snapped open her compact and applied a swath of pale peach to her lips, then tousled her hair with one hand. Grooming accomplished, she took a folder off a stack on her desk and handed it to her subordinate.

"While I'm up with the colonel, look over the surveillance reports on the Grappo clan's thugs and see if there's anything new we should be aware of."

"Aye, aye." Angelina cleared a space in front of her for the folder and yawned.

"Rough night?" said Natalia, quickly leafing through early bulletins to see if her summons might have been prompted by something there.

"Giuletta rescued a pair of stray kittens," Angelina said. "Newborns. We had to bottle feed them in our bed and not crush them when we all finally slept. Their mother had been poisoned."

"That's awful."

"There are sadists out there. If Giuletta keeps on like this, we're going to need a bigger place. Speaking of which, wouldn't you like a real adorable baby kitty."

"Tempting but I'd make a terrible mother. I'm hardly home."

"Have two. They'll keep each other company."

"I'll think about it."

"That's what you said the last time."

"When did Colonel Donati summon me?"

"About four minutes ago. I'll call up and say you're on the way."

Natalia thanked her and headed for the stairwell again. Emerging on the floor above, she hurried to the Colonel's office and paused in his ever open doorway. He had his back to her. His uniform jacket hung over an adjacent chairback, the dark blue wool setting off the gold of his rank and military branch insignia. On the windowsill rested his hat with the flaming grenade badge of the Carabinieri in gold, indicating his high rank

"Sir?"

No response. She rapped on the sign alongside the door that said *'Commander, 10th Carabinieri Battalion, Colonel Fabio Donati.'* This time he swiveled around, pulling out a white earpiece.

"Come in, Captain Monte. Sorry, Elisabetta gave me an early Christmas present -- Bach. Close the door if you don't mind."

Natalia did and took one of the leather chairs in front of his desk. Nice furniture was a perk she and Angelina didn't enjoy.

"Corporal Cavatelli said you wanted to speak with me."

"I just received a call from the Vatican. They are missing one of their properties. That work that's gone missing from the church of Sant'Angelo."

"I see. I just came from there. The good news is they didn't take the Donatello, if that's the Vatican's concern."

The colonel smiled. "The sculpted ornamentation would be difficult to steal from the sepulcher."

"What's missing," she said, "is a fifteenth century painting by Segli."

"I don't believe I know his work."

"Not a major work. Segli was a Neapolitan, which is likely the only reason for its display in Sant'Angelo. Gossip had it that Segli and the great Caravaggio shared a studio in Naples -- and maybe more. Segli's work was never a match for the master. I passed the missing canvas dozens of times in my student days and barely glanced at it."

"What was the subject?" the colonel said.

"Another of the interminable Ascensions, featuring the usual suspects. I have to get forensics over there," but the scene is thoroughly contaminated. For the time being, the story is the painting has been taken down for cleaning."

"The fellow at the Vatican claimed he remembered you from an investigation several years ago," Donati said. "A Signor Inozotti. Does the name ring a bell?"

"Inzotti," Natalia corrected him. "Yes, he's the curator of the Vatican's collection. He was a great help in my first art case when I worked in Rome -- the theft of a Tintoretto drawing from a museum in Calabria. It had been on loan from Vatican archives."

Colonel Donati pressed his splayed fingers together at the tips, a habit of his. "This Inzotti said you tracked it to an abandoned estate south of Palermo and rescued the drawing as well as a nearly starved German Shepherd."

A siren blared as a vehicle screeched up to a side door in the lot below. Doors slammed. Another suspect being brought in.

"Has Sant'Angelo received a ransom demand?" Donati asked.

"Not as yet. I think it will be a low figure, if it comes. The painting was only valued at three and a quarter million."

"What progress is there, if any?" said the colonel.

"All we know so far is that it likely happened early this morning."

"Who discovered it missing?"

"The priest," Natalia said, "Father Montalba. I assume we'll soon have a visit from officers of the Carabinieri Command for the Protection of Cultural Heritage."

"Undoubtedly. They'll swoop in and take over since the Vatican is involved, but your friend there wants you as their contact. So keep abreast of developments even if they assume the investigation. You're local, you know the scene. Your contacts might help. Lend a hand if they'll permit it."

"Yes, sir," she said, but doubted the CC/TPC men would. An elite Rome posting such as theirs had a way of swelling the ego.

Windy gusts stirred the bare linden tree that brushed the window. It portended a stormy afternoon. A small brown bird landed on the sill and peered in.

"Is Officer Cavatelli to be privy to this art theft investigation?" Natalia asked.

"I have no problem with it. If the Grappos decide to take out a few rivals, we might have to pull her away and let her help Stareno's group. Temporarily, of course. Meanwhile the Holy See wants discretion, discretion, discretion." He plucked a thread from his beautifully tailored uniform. "I have the utmost confidence in you, as I'm sure you know."

"Thank you, sir."

"Any questions?"

"No, sir."

"Any special plans for the Christmas holidays?"

"None so far. Call on my aunt is all."

"Elisabetta wants to have a few people over. She's already informed me that you and your corporal are on the list. Between us, it's her way of thanking you for putting up with me. I'll pass along the details as I get them."

"Thank you, sir. I'll inform Officer Cavatelli."

"Good. That's settled. I should warn you, Captain, my wife may try to introduce you to someone 'suitable,' as she put it. Oh, and she said to be sure to tell Officer Cavatelli *all* spouses are welcome. Keep me informed."

He plugged the earpiece back in and put his feet up on his immaculate desk. A little further and he'd tip over. Natalia stifled an impulse to warn him.

The fluorescent lights flickered on the landing as she walked down the stairs. Decent lighting would do a lot for the place, Natalia thought – not for the first time. The station's environment was plain ugly. The only grace notes were the mosaic tiles on the lobby walls. In all likelihood the station would remain drab. Their budget was stretched as it was. With so much of it tied up in remodeling their modest in-house barracks, the last thing the colonel would release discretionary funds for was décor. Maybe she should lobby the colonel's Milanese wife. Elisabetta firmly believed in the importance of good design. Lighting would be a start, along with comfortable seating in the reception area and a few toys for the children who were often brought along. A rug with cheerful colors would do a lot to lift spirits too. Natalia could easily imagine the colonel's wife arranging a fundraiser, a soiree with some of their deep-pocketed friends.

She grabbed her address wheel and started going through it. Her young partner relentlessly teased about her using it. Angelina's phone held all her information, personal and professional. Natalia hadn't made the transition. She still preferred her leather bound journal, and holding an actual book instead of a battery driven device.

"What smells so good?" Natalia said as her partner appeared with a telltale bag.

"I snuck out to the Arab's." Angelina handed Natalia a plastic cup. "Figured you could use it after your meeting with the colonel."

The Arab's tiny café was Casanova's go-to for coffee and snacks. It serviced mechanics from the garages and Carabinieri from Casanova. The hole-in-the-wall abutted a repair shop and stank of car grease and gasoline. Their coffee was delicious, however, and the owner's mother's pastries divine.

"You are a wonderful being," Natalia removed the foil from the lid and the acrid smell of espresso wafted up.

"What did the colonel want? Or is that classified?" Angelina asked, still smarting from having been excluded a month earlier from the distribution list of a confidential report on Camorra activities.

"Of course not," Natalia took a sip of coffee. "But let's close the door first."

Natalia gave her the run down on the stolen Segli.

"Inside job," Angelina said right off. "The caretakers maybe? Or volunteers."

Natalia waved off the suggestion. "Unlikely. They've been there since before I was born. They can barely walk, let alone climb up on a ladder or stool and boost a painting."

"They could be working with someone else."

"Impossible."

"Nothing is impossible, Captain. First lesson you taught me."

"So you *were* paying attention," Natalia laughed.

"From God's mouth," Angelina said. "By the way, I got the latest on the warring Grappo clan like you wanted." She pointed to a sheet of paper near Natalia's phone.

"Good girl." Natalia booted up her computer. "I'll look at it in a minute. God forbid we ever need something in a hurry."

"What are you looking for?"

"The colonel requested a list from Vatican security of all their art thefts going back a few years. I want you to go through it. See if there are any patterns in recent robberies -

– that sort of thing. I'll forward it to your e-mail once it arrives."

"Ahhhh," Angelina took a sip of her cappuccino. "Research. Makes a nice break from mangled corpses."

A head popped in the door -- the duty officer's. "That coffee smells fantastic. Mind if I have it while you're out? You've caught a killing."

Chapter 3

They weren't far from the market's center and the reported body when the traffic came to a standstill. The section was manned by Chinese merchants, their tables piled high with tee-shirts and scarves, and racks crammed with sweat shop clothes produced back in their home country. They avoided selling food. Although many had worked on that street for decades and spoke fluent Italian, they pretended they understood not a word so as to avoid dealing with the Camorra, beyond paying their *pezzo*.

They formed a tight-knit community. It's how they survived. Most of them lived in the Spanish Quarter. Centuries ago, the Quarter had garrisoned the Bourbons. Then it offered unobstructed views of the port and its surroundings. Nowadays the neighborhood wasn't so grand, dense as it was with ancient flats and tiny street-level apartments the locals called *bassi*. There was a smattering of shops and *trattorias* too, reached like the housing along a warren of stone stairways. Unlike the broad avenues of the well-heeled neighborhood on the ridge above, the Quarter's alleys corkscrewed and seemed to disappear. The twisting streets continued down into the flatland where the Montesanto open air market wound through narrow streets and alleys and spilled into hemmed-in plazas crammed with peddlers' tables and produce displays.

The traffic started and stopped almost immediately. By the elevated train station, passengers descended from the escalators and into the market. Shoppers hurried past through the wintry chill to make their purchases. Natalia sighed and hit the siren for a burst, to no effect. At the end of the block, a rose-colored cathedral caught the sun, its baroque facets casting odd shadows.

"We'll never get through this," Natalia said. "Go on ahead while I park." She pointed toward the right, "the square isn't far."

"Yes, Captain."

Angelina Cavatelli jumped out of the passenger seat and hurried away at a run. Natalia slowly eased the cruiser to the side and parked in a crossing grid, then walked quickly into the hodgepodge of street vendors hawking fish, vegetables, bread, fruit, milk, meat. A Chinaman arranged feather dusters and mops and whirligigs in large bins. His tortoise face regarded her for a moment as she squeezed past.

The ground was littered with rotted fruit, pulp and peels, making the stone squares slippery underfoot. A cat chewed on the carcass of a fish; leavings of the fish monger. A pile of watery ice smelled of the sea. Storm clouds turned the sky darker by the minute as she hurried on. An ambulance drove away slow and empty just as she reached the cramped plaza, still half filled with produce displays and vendors' stalls.

Corporal Cavatelli was taking the statement of a burly market woman. She had discovered the victim lying in the tiny alley in back of her stand.

"They left her like she was garbage," the woman said. "Who would do that to a child?"

The corpse was that of a young female, nineteen or twenty. Tiny. Not a hundred kilos. She lay on her back, half hidden by a fruit stand. A soiled work apron draped her face. Long tresses spread out from beneath it in a black halo. Natalia stepped closer and lifted the covering, surprised to recognize the street violinist who regularly played in the churchyards and plazas along Via Librai.

No fatal wound was immediately evident, though red streaked from one tiny point high on her throat. Corporal Cavatelli finished taking the woman's statement and suggested she finish packing up and go home. The open air market would be a crime scene for the time being. Natalia crouched by the body.

"Jesus," Angelina whispered and crossed herself. "Isn't that the musician?"

"Yes."

"Gypsy."

"Roma, yes. I think so."

"There's a suspect in custody" Angelina said, "her brother. Unfortunately, Police Officer Parati, over there, got a little carried away detaining him."

The corporal indicated a tall municipal policeman leaning against his blue and white cruiser, arms folded across the chest of his blue POLIZIA windbreaker. Slung over the hood of the car, face down, was a twenty-something youth with a dark pony tail and wearing a thin tee shirt made of shiny brown fabric. A tattoo was partially visible running up his neck. More tattooing adorned his upper arms. His hands were cuffed behind him. He peered sideways at Natalia as she approached.

The young man's face was swollen, his nose bloody. He was shivering from the cold and adrenalin, muttering what sounded like an incantation. The words were unintelligible. For a moment, Natalia wondered if he was speaking Latin, though it didn't sound like any she'd learned in school. In spite of his wounded face, Natalia could see he was as slender and handsome as his sibling: two beautiful kids, one dead, one beaten bloody.

"The victim is his sister," Angela repeated, walking alongside.

"Wait here," Natalia said.

The police officer grumbled something and looked unhappy. Natalia marched over and told him she was taking the boy into her custody lest he suffer more accidents, and if the young cop didn't like that, she would be happy to bring his behavior to the attention of his superiors and perhaps charge him.

"Charge me? For what? Knocking around a murderous fucking gypsy?"

"For abusing a prisoner."

"Bullshit."

"And for insubordination."

"He came at me with a knife." The officer brandished a plastic evidence bag. "It's right here."

"He looks like he came at you with his face. Was he cuffed already when you started in?"

"He assaulted me."

"I'm sure your dashboard camera will support your contention."

"He killed his sister."

"I assume you discussed your suspicions with him before you beat him."

"Waste of time. They don't speak Italian. Fucking parasites. I could've been killed."

"Why don't you get in your cruiser and go get those nasty injuries to your poor knuckles attended to?"

"It's my arrest."

"Get the hell out of here, Officer Parati. We don't assault suspects."

Parati weighed his options, mouth tight, staring down at the Carabiniere captain. Natalia leaned in toward him, face upturned into his.

"Push it and I'll write up the charges personally."

Parati was having a hard time working out the contingencies. Probably never dealt with a female Carabiniere before, much less one who outranked him. With a loud grunt, he opened his car door, slid in behind the wheel and slammed it shut. Natalia lifted the suspect off the hood. Parati revved the engine and drove off with siren wailing. Natalia brought the suspect back to the body.

"Look at this," Angelina led her to a pile of charred fabric a few feet from a trash fire. It was still smoking. Angelina had dragged a few swatches out of the ashes. "I think it's her jacket and scarf."

"Right."

Natalia had not encountered a Roma murder scene before. It was common knowledge Romany were doing jobs for the Camorra syndicates, moving drugs and driving loads of contraband cigarettes. Some had even broken away from their bosses and started up illicit ventures of their own. The Carabinieri thought it only a matter of time before there was a real bloodbath between the Roma interlopers and the Camorra clans, but this murdered young woman wasn't part of it.

"Corporal," Natalia said, "Keep an eye on the suspect. I'll be right back."

Taking her partner's flashlight, Natalia moved along the tight perimeter of the small square. A small group of shoppers stood gawking, though they kept their distance. A shopkeeper watched her pass from the safety of his doorway.

The street vendors and local residents knew better than to get involved and went about closing up for the day.

Despite the December chill, wet laundry hung like ghosts from balconies and windows, all of them shuttered. Had the girl cried out? Someone would have heard. Yet the chance of such a person coming forward was nil. The authorities were not to be cooperated with no matter the crime, especially murder.

Natalia scanned the street, strewn with wilted produce and bruised fruit, and examined the remaining displays of goods, noting the little alleyways the stands formed. The victim lay in what was left of one of them. The crowded market's noise and bustle had no doubt cloaked the murder. Nervy, whoever did it. No way an impulse killing.

More heavy clouds darkened the sky and the air grew colder. Dr. Francesca Agari arrived in her Alfa, red dash light pulsing. The mortuary van followed. Angelina held up something and waved it at Natalia as she returned.

"Found this in the dumpster just now." It was a violin case. "I think it maybe belonged to the girl." She opened it to show the interior. "No violin."

"The case is hers," Natalia said. "I've dropped coins in it myself often enough."

The Medical Examiner emerged from her car as mortuary workers in puffy white jumpsuits opened the back of their vehicle and pulled out a stretcher. More Carabinieri arrived to help secure the area. A body bag appeared by the corpse.

"Over here, Dr. Agari," Natalia called out. "We could use a set of lights."

One of the mortuary men climbed into the van to retrieve two stands and battery-operated floodlights, then handed out the stanchions and white curtain panels they would put up as a privacy barrier against gawkers. Francesca Agari approached, forensic case in hand, stylishly dressed in a charcoal jacket, beige scarf at her throat, and a grey pleated skirt with matching pumps.

"Captain Monte, Corporal Cavatelli."

Natalia responded and turned to the suspect. "Is that yours?" she pointed to an army jacket lying crumpled on the ground. He nodded yes. She quickly searched it and had Angelina release the suspect's arms so he could put it on.

"See if he wants to call someone."

Angelina acknowledged the order and cuffed the young man's hands in front. He took her phone after some hesitation and punched in a number. The morgue technicians finished positioning the lights so Doctor Agari could examine the victim more thoroughly.

Angelina retrieved her phone and checked the restraints again.

"Shall I recuff his hands behind him?

"No, corporal," Natalia said. Poor boy had already been through enough.

"He made a call," Angelina said. "Someone is coming."

"Let's hope the person can interpret."

Dr. Agari lifted back the apron's edge. The victim's eyes were a startling shade of blue. She gloved her hands and leaned over to gently close them.

"Not much blood," Natalia said, "a little on one hand. None on her face. Was she killed elsewhere?"

"No. Here. She bled a little from the wound there." Francesca pointed to a red spot under the chin. "What a beautiful child."

Natalia bent closer as Francesca tipped the body, exposing her throat more.

"There, see?" She leaned away so Natalia and Angelina could both get a better look.

Angelina said, "That? That little wound may have killed her?"

"Yes. Lividity is just setting in. Doctor Agari lifted the shirt tails. "See those large dark patches under the skin where blood settled along her right side? That's the side she was on when she expired."

Angelina said, "The woman who found her said she turned the victim onto her back thinking she might have fainted and gone unconscious.

"That fits," Francesca said.

"What killed her?" Natalia asked.

"I expect the needle-like instrument which made the puncture mark by her throat. I'd guess the killer pushed it right on into her brain. Quick and quiet. A professional hit."

"The brother had a knife," Natalia said. "No knife?"

"No."

The sky turned angrier.

"How long has she been dead?"

"Under two hours."

The morgue technicians finished erecting the privacy enclosure around them.

"Stabbed like that," Natalia said, "would she have cried out?"

"Probably not."

"We've seen her before," Angelina said.

"Really?" said Francesca. "You have a name for me?"

"No," Natalia said. "She's a street musician. Played the violin beautifully. Mostly outside churches. On the streets. What a shame. She was really accomplished."

Francesca took a swab of the girl's mouth and dropped the stick into a glass tube, stoppered it and wrote on its side with a marker.

There was a commotion. They heard a man jogging toward them, calling out, "Where is she?"

Natalia stepped out from behind the privacy screen and brought him to a halt, blocking his way to the body. "The Medical Examiner is with her now," she said, palms raised to fend him off.

"I'm her cousin," he said, distraught.

"Sir, it's best you see her later at the morgue." Natalia formally introduced herself. He did likewise. "Claudio Palumbo."

"The attorney?" Natalia said.

"Yes, I'm a lawyer."

"And Romy activist."

He pulled out an android phone and held an image up for Natalia to see. The pale corpse in the curtained area some yards from them was hard to reconcile with the lively young woman whose sapphire blue eyes peered out from the little window.

"It's her?" he said. "It's definitely her?"

Natalia nodded. "I'm very sorry."

He pocketed the phone. "Where is her brother?"

"First I need her full name, sir.

"Drina." He spelled it as she wrote.

"Drina what?"

"Just Drina. Roma use one name."

"Her next of kin?"

"Her mother, Zorka."

"Phone number?"

"She hasn't a phone."

"Address?"

"There are no street names or numbers where she lives in the encampment out at Annunziata." He took out a card, wrote on its back and added a crude map. "Here is her approximate location. May I suggest you let me inform her of this? I'll drive out and tell them. You'll have trouble locating her and it would be better coming from me anyway."

Natalia accepted the card. "All right. That would be appreciated. Please call us when you've informed her family."

"Her brother is here," he said.

Angelina, joining them. "He won't leave her."

"I need to see him," the lawyer pleaded.

"Maybe you should." Natalia turned and led him into the curtained area shielded from onlookers, not that there were many left. The few bystanders who remained were keeping well back from the crime scene tape that marked the forbidden area.

Claudio Palumbo knelt down and put his arms around his cousin. The young man whimpered and pressed his face into Palumbo's chest.

"*Koskozi*," Palumbo said to his cousin.

"What did you say to him?" Natalia asked.

"Courage," Palumbo answered. "I said, 'Courage.'"

The attorney tenderly ran a hand over the young man's face. "Who struck him? Why is he restrained?"

"He may have threatened a policeman when ordered away from the body," Natalia said. "He refused, allegedly pulled a knife. The investigating officer assumed he had killed her."

Claudio Palumbo said something to his cousin, who sat up and shouted: "*Hoffeno! Hok-hosnie mush.*"

"What is he saying?" Natalia asked.

"Policeman lie!" the boy yelled.

"The officer was first on the scene," Natalia said

Palumbo ran a hand through his hair, agitated. "There is no way Nuzi would menace police. First life lesson for every Roma male is step back from police. Never brandish a weapon."

"What was he doing carrying a knife?" Natalia asked.

"A lot of Roma carry them. We use our own cutlery — even when we are out."

Stiletto as cutlery? Natalia wondered. That was a new one. "I need to ask Nuzi a few questions, counselor."

"He understands but doesn't speak much Italian. I'll have to translate."

"Fine," she said.

Though in reality it was not fine. This man could interpret as creatively as he wished and she'd be none the wiser. What better opportunity for Palumbo to begin shaping his cousin's defense? Ordinarily, she could have brought him in and gotten an interpreter, but not one member of the Carabinieri or Naples' police spoke Romani.

"Did he throw the violin case into the trash?"

Claudio Palumbo posed the question to Nuzi in their language. The young man shook his head.

"What was he doing here in the first place?" Natalia asked. She waited again while Palumbo translated and heard him out.

"She called him. Asked him to meet her here."

"What time did he get the call?"

"He doesn't know exactly. Around noon. Says Drina sounded shaky. He got dressed and rushed over."

"Where does he live?"

"Annunziata."

"The Port of Torre Annunziata is a way from here. How did he get here so quickly?"

The lawyer translated the question. The young man pointed to a rusty Piaggio lying on its side. "*Motorino*," he said.

"He didn't kill her," Claudio Palumbo insisted. "Nuzi came because she asked him to. She was already dead

36

when he arrived. He stayed with her. We don't leave our dead. We are not the barbarians the media portrays us as."

"Please, counselor," Natalia said. "No one's implying any such thing."

The phone company's confirmation of the precise moment and location from which her brother spoke to her would establish his whereabouts and the intervening distance he'd covered. An exact time of death would help establish whether the brother could have gotten to the market quickly enough to strike her down. Angelina signaled that she needed to tell Natalia something.

"You'll excuse me a moment. I need to speak with my corporal. I'll have our pathologist examine Nuzi's injuries when she's finished."

Angelina produced the young man's cell phone. "He's telling the truth about getting a call from her. It came at a few minutes after noon." She consulted her notes. "Twelve twelve."

"Good. Bag it for evidence. What about her phone?"

"We haven't found it as yet."

"Have the other officers re − check the dumpster," Natalia said and returned to the dead girl's cousin. The brother sat next to his sister's body looking forlorn as Dr. Francesca did her work with Angelina following it closely.

Natalia flipped to a new page in her notebook. "You said he lives in the Roma camp at Annunziata?"

"They both do. Sometimes she stays in town at my place. He too."

"I see."

He flushed. "What are you suggesting?"

"Sir, you're being unnecessarily defensive. We're simply trying to establish what happened to your cousin, Mr. Palumbo. It's standard. We need to know where she was before this happened. Gather facts about her and her movements. I'm sure you're familiar with our methods."

He pushed his hands deep in his coat pockets. "Of course."

"Her brother agreed to meet her and rushed here, correct?" Natalia continued.

Palumbo nodded. "Nuzi worships her. They're very close."

"Does he know why she wanted to meet?"

"You already asked."

"Ask him again."

Nuzi's answer was longer this time.

"What's he saying?" Natalia asked.

"He says she sounded frightened, said she needed his help -- badly."

Francesca Agari summoned Natalia to her with a look. They all came closer to Dr. Agari and the body. A beautiful young woman mutilated and killed. At times Natalia disliked her job. Kneeling by the corpse, the pathologist drew their attention to a red ribbon knotted around her pinkie.

"Thieving magpie," Angelina said.

"What?" Natalia looked up.

"Gypsies are obsessed with the fingers. Each one signifies something. The pinkie symbolizes the magpie. I can't remember the others."

"Magpie. The chatty bird that likes shiny things," Natalia said. "How is it you know that?"

"I had a crush on a Roma boy when I was twelve."

"You know what the red ribbon's about?"

"No, Captain."

Had this young woman taken something that didn't belong to her? Natalia wondered. Was that the message of the ribbon? Certainly to leave a body on display in a public place generally meant to serve as a warning. But if putting the fear of God into the Roma was the intent, leaving her near her own community would have made more sense. Though the killer's ability to strike at will in a busy marketplace might serve just as well in conveying dread. No crime of impulse, this, Natalia thought, nor of passion. Cold and pre-meditated is what it was. Efficient and done with real stealth. Downright professional. Who had this young woman gotten involved with?

Claudio Palumbo turned away from the sight of his cousin's remains.

Natalia said, "Do you know what the ribbon around her pinkie signifies?"

"A gypsy thing."

"Her brother tied it there?"

"Yes." Claudio Colombo wiped at his tears.

"Why?"

"To help her navigate the hereafter."

Chapter 4

Natalia addressed Attorney Palumbo, sitting across from her in Interview Room 2, the victim's brother alongside him.

"Is it significant that her jacket and scarf were burned?" she asked.

"The clothes of the dead are unclean," Palumbo answered.

"Did her brother – did Nuzi throw her scarf and jacket on that fire?"

Palumbo asked. Nuzi answered.

"No," the boy said.

"So it was the person who killed your cousin who did it. He would seem to be familiar with gypsy customs."

"Or he was destroying evidence," Palumbo said.

Angelina interrupted and bent close. "Captain, Doctor Agari needs to speak with you."

"Excuse me. The corporal will stay with you. Interview paused at 18:07."

Natalia walked swiftly to her office to take the call.

"Natalia," Francesca Agari said, "I'm transmitting digital photos to you of the deceased and the crime scene."

"Doctor Agari, from your perspective, could this be a hate crime?

"Unlikely. Though I couldn't say for sure. But death was instantaneous. My guess is that someone didn't want her to suffer."

Natalia sighed. So … love could be the motive. Someone rejected – someone with a murderous temper. She thanked the Medical Examiner and rang off.

Angelina rushed into their office and over to her keyboard to tap instructions. "Come see this," she said, summoning Natalia over to her monitor. Together they peered at the screen.

"What am I supposed to be looking at?" Natalia said.

"This."

Angelina clicked on the triangle in the middle of a black box on the screen and a video started up, filling the space. It opened in a churchyard, Vivaldi playing on the sound track – a violin solo that sent a chill through Natalia. She didn't see Drina until she stepped out from the shadow into the sunlight. A purple scarf bound her thick lustrous hair. Cold reddened her cheeks. She wore a long white blouse with a silver vest over it, and a blue skirt that nearly reached the ground. Her eyes were shut tight. She could have stepped out of a Renaissance canvas.

A man sketched her as she played. The camera pulled closer to Drina and Natalia caught a glimpse of those sapphire eyes. Vivaldi's music soared, a heart rending flight – and stopped.

Her audience erupted, cheering and applauding. The camera panned down to coins being cast into her violin case, followed by euro notes, Canadian dollars, pounds, a travelers' check. A man squatted to empty his wallet, turning it upside down, bills floating into the red velvet case. The image froze as numbers in a tiny window at the bottom spun by in a blur.

"That's a counter," Angelina informed her boss. "Tallying the number of times it's viewed it. It's already in the thousands."

"What is this site?" Natalia said.

"Dittybop. My nieces are into it. Kids post their amateur videos."

"I've never seen it."

Angelina drew herself up. "May I show it to her brother and cousin?"

"Let's finish the interview first. We'll get nothing more from them after they see this."

Angelina agreed. Natalia followed her back toward the interview room with a heavy heart.

They reached number 2 and entered. Nuzi held his hands over a mug of steaming coffee. He shivered like he couldn't get warm enough.

Claudio Palumbo announced himself officially Nuzi's lawyer. Hoping she was not being swayed by the man's charm and good looks, Natalia granted his request to speak with his client alone in the interrogation room and followed her corporal out. Angelina turned back, puzzled.

"Why take the violin and leave the case? I mean, if you're making off with the instrument, why not take it away in the case. It doesn't entirely make sense."

Officers Rippi and Taleggio, who occupied the office next to Natalia and Angelina's, came off the elevator.

"What did we miss?" Rippi asked. "What have you got, corporal?"

"A girl murdered in the Montesanto market," Angelina answered.

"I thought you had a suspect in custody," Taleggio said.

The officers peered into the tiny interrogation room through the small pane in the door.

42

"Sounds like you could use a man's touch on this one," Taleggio teased, and cracked his knuckles.

"If we need your cerebral input, Sergeant, we'll ask," Natalia said.

"Just trying to help, ma'am." He held up both hands in surrender.

"Yeah," his partner chimed in. "And here I was going to offer to get you ladies a cup of Moroccan coffee from the Arab."

"No, thank you," Natalia said, warning in her tone. "Though we appreciate the thought ... Sergeant."

The men walked away, whispering to one another and laughing.

"I could have used more caffeine," Angelina said.

"Not if it came with that attitude."

"Listen to you -- always lecturing me about being diplomatic."

"Tell you what, I'll buy you coffee as soon as we're through here."

"Can I speak with you?" Claudio Palumbo said, coming out of the interrogation room.

"Certainly. Corporal Cavatelli, would you stay with Nuzi? This way."

Natalia led Claudio Palumbo through the bullpen and into her office. He sat down, pressed his palms to his eyes and didn't speak.

"What is it?" Natalia asked, leaning on her desk.

He opened his eyes. "I'd like to bring Nuzi home, with me. He's in no condition to be locked up."

"You're a lawyer. You know what the deal is. We haven't eliminated him as a suspect."

"There's no way on earth he murdered his sister."

"Her killer is very possibly a gypsy, wouldn't you say?"

"Plenty of Italians are familiar with our customs and language, including your corporal. Drina simply called her brother to meet her. She was dead when he got there. If he killed her, why on earth would he have stayed around to be arrested?"

"He hadn't planned on it," Natalia said, hypothesizing. "They met. Had an argument. It got out of control. Erupted."

"They've never had a cross word in their lives. He never ever lifted a hand to her and he never failed her, even in death. He stayed, tied that ribbon to her finger -- prayed over her. He wasn't concerned with perceptions. In our culture it's a sacrilege to leave a body unattended. You said yourself, the female vendor's statement about finding the body makes no mention of his being there. You don't have any hard evidence linking Nuzi to the crime, Captain. It would be irresponsible and cruel to hold him based on theoretical scenarios alone. He's grieving. If he were Italian he would already be free."

"I'll make you a deal," she said. "If I get the prosecutors to agree, I'll authorize his release. Whereupon his whereabouts will be your responsibility until Drina's killer is found."

"I would gladly accept. Thank you."

"Now, I have a few questions for you," Natalia said.

"What would you like to know?"

"Explain her living arrangements."

"Officially, she lived with her mom. And she slept there on occasion. But it's crowded – difficult to practice. And there's no privacy in gypsy communities. I have a guest room – large and peaceful. Once in a while she'd stay with me. I urged her to take advantage of it, but most times with her boyfriend."

"His name – the boyfriend?"

44

"Massimo Santini – Italian born and bred. Being among other Roma wasn't at all easy for her. She wasn't exactly welcome, mostly living apart as she did, not marrying when she was supposed to."

"How did she handle that — being ostracized?"

"It was difficult for her. I helped as much as I could."

"What can you tell me about her boyfriend?"

"Nothing really. Nuzi and I barely laid eyes on him. 'Maestro' she called him. I recently got the impression they'd broken up."

"When did you last see your cousin, Drina?"

"A week or two ago." He took a deep breath. "We argued about something petty. I never imagined they would be our last words." He started to tear up.

"Do you remember what you talked about?" "Besides our usual bickering? I told her she was wasting her time with the Maestro. She told me to mind my own business. Same as always. Nothing special. I take that back. There was the audition in Rome."

"Tell me about that," Natalia said.

"It's an annual. For young artists. First prize is a contract with a major orchestra, a big deal. She was nervous about making the cut. Here in Naples, she was among the very finest players. But in Rome she'd be up against others equally gifted. She knew that. To outsiders, Drina seemed so sure of herself. I knew better. I assured her she would make it, and I'd take her to dinner to celebrate when she did."

"Anything else? A conflict? Don't hold back, please. It won't do her any good."

"I urged her to stay away from Annunziata completely. She refused, again."

"Because she was in some kind of danger?"

"In Annunziata? No. The environment wasn't good for her. Like putting a flowering plant in a dark corner. No possibility to grow toward light."

"That's all?"

"Yes."

"Your cousin was a remarkable musician."

"We've been over that. A prodigy actually."

He seemed annoyed. Maybe it was the shock wearing off – reality setting in.

"Her violin case was at the scene but not the violin," Natalia continued.

"She told me once it was as valuable as a Stradivarius." Claudio Palumbo shifted in his chair.

"Really?" Natalia made a note. "How could she afford such an instrument?"

"She couldn't. Her teacher gave it to her on a kind of loan. I'm sure she was exaggerating its value."

He wrote down the name and address of the music teacher and passed it across.

"Did you inform her parents yet?" Natalia asked.

"No, I'll drive out there as soon as Nuzi's situation is settled tonight. There's just her mother. Her father and older brother died in the fire at Ponticelli."

Ponticelli was the gypsy camp torched by a mob several years back.

"That's terrible," Natalia said. "Poor girl. Did she have any friends other than her boyfriend? And you, of course."

"Drina was a private person. It was hard for her to trust outsiders – hard for all of us – even if you decide to live in the larger world. You leave what's familiar, though difficult, and once you leave you're no longer welcome there. Then you find out the larger world doesn't want you either. I wanted to spare her from that – offer her a safe passage."

46

"You were close to her," Natalia said.

"Since she was a kid, yeah. She saw I was able to get out, have a successful career. She wanted that for herself." He started to cry. "I am responsible for her death."

Natalia handed him the box of tissues as he fumbled for a handkerchief. "Sorry."

"Don't be sorry. This is difficult."

He blotted his eyes.

"We can continue this later," Natalia offered.

"No. I want to finish."

"Okay, if you're sure. Why is it you said you were responsible for her death?"

"If it hadn't been for me, she never would have left the community – or gone to school. I wanted her to have a chance at a decent life. If I hadn't encouraged her in that she would have married at thirteen or fourteen and had half a dozen children by now ... and she'd still be alive."

"We don't know that."

"No, we don't. But evidence suggests..."

"It's too early to talk about evidence or to make any assumptions, Signor Palumbo. I don't have to tell you, you've worked on criminal cases. Where were you before you got Nuzi's call?"

"At home. Taking it easy after lunch. I'd finished a long trial. I was still exhausted. Still am."

"Can anyone corroborate that? Your wife? Your partner?"

"I live alone."

"The concierge?"

"He saw me, yes. But you're not suggesting... Drina was my flesh and blood."

"I'm not suggesting anything, sir." Natalia started a new page of notes. "Your law specialty?"

"Corporate and estate mainly. Criminal cases when they come up."

"So you know we're following procedure here," Natalia said.

"Standard procedure, right. Rough up the gypsy."

"The officer was reprimanded at the scene," she said, not mentioning that she had done the reprimanding. "Meanwhile, I'm recommending Nuzi to your custody."

"I appreciate that. I keep thinking I'll wake up to find it's all been a terrible nightmare."

His shock and pain seemed genuine. He had cried, briefly, but generally he remained composed, unlike his younger cousin. Nuzi had broken down, sobbed by his sister's body, wept at the mention of her name.

"I'll need to talk with her mother at some point too," Natalia said. "It can wait for a day or so after you speak to her, but I'll need better directions to her residence if there really are no street names or numbers in gypsy communities."

"You are doing me a good turn, trying to let me take Nuzi home. Permit me to return the favor. Carabinieri are not exactly welcome at Annunziata. I'd be happy to accompany you."

"Thank you."

Now Claudio Palumbo began to weep. So she was wrong about the composure. It always came down to this in the end as the disbelief wore off and reality set in. She couldn't prevent tragedy. All she could do was witness the bloody aftermath and the toll on those left behind. Finding the killer couldn't bring back the loved one. To them, the finality seemed impossible — that the dead young woman would never play her beautiful music again or walk the streets of her difficult city, eat a peach, admire a newborn, a profusion of flowers, or touch her violin. She would never bite into a sweet melon or hear the church bells of Naples toll. Nor again know joy.

"If you'll wait with Nuzi," she said, "I'll call the prosecutor."

He nodded and returned to the interview room and his client.

As Angelina came back into their office, Natalia took a deep breath and stood up. "Palumbo says her violin is valuable."

"This couldn't be simple robbery," Angelina said, raising her hands in frustration. "They'd just snatch the violin and go. Not kill her for it."

"Nothing's impossible, I've been told," Natalia teased. "I'm going to spring Nuzi."

"You haven't even called the prosecutor. You're taking a chance, no?"

"Not much of one," Natalia said. "Mr. Palumbo is smart. He spotted the weakest point in the case against his cousin and went right for it."

"That being?"

"Your interview with the woman at the market who found the body. She made no mention of a young man or anyone else around the body. Nuzi wasn't there until sometime after the killing and the woman discovered the victim. Cut him loose."

Chapter 5

Natalia zipped up her insulated jacket, closed the door to the courtyard of her building and set off to see her pal. The hills, grey and barren, faded as evening came on. A band of swifts dove from a church tower. Bickering, they swooned into the linden trees. Lovely as they were, Natalia missed the songbirds that had vanished earlier that month and wouldn't re-appear until after the New Year. Winter was the season of revelations, she remembered her father often saying. The more birds that fled south from Naples, he'd often announce, the better it was to hear the melodies of those that stayed behind.

A few blocks along, a chestnut vendor did a brisk business, bagging treats as his customers warmed their hands over his fire. At a window table inside the Partenope Café the usual gaggle of widows enjoyed their evening coffees together. Crossing the street, she had Marco bag two rolls fresh from the oven that steamed the glass case outside his shop. She followed him in to ring up the sale. A wheel of *provelone* and a large sausage occupied the case at the back but apart for some canned goods, the shelves were empty. A bruised banana and a withered orange sat next to his register. How had he stayed in business, she momentarily wondered but instantly suppressed the thought. Marco was not in her precinct, she didn't want to know.

The winter equinox had just passed. Soon the days would start getting longer, and flowers bloom again. Tonight that seemed a long way off. Christmas preparations were underway – churches scrubbed, angels taken from their boxes and dusted off, along with handed down decorations. Her father's widowed sister had a wonderful collection of such lights and carved cherubs. Aunt Antonietta had promised them and several pieces of jewelry to Natalia because of her fondness for her niece and the fact that she was again feuding with every other member of the family. Antonietta spared noone except her granddaughter and Natalia. Every Christmas she gave her niece an envelope with ten euros to sneak to the child since she wasn't speaking to her daughter-in-law.

Antoinetta never forgot a slight nor did she forgive any. Natalia had always believed her aunt would have made a terrific *madrina,* running a criminal clan. She was sharp and imposed her will as a given right. In that way, she reminded Natalia of Lola Nuovaletta, her best friend who had dropped out of school and been taken into the family business after high school. While Mariel and Natalia dutifully graduated from the Sacred Heart of Jesus and went off to university, Lola claimed her legacy in the Naples underworld.

Natalia's personal connections to the less than proper citizenry had profited the law enough times that her superior turned a blind eye to these associations. There was an understanding. The colonel wouldn't ask her about them and she would remain discreet in her contacts. It was an arrangement not recognized by her colleague, Marshal of the Carabinieri Cervino. He kept bringing her 'known associates' to the attention of the colonel and anyone else at the station who would listen. So far, Colonel Fabio had not acted on the allegations, but they had become almost common knowledge. Regardless, Natalia could not abandon her oldest friend anymore than she could her lovably cantankerous aunt. Having once denied her street cleaner father on a grade school outing, she had vowed she would never shame herself like that again, no matter what. Nothing was worth the hurt look in his eyes when she skipped by with her schoolmates and refused his greeting.

Reaching her destination, Natalia buzzed and stuck out her tongue at Lola's surveillance camera, scanning overhead. Her friend answered the door in four inch red heels, Micu in her arms, barking. Owner and pet were resplendent in matching pink cashmere sweaters.

"Look who came to visit." Lola kissed the dog's mouth and pointed it toward Natalia.

Natalia averted her face and patted the dog's head instead.

"I just got back from some serious shopping," Lola said and led the way to the living room where she sank into a salmon colored armchair and immediately pulled the red stilettos off her feet. Isabella greeted Natalia and retreated to another room. Lola dropped the shoes on the lemon rug with relief.

"These fucking things are killing me. Five hundred euros and I'm bleeding?" She dumped the dog in Natalia's lap and dug into one of the shopping bags.

"You like?" She pulled out clothes. "Look at this. Adorable, right?"

The silver and grey dress looked shredded around the hem.

"It's a Tuffo," Lola chirped, proudly.

"Tuffo?"

"A Milan designer who relocated to Naples last year -- for inspiration. Real exclusive. You can't hardly get an appointment at his studio without being referred. Guess what I paid?"

"Three hundred euros?"

"You're kidding, right? You can't get one of his pieces for under a thousand." She tossed the dress back into the bag. "Got them down to eight fifty."

"It looks like something you rescued from a dumpster."

"You're beginning to sound like one of those *parentis.*"

The venerable widows were a Naples' institution. They huddled in prayer near the main altar of the Duomo once a year to make sure San Gennaro's dry, powdery blood, miraculously liquefied again for the presiding priests.

"Is that supposed to mean something?" Natalia said.

"Just trying to help."

"You want to help, tell me whose gang is collecting the *pezzo* at the Montesanto market these days."

"Where that gypsy kid died? Bianca's people, I think. It's her turf."

Lola retrieved the skimpy dress and held it up against herself.

"Eight fifty, huh?" Natalia teased.

"If you weren't so high and mighty, you could afford couture now and then too."

"Spare me the lecture, okay?"

"Listen to me, Nat. You put your life on the line for what – so we can drop roses on your flag draped casket? You were the smartest of us and you're tossing your life away."

"Mariel is the intelligent one. How many academic prizes did she win from grade school on?"

"Book smart maybe. But you've got the nose for the street and the rarest thing of all -- common sense. I love Em like a sister but she lives a different life from us. Always has."

"Hey, her parents"

"Died when she was young. Yeah, yeah. Mariel had it rough, I know. But she always had her books and fancy clothes. Money, Nat. Gold fixtures in the bathroom. Season tickets to the opera, fresh flowers from Valentino's every week. I wanted the best too and got it. I want it for you."

"I'm doing alright," Natalia said.

"Really? Your lousy apartment? Your magnificent salary? Or is it the fancy designer uniforms?" Lola nuzzled the dog asleep in her lap, and kissed the slumbering pooch. "She doesn't get it, does she? It's a matter of respect, right sweetheart?"

"Respect?" Natalia said. "People being scared of you?"

"If that's what it takes to get what I want."

A maid rolled in a cart with a bottle of wine and two delicate wine glasses.

"You're gonna love this *vino*," Lola said. "I'll pour," she informed the maid.

"Yes Signora."

"She's new," Natalia observed as the young woman did a half curtsy and left the room.

"Sofia had a medical issue. I gave her the month off. Mmm," she swirled her glass and sampled. "What do you think?"

"Pretty good," Natalia said. "Interesting aroma."

"A musty palette. It's vintage."

Natalia winced. "Musty pallet? That sounds like an old couch."

The dog nuzzled Natalia's shoulder bag.

"Muci's after something," Lola said, pulling her back.

"I nearly forgot. Your favorite rolls." Natalia took out the bag. "Still warm."

Lola made a face. "They're made from white flour."

"Yeah. So?"

"Glycemic index. Dominick and me, we're only eating whole grains."

"I thought you were ditching him," Natalia said.

"Don't start, okay? I mean, where's your Mr. Pino these days — waiting in a cave somewhere for the second coming of Buddha?"

Pino had wreaked havoc in her life and broken her heart, then retreated to the country to deal with some heavy karma.

"Yeah," Natalia conceded, "a stretch in a cave might not be a bad idea for him."

She didn't want to get into her former boyfriend with Lola. Besides not wanting to deal with painful memories, Signora Nuovaletta's input wouldn't help.

"Going into law enforcement?" Natalia lifted two silver handcuffs from a woven basket on Lola's coffee table.

Lola smiled. "Dominick likes to spice things up, you know?" She and Micu rubbed noses. "Did I tell you, my *nani* got a dog?"

"I didn't know your grandmother liked pets at all."

"She doesn't. But you should see her with her new baby. She named him Pippo."

"Pippo? What kind of a name is that for a dog?"

"She's had him a month and he already looks like a sausage. I told her to stop feeding him so much or he's going to have a heart attack. So she calls me up and says she did what I told her and put him on a diet. When the little beast turned up his nose at his health food, she cooks him a major steak, cuts it up and serves it to him on a plate."

"Same old Rosalia," Natalia laughed.

"The woman's stubborn. Like you."

"She's eighty nine, Lolly. Maybe she's earned it."

"Before I forget" Lola quickly rose and headed toward the bedroom.

"Loll," Natalia said. "Is the Montesanto market still your boss's territory?"

"No. Lenny DePretis has it. Some deal they cut. Be right back."

Natalia sank into Lola's gigantic grey sectional and leaned her head against a lush turquoise pillow. The dog trotted over and eyed her lap.

"Don't even think about it," she said. Micu scooted after his mistress.

Lola and her couture, Natalia chuckled. Although there was something to what she'd said. Natalia *was* starting to look frumpy. Lola dressed lavishly, buying new outfits at whim. Several times a year Mariel invested in a few good pieces for herself. The only name designer outfit Natalia owned was her uniform. Armani and Valentino both had contributed their talents. Otherwise, she faded into the woodwork with her bland civilian threads. But unlike her flashy friend, Natalia had no desire or need to draw attention to herself – profession notwithstanding.

Efforts to upgrade her wardrobe never worked. Why would they now? She hated shopping. Growing up, new clothes had been an unnecessary luxury she'd learned not to pine for. If a special outfit was required, her mother whipped out her measuring tape and took the cover off her trusty sewing machine. From first communion to university graduation, she had made all of Natalia's clothes.

Her last dresses were the bridesmaids' gowns Natalia and Mariel wore to Lola's wedding. Natalia remembered exactly the pale blue chiffon edged in purple. Lovely as they were, she and Mariel might as well have vanished as Lola entered the cathedral in a cloud of tulle and silk, her veil encrusted with pearls and diamonds, and two attendants bearing the long, heavy train. The priest actually blushed when the veil came off the neckline was such a scandal. Natalia and Mariel had cracked up, laughing again when the white doves were released and flew up to the stained glass windows and out the cathedral's huge open doorway.

Lola came back, carrying a good sized painting. "What do you think?" she said, propping it on the couch next to Natalia.

"Nice. Since when do you own a Guttuso? I've never seen one this close up."

"Impressive, huh? It's supposed to be Sicily." Lola gave her a dubious look. "You could've fooled me. It's a field or something."

Ironically, in Natalia's first year assigned to the art squad in Rome, a case had taken her to Guttuso's hometown to track down a missing Rembrandt drawing. Guttuso's birthplace was bleak, full of factories and abandoned lots where apple orchards once stood. The Mafia had extorted a fortune from farmers for every drop of irrigation water. It drove them out. The apples and farmers were long gone, the Mafia parasites moved on to other hosts.

"What's it supposed to be?" Lola said, indicating the canvas.

Natalia tried to explain the composition to her friend – how the oranges and yellows represented sunlight, and the darker strokes were lemon groves and olive trees.

Lola squinted at the painting. "Looks like something my kid did in second grade."

"Guttusos are hard to come by," Natalia said. "They're either in museums or private collections these days. They rarely come on the market."

"Annalisa said it complements the couch."

"Annalisa?"

"Annalisa Conti – a friend with an art gallery." Lola dug in a shopping bag for her handbag -- a glittery yellow pouch with chrome handles.

"How many handbags do you own?" Natalia said.

"As many as I want, Missy. It's a matter of color coordination, which you could use a little of, by the way."

"You've got a new decorator."

"No. She gifted me a session."

"That was generous. Did Annalisa Conti sell you the painting?"

"It's a loaner from her gallery. I'm living with it for a while, until I can decide if I want to keep it. Meanwhile I'm having the place redone. She suggested a muted scheme. Whites and beiges with a dash of black ... to set off the collection."

"So you're a collector now?"

"You gotta start somewhere. And I don't mean those dark and dusty masterworks you and Mariel are always swooning over."

"You mean like Rembrandt?"

"Just because I didn't go to college and study art like you and Em, doesn't mean I don't have taste."

"Of course not. You do."

"Seriously, you like the painting?"

"It's ... dynamic."

Lola gasped. "That's what Annalisa said -- dynamic. Exact word! Dominick hates it. Tell you the truth, I'm not crazy about it either. You interested?"

Natalia laughed. "I'm afraid a Guttuso is over my budget."

"I meant as a gift. I'm serious. I'd like to buy it from her but I don't want to live with it."

Natalia went over and hugged her friend. "I can't," she said, "You know I can't," and kissed her cheek. "But thank you, *Cara*."

"Nat, stay for dinner. It's late. It'll beat whatever you've got in your icebox. Please, please. Besides, the *polizi* haven't got me staked out tonight."

"How do you know?"

"I know."

"Okay. I'd love to. We can catch up. I can see my goddaughter."

"Good. She'll be home right after her music lesson. She's missed you." Lola looked wistful. "Me too."

***

Natalia left right after dinner to finish one last bit of work. She didn't have far to go for it.

As Natalia rang the doorbell, down the hall, a different front door opened a crack and a wispy haired woman peered out, only to quickly slam it shut.

The young man who stepped out of his doorway looked sleepy, like he'd just gotten up from dozing. His hair was tangled, his jeans speckled with paint, and he was naked to the waist.

Angelina would have called a pretty boy, with his lanky build, dusky hair, and olive skin.

"Just a minute," he said and closed the door. When he re-opened it, he was wearing a shirt.

Natalia showed her ID and introduced herself as Carabinieri. He invited her in. The studio reeked of turpentine. He was good, she thought – if the nearly finished canvas on his easel was any indication. His female subject faced out from the painting, each line delineated perfectly. Her eyes were vivid and alive. The background was purposely muddy so that the viewer was drawn to the figure – Drina. The artist had created the illusion of a model emerging from the canvas.

"You are Massimo Santini?" Natalia said.

"*Si.*"

Surprised but not nervous, she noted. He looked a bit younger than his ex-girlfriend. Natalia wondered if he'd had many bad things happen to him. Probably not, judging from his lack of reaction to the authorities at his door. Bad experiences tended to accrue with age anyway, along with wariness.

Massimo Santini wiped his hands on his jeans. He obviously lived and worked in this small space. A bed that doubled as a couch. A tiny refrigerator and a hotplate. A series of large charcoal drawings were taped along the wall. More nudes. A figurative artist, *Signor* Santini. Old fashioned. Representational work hadn't been in vogue when Natalia was at university reading art history.

Had the dead girl been the model for these other nudes too? It was hard to tell. The figure faced nearly away in each. Certainly it could have been her. The model had the dead girl's hair, build and erect posture. Posing nude for a *gadje* would have been forbidden in her community, where women were kept well covered and only permitted to bare themselves for their husbands. Had someone from the Annunziata encampment found out what she'd been doing?

Nuzi had sworn he told no one of his sister's romance with Massimo. Then again, he or his uncle had said the youngsters had broken off their romance months ago. Nuzi became even more distraught when Angelina posited that someone might have found out and pressed him to forbid her relationship, or else. He insisted not. Angelina persisted. Had he tried to prevent her punishment and gotten there too late? Again he denied it.

The Roma was a closed society. Secret. Natalia imagined all kinds of justice was meted out with the larger world none the wiser. This assassination in broad daylight in a busy market – was it a warning to other girls who might have ideas of betraying their heritage and baring themselves for *gadje*?

"Is something wrong?" the boyfriend asked, a hint of nervousness now. "What is it you want?"

Natalia wasn't sure how to start. You'd think with all her experience she would. What made it harder was his look of innocence while asking to hear the unbearable.

She steeled herself and in the most calculated way told him Drina was dead, killed, stabbed to death in the Montesanto market.

His face went white and he started trembling. Natalia pulled a paint-splashed high stool over from his worktable. A sob caught in his throat.

"You'd better sit down." He did.

When he'd recovered enough to talk, Natalia asked when he'd last seen his girlfriend.

"Early last week. I was busy preparing for my show at school and she for an audition."

"Was that unusual -- not seeing each other every day?"

"No. We had agreed we both needed breathing space."

"You hadn't argued? Broken up?"

"No. Now and then we'd have a spat, but nothing ever serious. We each needed our space. You can see …" he gestured to the room. "I needed to paint, and she to practice. We were taking a break from one another, that's all." Tears started. "I adored her."

Natalia gave him a moment to collect himself, and asked how they'd met.

He'd noticed her playing on the street a couple of years ago, her music was something "magnificent," and she, likewise. He asked if she'd mind his sketching her. One thing led to another…

He started to sob quietly.

"Do you want me to come back another time?" Natalia asked. Poor kid, she thought.

"No, I'm … No."

She'd come prepared and passed him some tissues. "You're sure?"

"Yes," he snuffled. "Where is she? I'd like to see her."

"She's at the morgue. It might not be a good idea just now, even if you were permitted to. Do you have someone to call? You shouldn't be alone with this news."

He wiped his eyes. "I'll be okay. I'd rather be by myself actually."

"Do you mind? I have some more questions?"

"No."

"Did she ever talk about people in her community?"

"Her brother, her mother a little. And her cousin, this lawyer. She thought the sun rose and set with him."

Massimo was jealous, Natalia realized.

"Were you in a monogamous relationship?" she asked.

He colored. "Yes."

"You're sure? She wasn't intimate with anyone else?"

"We gave our word. She never lied, not about anything."

"Can you say where you were between noon and three o'clock today?"

"Is that… you suspect me?"

"I have to ask. Lovers, next of kin… You understand."

He swallowed. "Life drawing at the university. We had a model at lunchtime."

"Can someone confirm you were there?"

He nodded and dictated the name of the instructor and opened his sketchbook to the pose he had rendered of a very full bodied model.

"Are there any of Drina's possessions here? Clothes, books, notes, letters?"

"No. She wouldn't even leave her toothbrush. She said she didn't feel comfortable. She worried someone would find out and we'd be harassed. We had to be careful, she insisted. But I wondered if that was the truth."

"How do you mean?" Natalia asked.

"I'm not sure. I was afraid it was an excuse – that she didn't love me as much as I did her, and that was her way of keeping her distance. My dream was to settle down with her – children, the works. Not right away, but after I'd finished school, had a few shows – after I could make some money so we could live decently. But Drina? She liked the freedom to come and go. Children didn't delight her. She was like an uncaged bird – flitting from place to place, never still. Maybe her background, coming from that place, I don't know."

"Did you ever visit her home?"

"No, never. I was curious. She wouldn't allow me to go with her, and she forbade me to go alone. One time I accused her of having a gypsy husband and a few children hidden there. She slapped me."

Natalia regarded him. The young man had been in love that was certain and the object of his passion had not returned the intensity in kind. Drina's passion was her music, Natalia surmised. Massimo must have been disappointed. Disappointed enough to kill? Was this young man capable of destroying her? His soft, sorrowful eyes said no. Still, until her murderer was found, he'd stay on the list. Natalia handed over her card and encouraged him to call if anything at all occurred to him that might be of help, then left.

She considered a drink at the corner café then thought better of it. A skinny little child with wild hair and freckles moved quietly among the tables, apparently alone. Most of the customers ignored her and her plea for money scrawled on a piece of cardboard. Only one woman dropped a few coins into her grimy palm. Up close the child looked no more than six.

A block further on Natalia saw the gypsy girl from the café again. She was sitting on a curb next to an older woman in a long purple dress, who was counting coins and euro notes. The woman struck her hard and shouted, "*Mang!*" and struck her again. The girl's arm rose against the blows but she didn't make a sound as she was beaten across the shoulders and back. The young face filled with humiliation and hurt.

"Hey!" Natalia shouted and moved toward the woman, who grabbed the girl sharply and hustled her away down a dark passage. Natalia hurried to the alleyway where they'd disappeared but they were gone.

She stopped to catch her breath. There wasn't much point to chasing after them. Even if she caught up, what could she do? Put the grandmother in jail? Send the child to foster parents? Not likely. Gypsies weren't welcome anywhere − not jail, not youth hostels, orphanages or hospitals, or schools either. Some life.

What had been Drina's lot at that age, Natalia wondered, before Claudio Palumbo intervened?

Chapter 6

The police were directing the morning traffic away from Via Tribunali as she walked toward Casanova and the station. The black clad widows were positioned in their customary places on the bench in front of Da Fenzatta's butcher shop, waiting for a funeral procession to pass. Funeral rituals and ossuaries generally held a fascination for Neapolitans. It even crept into street games. When Natalia and her friends were children, she partook by dutifully accepting her turn playing dead. The kids would tuck their hands under the drafted corpse, chanting – "Stiff as a board, light as a feather." When the dearly departed raised an arm, the rest would shriek and run.

Greeting the widows, Natalia resumed her stroll toward work, passing worshippers coming out of morning mass from the centuries old San Bartolomeo. A throng of young people was assembled on the sidewalk outside, holding a vigil amidst flowers and votive candles massed in front of the gates where a large photo of Drina occupied a place of honor.

Reaching Casanova Station, she took the stairs. The officer at the reception desk was too overwhelmed with calls to even greet her. In the cubicles beyond, *Carabinieri* in shirt sleeves stood about, staring intently at computer screens. Angelina was in front of her screen too, arms crossed, studying her monitor.

"What's going on?" Natalia said, entering their office.

"That video yesterday of our victim playing the violin? It's not the only one. There are more, all shot by tourists and passersby. Our girl traveled. The last one I saw just now was shot in France."

"Are you saying she actually played in the streets in France?"

"Apparently she and her violin went there on a personal pilgrimage last summer. RAI TV ran one of the tapes on their morning newscasts. A record producer just called, begging for contact information for her parents or family."

"Her mother doesn't even have a phone."

"That's what I told the man. He didn't believe me." Angelina took a deep breath and slumped back. "I said I'd check and get back to him. Here, take a look," she said, and turned the screen so Natalia could see too.

Drina stood in the center aisle of a simple church made of huge, rough stone, violin under her chin. She closed her eyes and started to play a Viotti concerto familiar to Natalia but the rendition was so dazzling she could have sworn she'd never heard it before.

"Angelina, do you know what '*mang*' means in Romani?"

"Yeah. 'Keep begging' Why are you asking?"

"I heard an old grandmother shout it at a young girl as she knocked her about."

A sergeant appeared at the door.

"Excuse me, Colonel Donati wants you immediately, Captain."

Dashing upstairs, Natalia found the colonel on his feet, speaking to a couple of officers gathered around his desk. She didn't recognize them. Donati stopped and warmly included her. They had just arrived from the special art detachment of the Carabinieri Command in Rome. They'd come to take over the Segli case as she'd predicted.

Colonel Fabio introduced her to Captain Villari and his lieutenant. The captain and Natalia shook hands. He was a northerner without a doubt – the pale coloring, the slim build and light colored eyes. Colonel Donati asked her to review the facts of the robbery while copies were made for them of Natalia's preliminary report. She filled them in and turned her hand written notes over to the captain.

Rushing two officers to Naples to investigate a less than significant art theft was excessive, especially given the relatively low value and quality of the missing piece. But as she well knew, no effort was ever spared when Church antiquities or art were involved.

Captain Villari asked if the thieves had slipped anything into the space where the Segli had hung. Colonel Donati looked momentarily puzzled and Natalia explained that it was a common deception employed by art thieves to delay detection of their crime. Most parishioners were getting on in years and paid little attention to the reliquaries and works of art that surrounded them, and tourists didn't always know what they were looking at. No, Natalia reported: nothing had been left in its place as a disguise.

Captain Villari took an interest in the man who might have been in the confessional when the Segli went missing. Natalia offered to pursue his identity further. The captain declined, saying it was unlikely the priest would reveal it and their Vatican liaison would likely object if an issue were made of it.

Colonel Donati said, "One thing I don't understand. Why choose a modest work by a relatively unknown artist when a much more valuable art piece hangs nearby."

Captain Villari smiled. "It happens from time to time, especially with novices. Cutting the painting from its frame suggests that might be true in this instance. In their nervousness, they'll often rush and leave a trail of clues that leads to quick apprehension. Not the case here, unfortunately. If they have no criminal history, then it will be challenging to trace the crime. Plus, the inexperienced thief may not know how to dispose of the piece and hide the prize away for a long time while they figure out what to do."

"Likewise," Natalia said, "if the thief snatched the painting for his own private viewing and pleasure, he could be difficult to track down."

"True. The art might not see the light of day for years," Villari added. "Speaking of time, Colonel Donati, might we have some of Captain Monte's? Would you permit her to direct us to the church where the theft occurred?"

"Of course."

Captain Villari shook the colonel's hand upon leaving and passed by Natalia, saying, "We'll meet you downstairs. Look for a large blue van."

"Captain Monte, a moment," Colonel Donati said, and gracefully resumed his seat. "As you predicted – Rome has taken this out of our hands. Perhaps for the better. Meanwhile our gypsy violinist is getting a great deal of attention. We're about to be inundated." He indicated a stack of call slips. "These were waiting for me when I got in. Command Headquarters, the Holy See... I thought the Vatican might be calling about the missing painting, but no. About our young gypsy." He picked up the top of the pile. "The mayor, the media, and our concerned citizens."

"Yes, sir," she said. "I'm not sure I know what I should do next."

"Change into uniform. You have a spare here, I assume?"

Their dark blue Mercedes 3000 van had a high roof and red band that ran across its sides horizontally. 'CARABINIERI' was printed in large white letters and 'Mobile Art Lab' in a small font underneath.

The spacious cab could hold five. The passenger seat up front had been saved for her. The rear contained the lab itself. The lieutenant behind the wheel greeted her as she got in and asked for directions. Natalia casually inquired what the mobile laboratory held.

"Mostly testing equipment we use to date paints, inks, resins, canvas, frames. A portable X-ray machine for seeing beneath. Two computer stations in there link to databases we use when we're researching an artifact or authenticating a painting."

Nice to have their budget, Natalia thought as they drove to Sant'Angelo, with her navigating. As they approached the church, the pedestrian traffic on Via Librai thickened. Their drive resorted to the siren and flashing emergency lights as he inched their vehicle through the crowd, honking as he went. Naples' drivers seemed unimpressed.

Finally giving up, the lieutenant parked and the officers joined the civilians ebbing into the plaza. Most of the crowd were young, in their teens and early twenties, and carrying candles. Nearly all bore flowers they deposited near the front steps of the cathedral before an improvised shrine honoring the violinist. A good many remained there outside. Only the Carabinieri crossed the street to the smaller Sant'Angelo church to which Natalia led them.

While her colleagues went in to meet with Father Montalba, Natalia lingered on the top step out front and stood looking over the street and the people crowding it. Next to her, a couple of sweepers in dayglo green uniforms and fluorescent jackets leaned on their orange brooms, smoking.

"Natalia Monte?" said the husky one nearest.

"Sergio!" she exclaimed. The man had worked with her father.

"I heard you had become a Carabinieri but I hardly believed it. My God. A captain no less. Your papa would be proud."

Natalia thanked him and asked after his family. It had been a while. She hadn't seen him since her father passed.

"Are you here because of this?" he said, pointing to the young people shuffling through the plaza across the narrow road and into the big church, or stopping outside at the shrine enveloped in a sea of blossoms.

"No," she said. "I'm here escorting some Carabinieri from Rome."

"Ah."

"Monday morning, were you here by any chance?" she asked.

"Yes, around six thirty, seven o'clock. We do this area before the churches open."

"Did anyone come out of Sant'Angelo at that hour?"

Sergio bobbed his head, glancing over to see how close his co-worker was.

"It could be important to me," Natalia said.

Sergio spoke softly. "This can't come back to me."

"It won't."

"Swear?"

"On my father's grave."

"Lenny DePretis."

"You're sure?"

"He's here once a month like clockwork. Always a Monday."

Natalia didn't say anything more or show any reaction. Captain Villari came out and his lieutenant followed, looking a bit dejected and carrying a large plastic-wrapped square: the empty frame. Natalia touched Sergio's arm to bid goodbye and descended the steps to follow them back to the van.

"No luck at all," Captain Villari informed her. "No guards, no surveillance cameras." He shook his head. "You were right. The scene has been completely compromised."

"Unfortunate," she said. "Was Monsignor Montalba cooperative?"

"Cordial but otherwise … not so much. I was hoping he might give us the identity of the penitent whose confession he heard Monday morning. He refused."

Natalia wasn't surprised. Since the archbishop had banned the town's criminal families from important church functions, their weekly offerings and gifts to clerics had only amplified and become more lavish. She doubted Father Montalba was an exception. A wealthy benefactor like DePretis would always be accommodated no matter what sins he came to be absolved of.

The lieutenant locked the empty frame in the mobile lab while the captains climbed back in their seats. At Casanova Station she took the captain aside and told him what she'd learned.

"Lenny DePretis," Villari repeated. "Who is he?"

"A Camorra godfather, likeable and dangerous."

"And you learned this how?"

"From a melodious bird wintering over."

***

Natalia and Captain Villari set out alone, agreeing that a small presence might serve their purposes better than a

71

mob of officers descending. She drove the Alfa cruiser, following the traffic lights and signs.

The captain asked her what she knew about Depretis.

"He's about forty. Handsome despite a facial scar. Reportedly came from the docklands of Bari. Little schooling. Worked as a stevedore for a while. Some Neapolitan's cousin. He turned up in Naples sixteen years ago. Keeps to himself."

She filled him in on what she knew of his career, that he smuggled drugs from South America to Mexico, and from there to international destinations – including Naples. Lenny DePretis had amassed a lot of influence and territory. He liked opera, gourmet cooking, street food and making money, lots of it.

"He was unorthodox and rose quickly in the criminal ranks," she said.

"Unorthodox how?" Captain Villari sat back.

"A decade ago he married one of the Montecino clan's women in a ceremony at the Duomo. Months later he caught his wife with her chauffer. DePretis never touched her, just quietly divorced her -- very uncharacteristic of his Catholic peers. What happened to the chauffeur is less clear. The man fled or was disappeared. In either case, no object lessons were left dead in the street. All very discreetly done."

"Interesting," said the captain. "Not your typical Camorra boss."

"We're here."

"Did you know," Villari said, "His primary residence is here, but he owns an apartment on Place des Vosges in the most expensive neighborhood in Paris? Has a modest estate outside London and a crumbling palace in Bucharest."

Villari tapped something into the screen of his digital phone and passed it over.

"And here I thought he was a simple man," she said, looking at a sprawling marble residence that made Camorra mansions look like gate houses.

"That's the little place in Bucharest. For the past couple of years he's been divesting himself of businesses." Villari consulted his notes. "Three years ago he opened an art gallery in London. Milan soon after that, then Venice. And now he's put money into Annalisa Conti's gallery here in Naples. We've been interested in his interest in art for some time."

Lenny DePretis' residence was modern, a grey stone and glass affair, quite understated. Not the usual mobster's style at all. If he was surprised to see two Carabinieri captains on his doorstep, he didn't show it as he tucked his blue and white striped shirt tails into his pants and asked them in. No obvious security, no goons.

He looked damp, like he'd just gotten out of the shower. His thick black hair didn't have much grey. A stocky man, DePretis' brown eyes were a surprise. They were soft, almost sad. They passed over her face, her figure and came back to her eyes.

Natalia and Villari offered their credentials but he waved them away and asked them in. DePretis led the way into the enormous living room and a bank of black leather sectional furniture, all of it modern, in keeping with the architecture. A wall of windows looked out on a Japanese garden and a lone bush with tiny crimson berries, shiny and wet from the earlier frost.

One long white wall was a gigantic floor to ceiling bookcase, completely filled. At the touch of a remote the shelves slowly disappeared behind high white panels that pivoted shut. Natalia wondered if there might be art on the opposite wall similarly hidden from view. The only artwork in the room was a Black Madonna sculpture carved from ebony wood.

Captain Villari told DePretis they had information that two days earlier he had been at the chapel of Sant'Angelo a Nilo around 0600 where a theft had occurred around that time. They wished to ask him some questions as he might be a possible witness.

"Really?" DePretis pushed aside a pair of bifocals. "Must have been a pretty big theft. What was stolen?"

Villari shifted uncomfortably. "We're not at liberty to say."

DePretis laughed. "Forgive me. How then are we to proceed?"

"Were you in the Brancaccio Chapel of Sant' Angelo Monday morning?" Natalia asked.

"I may have been, yes."

"So you were there."

"Possibly. How is it you came to believe I was?"

"It's confidential," Villari said, "the source."

"*Were* you there," Natalia said, "meditating?"

"I can't help you without knowing what it is you want me to speak about."

"Did you see anyone on the premises other than the pastor?" Natalia asked.

"No."

"Did you hear anything unusual while you were there?" she continued.

"No. It was silent as a tomb." He took a deep breath. "I saw no one suspicious. I heard nothing and saw nothing. Did they make off with the altar pieces?"

"The Segli," Natalia said.

Villari looked at her, surprised – or perhaps alarmed.

"The Segli *Ascension*?" DePretis exclaimed. He shook his head in disbelief. "Why don't I write the monsignor a check right now so he can buy some real art. Oh – I forgot. The archbishop would never allow that."

"This is a serious matter, Mr. DePretis." Captain Villari reminded him.

"Of course, of course. We wouldn't want to embarrass the Church or endanger the recovery of this … treasure."

"Might your driver or associates have seen anyone leaving Sant' Angelo while you were in the chapel?"

"Not possible. I arrived alone, I left alone." He gripped his knees and sat forward. "I'm sorry I can't help you," he said, and stood. "Forgive me. I have an appointment."

Natalia and the captain rose with him. In the huge foyer he turned to Natalia.

"I've heard about you, Captain Monte, and I'm glad we have finally met. I hope to become better acquainted on a more convivial occasion."

"You're very confident interviewing Camorra, captain." Villari looked over at her as they returned to the car. "Judging from his living circumstances, I'd say Leonardo DePretis certainly has the means to have his way with the Monsignor and make his confessions without being observed, coming or going. Still, I wonder why he is so guarded about his time with Montalba. I thought Camorra generally considered themselves religious."

"They tend to, yes. DePretis not so much. But from what I gather, he considers himself spiritual – a private audience with a priest – why not? You saw – no bodyguards visible – he likes his unguarded private moments. Unfortunately, after our visit, confession at the Sant'Angelo can't be among them. His movements are known. Whatever he is, he's never struck me as a man with a death wish."

Chapter 7

Dr. Francesca Agari pulled the sheet away from the girl. Drina's face wore a tinge of blue. Her beauty had suffered but hadn't been erased.

"Time of death was in the afternoon, between one and three. Cause of death: a large needle-like tool or awl piercing her brain."

"Unusual?"

"These days, yes. Back in the 1940s and '50s, ice picks were a favorite killing instrument of particular *Mafiosi*. Knitting needles too. This weapon is a refinement on that. Look for a cobbler's or a woodworker's tool," she said. "One with a hefty grip – they needed leverage, obviously."

"Your criminalists find any blood on the violin case?"

"No. You have a theory of the crime yet?" Dottore Agari asked.

Natalia covered her nose and shook her head no. The smell of formaldehyde was getting to her. Lifeless bodies filled a dozen drawers in the refrigeration units along the wall. The Medical Examiner remained poised in the midst of them, undaunted and unflappable as always – unfazed by the chemical odor and the beautiful corpse that lay before them.

Francesca Agari pushed strands of her hair out of her eyes with a perfumed wrist.

"We're running a couple more tests. A more sensitive second toxicity screen of her blood. So far nothing. I should have the certificate in a day or two." She snapped off her latex gloves. "Anything from your end?"

"Nothing as yet. Her violin is still missing, but whether that's significant …" Natalia shrugged.

"Not your typical robbery," Doctor Agari said as she draped the body to the neck.

"Exactly," Natalia agreed. "Robbers could have taken the girl's violin without killing her. They could have just followed her down an alley – showed a weapon."

Doctor Agari's assistant slid Drina back into the vault. Natalia contemplated the closed drawer.

"She wasn't much more than a girl."

Dottore Agari leaned a hand on the autopsy table, holding the other against her hip. "Who could do this terrible thing?"

"Doesn't seem like a crime of passion," Natalia said. "The killer was much too efficient."

Dottore Agari's mobile phone pinged and she pulled it out. A quick glance and she slipped it back into her lab coat. "Enough death," she said. "Anything interesting going on in your life?"

"No," Natalia answered, slightly surprised at the sudden shift. "Yours?"

"I don't have a life," Francesca sighed. "Less complicated that way."

"Sorry I didn't mean to intrude."

"Not at all. It's actually comforting to know someone cares enough to ask."

Natalia returned to Casanova and collected Angelina. Together they drove back to the scene of the murder. They found the market in full swing. Scarlet flowering plants and poinsettias dotted the cobblestones, as they did each

December. The ornamented market stalls were filled with dark green squash and apples. Stacks of potatoes and a oranges from Sicily animated the tables with color. Such a vibrant place, it was hard to imagine a young woman had been slain a few yards from here.

Candy-colored jerseys and scarves were laid out on tables and displayed on racks. A grizzled man dumped mussels onto a large bed of ice. A red-haired beauty busily arranged tubs of flowers.

Vendors' spots were handed down from generation to generation. Outsiders were not welcome. And that went double for agents of the state like the *Arma dei Carabinieri.*

Angelina approached a woman unpacking a box of fruit. Natalia stood aside as her corporal questioned the seller.

"No. *Niente.*" The woman picked up a cherry, sucked the flesh and spit out the pit.

Angelina pushed a photo at her. "Look," she insisted.

The woman ignored her.

"I'm eighty years old."

"I don't follow," Angelina said. "You can't see?"

"You want to live to my age, you mind your business. A gypsy -- right?"

"She was Roma, yes," Angelina said. "A talented musician."

"Where are you from?" she asked.

"Palermo."

"Palermo," she repeated. "I had an uncle from there. The girl – she has nothing to do with us. You'd better get out of here."

A man approached the stall. He wore tight leather pants and a matching jacket with the image of a falcon punched into the front with metal studs. *"Nonna,"* he said. Grandmother.

"What you want?" the woman snapped.

"Nice way to talk to your grandson." He grabbed a handful of cherries and smiled at Angelina, flashing lots of gold teeth.

"I know you, you son of a bitch. You and your father, you're the same. You come when you want something." She crumpled a twenty euro note and threw it at him. "Get out of here."

He picked up the balled money and tried to kiss her. She flinched away. He disappeared into the crowd, sneering.

"Let's try a couple more," Natalia said to Angelina.

They approached a large bald man. In spite of the cold, he was wearing only a t-shirt. His arms were covered in tattoos. Natalia held out the picture of a smiling Drina.

"You remember seeing her?"

"Nah." He picked up a crate of red apples and set them on his table. "That the woman who was found dead here?"

"Yes," Natalia said.

He didn't seem concerned. Natalia wasn't surprised. The prevailing attitude among the public was that the Roma deserved whatever bad luck came their way. The press and television newscasts took a hard line against the Roma too, which suited the police and city authorities. The ugly truth was, no one wanted them around. Recently the director of tourism, reputedly a member of the fascist Nuova Forza Party, brandished a letter on television that he'd gotten from a German tourist who complained of being pestered by impoverished children while trying to enjoy the sights at Pompeii. "In these economic times we cannot afford to be held hostage to these criminals," the tourism director had announced at a noon news conference.

Natalia and Angelina tried several more vendors, all with the same result. No one had seen, no one had heard, no one knew the girl murdered yards from them. Worse, no one cared.

As they came to the end of a market aisle, Angelina said, "Look."

The makeshift alley where Drina's body had been, now filled with flowers and candles in flame.

***

On the trip back to the station they got stopped by a wedding procession. The bride led the way, resplendent in white satin and lace. The fact that it was barely 4 degrees Celsius did nothing to diminish her joy. A photographer and videographer preceded her, along with her bridesmaids. The photographer stopped to pose them in front of the bust of Pucinella as they opened their overcoats to show off their dresses. Natalia accelerated past.

She had a message from Claudio Palumbo on her desk. If it fit with her schedule, he'd pick her up later and bring her to meet with Drina's mother. He suggested they use his car. Law enforcement was not welcome in the Roma camp. There was a good chance someone would take the opportunity to strip off parts or even steal the whole vehicle while they were visiting the poor girl's mother.

Natalia well believed it. Her one previous experience of a Roma encampment was the report of a man stabbing his wife. The mobile call came from somewhere in the gypsy slums in the Poggioreale district. Since situations involving Italian citizens took precedence over any concerning the Roma, individual officers were left to decide how to respond to such summons. Mostly they didn't.

Natalia and a male colleague drove with sirens blaring. In minutes they reached the Via del Riposo cemetery, so crowded its giant mausoleums overhung the wall. They bumped off the main highway onto a dirt road behind the cemetery and soon passed hills of rotting garbage in the city dump until they came upon an opening that led through to a shanty town.

Cooking fires spiraled black smoke, set off against the bizarre smoldering background. Dante instantly came to mind. A young man in a jumpsuit appeared in the entrance to a hovel. He pulled out an ear bud and waved a flat white phone at them. They pulled up and got out. Scrawny dogs eyed them as the residents appeared: gaunt women, scruffy men, small children clinging to their mothers, all with that same hostile expression in their eyes. Before she and the sergeant had gone fifteen feet, a stocky man approached, a village elder from the look of him.

Natalia said, "*Buon Giorno.*"

He didn't answer. The men around him closed ranks.

"We need to talk," Natalia said.

She and the old man stood away from the others. She explained someone had called about a stabbing. He said nothing. "Is everything all right here?" she inquired. "Does anyone speak Italian?" she said to the crowd growing behind him as he remained silent.

A withered woman approached and said something to the Carabinieri sergeant accompanying Natalia.

"What did she say, Sergeant?" Natalia asked.

"I don't know." He put a hand on his holster. "But I get the strong impression she wants us gone. They all do."

"Go," the elderly woman growled in a hoarse voice and shooed them with her aged hand. "Go out!"

Natalia scanned the crowd for any locals trying to signal they needed help. Defiant faces stared back. Natalia and the sergeant backed away, returning cautiously to their car. Whatever had taken place would stay within the confines of the encampment. They would learn nothing by staying.

Retracing their route, Natalia drove around the rear of the camp and exited. The Roma shanty town receded in the rearview mirrors. A hundred yards farther on, a man on a tractor ploughed a lush green field bordered by flowers and abutting a car dealership. He could have been toiling on another planet. Reaching the highway, they headed home. The memory of that day made her apprehensive about paying another visit to the Roma.

"Captain," Angelina said, then a second time. "Captain."

"What?"

"Mr. Palumbo is waiting downstairs."

"Thanks," Natalia said, and got her things.

A cold rain flooded the street. The lawyer sprang open a large umbrella as she exited the building in civilian clothes but under a Carabinieri slicker. He escorted her to his car, a silver Ferrari, its windows tinted to shield against glare and perhaps prying eyes as well.

His practice must be doing well, Natalia thought as she slid onto the buttery leather. He quickly went around to the driver's side and got behind the wheel. As they pulled out, the rain intensified and fell in icy sheets. The wipers flashed back and forth across the windshield. At the touch of a button the car flooded with music.

"This was the only thing we disagreed about -- Drina and I. She insisted Bach was the most romantic composer. He is wonderful of course. But I insisted it was Shubert."

They moved rapidly through traffic despite the weather. The Ferrari held the road well.

The port of Torre Annunziata sat at the foot of Mount Vesuvius. To the north of the pretty seaside town was Annunziata Nord, a decades old temporary Roma community. It had existed for over thirty years but she'd never been to it or ever seen it. After the 1984 earthquake, local residents fled the area, and the government allowed the Roma to move into some abandoned brick shells.

"That's one of my next projects," Claudio Palumbo announced as they left the highway and rumbled through several potholes. "The mayor insists the Roma don't pay taxes so they're not entitled to a decent road or any signage. I told him the Camorra never pays a cent in taxes, yet they are provided with roads and electricity and anything else they desire."

"What did he say to that?" Natalia said.

"Not much. You know you are nothing when the mayor doesn't even bother to intimate he might entertain a bribe. The Africans have a shitty life for sure, but at least Neapolitans will rent them a room and they can sit in a café, enjoy a pizza without being chased away. They give the Camorra their *pezzo* cut and are left alone, free to sell their knock-offs on the street. The *camorristas* even provide transportation for their African workers. No buses even service our community."

"You seem to think Africans have it better than the gypsies," she said.

"For sure. Plus they have roots, a country. They belong somewhere."

The Ferrari eased around the carcass of a Fiat Punto.

The Roma had done their best with not much. Some brick shells were finished properly with mortar and stucco, others with tarpaper and cardboard. More recent shelters had been erected from plywood, discarded pallets and roofs improvised from corrugated metal and tarps. Annunziata

Nord could only be described as grim. Scrap metal lay everywhere, scavenged from discarded industrial and construction waste: piping, wire, rolls of home insulation that looked like bedding. Car batteries were strewn about, lots of liquor bottles, used mattresses, rusted bicycles, old doors, sagging couches, broiling pans. No signs of running water or electricity in the shanty area, only open sewers and hard packed dirt. It was hard for Natalia to imagine any music coming from this place, let alone Bach and Schubert. Somewhere, a generator hummed.

There were impoverished sections in and around Naples but all were brightened in small ways -- pots of geraniums on rusted balconies, colored underwear fluttering on clothes lines. From the most humble shelter, Mario Lanza's voice might suddenly burst forth singing an aria. There was not one dab of color here, other than a maroon car sitting on cement blocks. Surely, living in a landscape of such despair and destitution would dampen the soul of anyone. How could Drina's talent have been nurtured in this place?

They pulled up near a tidy yard in front of a small brick house with a front door that had once been yellow.

"I should have warned you about the mud," Claudio cautioned and got out. "I'll come around."

He opened her door and held the umbrella overhead. She stepped across an oily puddle and an empty metal box. A collection of ragged young boys surrounded them. Natalia gripped her shoulder bag.

"It's okay," Claudio Palumbo said as the tiniest stuck out his tongue at Natalia. He was cute, with his freckled face and wild hair. Natalia attempted a smile. He flicked a V with his fingers, signaling *Vaffanculo*. Fuck off.

Palumbo admonished him. The boy spat and ran away. The oldest stood his ground and took a swig from a bottle of Peronie.

"You know what he's drinking?" Claudio asked.

"Beer?"

"Moonshine, ninety proof. Guaranteed to rot your brain and liver. These gentlemen will watch my car," he explained, "not that I'm worried. It gives them something to do to make some money, besides picking pockets."

Natalia scanned the drab surroundings.

"Grim, isn't it?" Claudio Palumbo said. "They are almost proud of it. We have a saying: *I do not wish to live like a baptized person. I wish to live like a dog in the woods.*"

"How do you say hello in Romani?"

"*Koshto divvus.*"

Claudio pushed open a wooden gate and they stepped into the yard in front of Drina's house. A few tufts of grass grew up out of a plastic tricycle lying on its side.

"My aunt's name is Zorka but don't use it. Adults aren't addressed by name."

"How do you address her?" Natalia said.

"I say, 'My Aunt, how are you?' Like that."

The steps up to the door were made of concrete blocks. A crude plastic awning hung over the porch. A rose bush grew thorns, its only creamy blossom splayed open. Claudio closed his umbrella and rested it upright on the porch. He opened the front door without knocking and called out something in Romani.

"Come." He urged Natalia forward. "It's alright."

The interior was a pleasant surprise. The small kitchen area had all modern appliances and a cheery window with a gingham curtain. A bright crimson cloth covered the lone table. In the middle of it, a small carving of Jesus leaned against a crystal sugar bowl.

"Come," Claudio took her arm and guided her into the living room part. A deep blue carpet covered a large portion of the concrete floor. The furniture was basic but not cheap: an overstuffed couch occupied by a large woman; beside her, a man in a beige recliner. He had an elaborate mustache and a cigar clamped in his teeth. His green military field jacket contrasted filthy, striped pajama bottoms.

The woman had to be Drina's mother but her father was long dead. So who was the eccentric looking male flicking ash on the floor? The man had massive, grimy hands. One of his pinkie nails was curved and long, like a claw. He stood and said something angry to Claudio, who responded at length.

"He'll behave," Claudio said to her, and ushered Natalia further into the living room. "I told him you needed to talk with Drina's mother or the place could wind up swarming with cops."

The man dropped back into the recliner.

"Let me talk to her before I introduce you," Claudio said, "She's not used to outsiders."

He brought a chair over for Natalia and she sat. The room was stifling: a large electric heater was running full out. The windows, she noticed, were sealed shut. Claudio Palumbo knelt on one knee and took his aunt's hand as he whispered something in Romani. She had on a pair of black silk slippers, a long flowered skirt and a bulky red sweater. A dark shawl draped her head. It seemed the only sign of mourning. The woman leaned past him and addressed Natalia in Romani.

"She's thanking your legs for carrying you here," Claudio said.

"*Koshto divvus*," Natalia said.

"*Sarshin*," the woman replied, and warmly added something. "She wants to know if you'd like a drink of vodka."

"Tell her thank you, but I'm not permitted to drink when I'm on duty. Please extend her my heartfelt sympathies for her great loss."

Claudio did, at some length. When he finished, Natalia said, "Would you ask if I may see her daughter's room?"

Claudio translated. The woman hauled herself up and Natalia followed. She led the way to a small, sparse room barely walled off by plywood and a cloth curtain over the empty doorway. An Indian cotton spread covered the narrow bed and a small trunk lay open on the floor, skirts and blouses neatly folded inside. A disc player occupied the space beside it. Near the window, a stand overflowed with sheet music. A pink and green scarf was casually draped over it. Natalia rifled through the paper: Bach and some early liturgical pieces, composers unknown.

A violet occupied the window sill. The walls were bare except for a cross and a faded poster of Saint Patrick, depicted as a curly haired man with dark eyes and a thick beard. He wore green vestments and red shoes, and a red crown topped with a gold cross studded with jewels. Natalia remembered he had traveled with missionary caravans. A wanderer. No wonder Roma identified with him.

Was Drina a practicing Catholic, she wondered, or just observing customs?

The portrait of a dark skinned Saint Sarah hung on the facing wall. Claudio slipped into the room behind her.

"Ah," he said, "Saint Sarah – Egyptian maid of Jesus' aunt."

"Yes," Natalia said. "And Saint Patrick over there. Was Drina religious?"

"Not especially. We cover our bases as you may or may not know Drina," he whispered. "Officer Monte, I'm sorry, I can't stay in here."

The possessions of the dead had a way of triggering memories − returning the departed to life − at least in the mind's eye. Natalia could imagine Drina striding into the day, pink and green scarf fluttering. No more.

A straw basket on a makeshift bureau held rings and shiny bracelets and a postcard she'd bought and written to her mother from France but never sent. Perhaps because it required a street address. A couple of photographs were propped up against the mirror. In one, a smiling Drina held aloft her violin like a trophy. The Eiffel Tower loomed behind her. The other snapshot, taken years earlier, showed her as a girl of ten in a pink organza dress. It had a cummerbund embroidered with roses. Beside her, stood her Uncle Claudio in cap and gown, the royal blue velvet cape indicating he had graduated with high honors.

A stack of books was piled on the floor next to the bed. A biography of Paganini, the famous violinist from Genoa. An expensive picture book heavily illustrated with images of Stradivarius violins. Perhaps a gift from her lawyer uncle or her music teacher. Natalia sat on the bed and went through the images. Of the famed instruments, only 650 remained in existence, each valued from a few million euros to fifteen million. As Natalia knew from her once upon a time musician boyfriend, the most expensive instruments in existence. Lucky were those few fortunate enough to possess one.

He'd told her that the lay audience couldn't tell the difference between music produced on a fine violin or the same music played on a Strad. But to the musician, he claimed, the difference was amazing. The girl was a dreamer, Natalia concluded, and returned to the living room and Claudio Palumbo.

"Please, tell your aunt again," Natalia said to him, "that I'm sorry for the loss of her magnificent daughter."

Claudio translated and the mother started to cry. The man in the recliner shifted uncomfortably. He muttered something and spat. A gob of yellow phlegm landed near Natalia's feet.

Claudio muttered a warning and turned to Natalia. "Please accept my apologies. He's not been house broken or civilized." He said something more in Roman that made the man bristle.

Natalia estimated Claudio Palumbo was ten or fifteen years older than his talented cousin. She was close to Natalia's age or even younger. Which meant that Drina's mother must have had her daughter when she was a teenager. Yet she looked old enough to be her child's grandmother. There was no sign of the ethereal beauty that had been her daughter in this worn and grieving woman.

"Would you ask her the last time her daughter came here?" Natalia asked.

Claudio repeated the question. Drina's mother shot a look at the glowering man who rocked forward in the recliner. For a moment, Natalia wasn't certain she was going to answer, but she pressed her hands to her face and sat up, said a few words and started to weep again.

"This isn't easy for her," Claudio said.

"Tell her I appreciate her talking to us."

Claudio again translated and she gave Natalia a weak smile.

"She says her child was here last week, on Tuesday."

"Is she sure?" Natalia asked.

"She's sure."

"Could you ask if she seemed upset in any way? Afraid?"

The mother seemed agitated. She said a few words, then stopped.

"What?" Natalia said. "What did she say?"

Claudio dropped his voice. "A week before Drina was killed, my aunt dreamed of ravens. When she told Drina she had dreamt this warning, her daughter laughed at her and said she wasn't to believe such omens."

"What do ravens foreshadow?" Natalia said.

"Death."

"What else was she saying?"

"She told me to take you out of here. That *gadje* like you bring bad luck." Claudio pointed back at Gregor with his eyes, and whispered, "That was said for his benefit. She wants to cooperate."

"Thank her for me."

Natalia stood. Pointedly ignoring the crude man, Claudio took an envelope out of his breast pocket and laid it on his aunt's lap. The man took a hand rolled cigarette from a case and struck a match on the concrete floor.

Natalia and Claudio said goodbye and left. They lingered on the tiny porch. Rain clattered onto the plastic awning and splattered the muddy puddles. The lawyer's hair, Natalia noticed, was curled tight in the humidity. Such an appealing man, she thought.

"There's no evidence linking Nuzi with his sister's death," she said. "At this point he's not a suspect."

"I appreciate your telling me. I'd like him to stay with me for a few more days until she's buried. He's having a tough time – blames himself for not getting to her sooner. Thinks maybe she could have been saved. Do you mind if I smoke?" Claudio took a pack out of his raincoat pocket.

"No, it's fine."

"I don't smoke as a rule. Only when I visit here."

"Who was that man with your aunt?" Natalia said.

"Gregor. A camp leader. You can tell he's important from his fat and all the gold around his neck and in his mouth."

"Is he a relative?"

"He took Zorka and her children under his wing when they moved here after the fire at their camp. He's not all bad, appearances to the contrary. He fancies himself Nuzi's and Drina's uncle. He and his wife have one child – a boy. He thinks his wife wasn't able to give him more children. He doesn't know she had an abortion every time she got pregnant and ended the last two pregnancies herself with a pill."

"That's horrible."

"Yes it is. Gregor doted on Drina and she loved him. She had no father and he was kind to her. She reciprocated by being the best child earner in the community."

"Doing what?"

"What do you think?" Claudio lit a fresh cigarette. "Begging when she was young. When she got old enough – picking pockets and knapsacks, pilfering tips from outdoor cafes, swiping bills at automated cash machines. Zorka didn't like it but what could she do? She owed him so much for rescuing her and her kids after her husband and son died. I ruined everything."

"How?"

"I got her into grade school. She quickly learned to read and there was no turning back. Gregor knew it.

"He exploited her as a child."

"Not in the eyes of the Romani. It's complicated. Whatever good there is in him, she was the beneficiary. He bought her beautiful clothes that made others jealous and indulged her at every opportunity. What did she need to go to school for? She was going to be a gypsy wife, marry his son in fact, be his daughter-in-law, mother of his grandchildren. Her destiny was to make babies and prepare food, take care of her husband. When I prevailed, he was furious. He agitated to have me banned. But I'd helped too many people. It didn't happen."

"Who is his son?" Natalia asked, as she fumbled for her notebook.

"He's called Mario. But you don't have to write it down. He was paroled and shipped to Bucharest a couple of years ago by Immigration. If he sets foot on Italian soil, they'll throw him in prison again."

"Again?"

"He and Nuzi got caught setting fires during the city's garbage strike. The authorities wanted to deport Nuzi too. Just put him on a plane and send him away. Imagine, he was born here, has never been to Romania, doesn't speak the language. He was let out of Poggio Reale and put on a bus waiting to take him to the airport. Him and a dozen other deportees. I was able to pull some strings and stop it. Mario wasn't as fortunate. I tried to intervene but couldn't do anything for him. Although maybe his getting deported was lucky. There was a Roma kid he ran with. An Italian enticed the boy to do for the Camorra. The young man got ambitious and made a private side deal with a supplier. The next time he went to deliver money to his boss, they seized him."

"He's dead?" Natalia asked.

"Worse. They burned him with acid. Wrapped him in a blanket and dumped him in front of the hospital. A doctor friend of mine arranged to airlift him to Rome. He's alive but has no face to speak of."

"Did Mario communicate with Drina after he was hustled back to Romania"

"That I couldn't tell you. She and I were close but we didn't share everything."

"Did he expect to marry Drina at some point?"

"Perhaps. It's unlikely he still holds out hope, but who knows."

"Did he presume the marriage would take place eventually?"

"I don't think he ever gave up on the idea. He wanted to send Drina to Romania to join his son. He thought she'd come to her senses if she went. Can you imagine? Bad enough she had to grow up here. There was no way she was going to marry into this life, be a *boria*, stuck for good."

"*Boria*?" Natalia took out her pen.

"A Roma bride. You know, married at thirteen and bearing a child every year thereafter.

"Could Drina still have been doing work for Gregor?"

"Now? Absolutely not. She was way too old for that life anyway. It ends at fourteen when a kid loses legal immunity as a minor. She stopped at ten when she enrolled in school."

A sophisticated man, Natalia thought, this Claudio Palumbo, but in some ways naïve. Or maybe he just had a blind spot where his niece was concerned. Natalia's years as a *Carabiniere* had certainly exposed her to duplicity. Divided loyalties often came with a cost, as she herself well knew.

"Everyone here was shocked by Drina's attitude," Claudio said, breaking into Natalia's thoughts. "To spurn Gregor's plans for her, a man of such means. No one could fathom it."

"Means?" Natalia said.

"I suppose you wouldn't ever guess looking at him, Gregor is well off."

"How is that?"

"He toyed with engines all through his youth, developed into a genius of a mechanic. He scours junkyards for bodies, wrecked engines, chassis, transmissions, and resurrects fantastic cars from the scrap, from nothing. The scrap dealers call him Doctor Frankenstein. By the time he finishes restoring a car, he has orders waiting. His son Mario worked with him before he got himself expelled from Italy."

"Gregor appears to have a temper."

"He never laid a finger on Drina, I can assure you. He loved her like a daughter."

"How did Drina become such a virtuoso?"

"She's played the violin since she could walk. At nine she was on her way to becoming concert material. Gregor didn't like that either and tried to interfere. I threatened him about some of his activities and he backed down."

"Where did she study?"

"At first with her grandmother. Drina played from the moment she could hold a baby violin. Her people were harpists going back centuries. Zorka used to play at weddings and celebrations. This was before the fire her husband died in. Her harps and violin burned too. I told her I'd replace them but she declined. Said she was content to sit and smoke her pipe and listen to Drina."

"Did she want Drina to come back to the life here?"

"She wanted her daughter to succeed, to be free to have what she never would. Zorka couldn't express that publicly, but I knew. She idolized the great Papusza."

"The Doll," Natalia said.

"You know of her?"

"Your most celebrated singer, yes."

"She taught herself to read," Claudio said, "wrote poetry, songs, many of them about gypsy life, and performed all over Europe. She got taken up by the *gadje*."

"She became famous," Natalia recalled, "toured and traveled all over Europe."

"She was condemned as *mahrine* -- unclean -- and shunned by Roma. She died alone, heartbroken." He glanced at her. "It's what made me fear for Drina. Are you married?" he said.

Caught off guard, Natalia colored. "No."

"Sorry. I didn't mean to intrude. It's hard to be married if you have a demanding career, I know. I haven't been able to manage it. My cousin, she wanted to experience the world, but most especially she wanted music. She felt it her destiny."

"Was either her brother Nuzi or her suitor Mario involved with the Camorra, beyond setting garbage fires for them when their haulers went on strike?"

"Nuzi, never. Mario? Probably."

"Trafficking drugs?"

"That would be pretty serious. I don't know. I didn't have much contact with him."

"Don't know or don't want to say?"

He remained silent.

"Signor Palumbo, if you want us to find out who killed your cousin …"

A rain drop struck his cigarette and put it out. "It's not relevant to this case."

"You can't know that, unless you know who killed Drina."

"I don't know who or even why."

"You need to be truthful with me," she said, staring him down, "otherwise I'm going to wonder what you're hiding."

"You're right. Sorry. I haven't lived as a Roma for many years. Still, it conditions you."

"I understand. Of my two oldest and best friends, one is Camorra, born and bred. It is also a closed society full of secrets and ritual."

"Did you ever want to join," he said, "be Camorra yourself?"

"Sure."

Palumbo looked at her skeptically. "Seriously?"

"Yeah, when I was a kid. Whenever the heads of clans went to prison or were killed, their women took over. I wanted to be like them, have the clothes, the money, the freedom. The glamor. That's all I saw. Until one day I had to step over Anna Chimenti's body parts in order to get to school. They'd planted a bomb in her car. You couldn't identify any part of her exactly, except a pair of high heeled pink boots in the next block. Her bloody feet were still in them."

Claudio Palumbo tossed away his wet cigarette. "I like you, Captain Monte."

Natalia was taken aback. "I'm… I'll need a photograph of Mario."

"I'm sure Nuzi will have one."

"Just one more question…"

"As many as you like," he looked directly at her.

"I was wondering why your Drina had a poster of St. Patrick on her wall. . . I figured it was because he was a wanderer."

"The snakes." Claudio Palumbo said.

"He chased the snakes from Ireland," Natalia said. "That I knew. I don't understand the connection."

"We have a phobia about snakes. It's a cultural thing. They are considered unclean because they consume other animals' skins, like rats, and shed their own. They shed their skin eat the skin of others. In fact we consider it bad luck to say the word out loud."

"I'd never heard that."

"There are many such beliefs. Especially about animals. Those dogs?" He pointed to a huddle of boney creatures outside his aunt's gate. "No one here would consider taking animals inside, into their families. Roma will feed them scraps but that's about it. They are *rikono*. How can I explain? You share the world with them, you have a relationship with them but not like you would with pets."

"So domestic pets they see as a luxury?" Natalia said.

"Yes. And obligation. We barely fed ourselves for centuries. Even now. When I was a boy, I was lucky if I got a cup of watery soup for dinner with an occasional scrap of fat floating in it. Hunger doesn't do much to engender compassion or attachment to other creatures."

"Deprivation will do that," she agreed.

"Things are relatively better now but Roma still won't let a cat or dog inside their homes. You know what Gandhi said about a people that doesn't look after its animals?"

"That they are not a civil society," Natalia responded.

"You knew," he said, impressed.

"My friend Pino made a point of it once."

As they left the porch, a woman hurried past, dripping wet, carrying several heavy grocery bags. Green spikes of onions stuck out of one.

"Maria?" Claudio called out. The woman kept walking. "Nuzi's wife," he explained as she hurried on.

Natalia stared after her. "You didn't mention Nuzi is married. Why didn't she speak to you?"

"Because I'm with a *gadje*." He opened the umbrella and led the way toward the car. "Sorry about the mud."

"These shoes are old," Natalia said, "it doesn't matter. What about yours?" She indicated his expensive patent leather boots.

"I have several pairs. We Roma make a fetish of our footwear. A gypsy will buy shoes before food, or nick them."

"Nuzi and his wife, they live with your aunt?"

"Next door," he indicated a small concrete shed. "She and Nuzi have two kids."

"He's a child himself," said Natalia.

"So is she. He was a father at fourteen."

As they approached the car, the seated boys got up from their crates parked under their tree, into which they'd thrown cardboard slabs and a rubber exercise mat draped with a plastic sheet, improvising a shelter from the downpour. They looked like wild things, drenched up to their knees, beautiful but scrawny and very unkempt. Natalia's grandmother would have scrubbed them and fattened them up in no time. But what her *nonna* thought about gypsies, Natalia had no idea, except that she had raised Natalia's father and he was the most tolerant and gentle person ever.

Claudio Palumbo handed them a few euros and gave the smallest a hug.

"That was me, once upon a time," he said as they settled into the car. "I do what little I can, but I'm afraid they'll waste away in this place. Many of their mothers want them to get an education, go to school. The fathers forbid it. Nowadays the bureaucrats discourage enrolling them and block their parents from obtaining citizenship."

"That can't be legal," Natalia said.

"It isn't. But as you know, the law requires everyone to have a legal residence – an address. As they'd prefer for all of us to go back to where we came from, they are happy for

Roma to live like squatters, without fixed addresses or even street numbers. That way they can expel as many of us as they want when they want. Or knock down the makeshift housing at will."

"Even yours?" I have a bank account, a tony address. There isn't much they could do to me. Gypsies don't believe in keeping their money in *gadje* institutions like banks. They don't trust them. I'm an exception, obviously. Suspicion keeps Roma on the margins. It's a vicious circle, really. They dropped out of society a thousand years ago and have remained as outcasts."

When he started the engine the ring leader of the boys stepped back under the makeshift shelter suspended from the tree. Palumbo backed out, watching them in the rear view mirror, and shifted into forward gear.

"I'll talk to Social Services," Natalia said as they bumped over the muddy track they had arrived on.

"Don't bother. I've approached their parents endlessly about the importance of schooling. The women say yes, maybe. The men say absolutely not. It breaks my heart. Those boys back there? They don't even know how to read a clock, much less a book. Besides, schools don't want them."

Natalia glanced at her escort. It was hard to see the handsome, self-assured man in those lost boys. The rain fell harder. The windshield wipers thrummed. A group of Roma trudged past, going the other way, toward home. Claudio Palumbo slowed so as not to splash them and tapped the console. Instantly, a Bach cantata enveloped them. Such a charming man – it seemed to come effortlessly to him.

"She worshipped Bach," Claudio said. "Do you know the gypsy connection?"

Natalia shook her head.

"Wilhelm Freiderich, Johann's eldest, was the organist at a church in La Halle. He ran away to follow a band of gypsies." He glanced at her. "Romantic, no?"

Natalia avoided his gaze. Was Claudio Palumbo flirting with her?

"Your cousin," she said, "had an interesting assortment of books."

"I'm not surprised. She loved to read."

"She was at your law school graduation. She had the photo on her dresser."

"Yes," he said. "Such a happy day. It seems like a million years ago."

"What is the significance of Saint Sarah? Jesus's maid, you said?"

"Why do you ask?" he seemed surprised.

"I need to understand the victim if I am going to find out who killed her."

"Of course. Sarah begged alms like a gypsy. She's also Kali, the Roma goddess of fate."

"I see," Natalia said. "More layers of secrets."

"We are raised to believe in portents and signs. Babies are swaddled in red, smeared with foul things."

"To prevent the evil eye," Natalia said.

"Exactly. Our thinking is stuck somewhere in the Middle Ages. That's why I begged her to finish school, to go to a conservatory for her music."

"Was Drina superstitious?"

"No more than you or I."

"She resisted your advice to finish school – why?"

"She wanted no part of a *gadje* institution. It was incredibly frustrating. She was so smart and she liked nice things, yet wouldn't bend an inch to do the thing required to get them. At sixteen she went back to the streets to play her music for coins. Now I'm getting calls every hour from record companies trying to get a hold of her taped performances. They don't care about the quality, their technology can fix that. When she was alive, no one was interested. Dead, she's about to become famous. It's so strange."

"It would be nice to have her work well recorded," Natalia said. "Permanent."

"You're right." He swerved to avoid a puddle, edged to the side of the road and stopped. "Sometimes I wonder if her musical gift was a curse. If she hadn't been so gifted she might not have gone on with her academic studies and gone back to the Roma instead to be a teen bride. But she'd still be alive."

"You were close to your cousin," Natalia said.

"We were."

"You saw each other regularly?"

"Every week. We talked on the phone every day."

"You had no idea she was in any kind of trouble?"

"No."

"Was she depressed recently?" Natalia asked.

"On the contrary. She seemed buoyant — happier than I've ever known her."

"Perhaps a romance made her happy."

"Could be. We didn't discuss our private lives."

"And yet you spoke nearly every day?"

"What are you implying?"

"I'm not — not anything. It's just curious how close you were, but you didn't share important information."

He started the engine and sped up as they eased onto the service road. Natalia inhaled the acrid smell of rubbish smoldering in the rain.

"Our survival depends on secrecy," he said.

"To keep secrets from outsiders — I get that. But you were her flesh and blood uncle. Her beloved benefactor."

"Captain, can I buy you breakfast, or lunch maybe?" Claudio Palumbo said, glancing at his wristwatch.

"I would like that but duty requires me to get back to the station."

"Perhaps another time," he said.

"I will look forward to it."

In seconds, the hovels of Annunziata were a mirage. The car speeded up into the road traffic. Trucks roared by and Naples loomed in the distance.

Chapter 8

He dropped Natalia at the tiny café she directed him to near her *Carabinieri* station. She needed the caffeine and a moment to think, undistracted by the demands that awaited her at Casanova. The rain had stopped but the wind blowing inland was cold. A pair of Germans sat at an outside table with their coffees, smoking. She sat on a high stool in the window, opened a sugar packet and poured it into the foam of her cappuccino. The first sip immediately cleared her head.

Drina had her mother's moral support and her brother's, and that of Claudio. But had her defiance of Roma custom dishonored or angered somebody enough to take her life? Someone like Gregor, a nasty specimen. Unlike Nuzi, he appeared to have the strength and seemed hard enough to have done it. According to Claudio, Gregor only left the compound to trawl for auto parts. Easy enough for him to divert from his salvaging routine unnoticed. Drina had deeply hurt and angered him with her rebellion. Of that there was little doubt. But she'd been living an independent existence for years. Why would he turn on her now? Had Drina been seen with her *gadje* boyfriend or had she rejected an arranged marriage a second time? Had something slighted Gregor again – something that demanded a cleansing vengeance? Had his son snuck back into the country and found her with another man?

Perhaps Gregor had himself harbored a deep-seated affection for the girl he'd known since she was little. Did he hope to marry her off to his son to bring her even closer to himself, make her a part of his family?

Annunziata was a small closed world like the one Natalia had grown up in. Surely everyone knew everyone's business in both. For the people on top and in charge that was perfect. Vigilance and mistrust of the outside impeded change and blocked interference, protecting the status quo and, thus, their power. Those who rejected the group were shunned as traitors. Was Drina's defection seen as a betrayal sufficient to call down bloody retribution?

Across from the cafe a funeral cortege was getting under way. Natalia watched as they slid the coffin off the metal rack mounted in the back of the black van and into a polished hearse. The family standing nearby looked poor, but they would use up all their savings if needed and bury their loved one in lavish style. Death and its attendant symbols were endemic to Neapolitans. The Roman Church was preoccupied with death, the faithful reminded daily of their approaching demise as they recited their rosaries over and over: *"... pray for us sinners, now and at the hour of our death."*

The Greeks had named Mount Vesuvius. It meant "The Gates of Hell." Natalia once asked Sister Benedicta how the poor victims at Pompeii could have made the passage to heaven if they had so clearly entered hell first. The good sister explained it was the spirit that did the traveling – not the flesh. Natalia wasn't convinced.

The mourners getting into the lined up limousines appeared undernourished, their clothing mismatched and cloth coats tattered from too many winters. A young girl cradled an infant. The baby started to shriek. If things

104

didn't get better soon, more would go hungry. Natalia knew families where adults ate only one real meal a day.

Gathering her things, she went up to the station. Her shift had left for the day. The next was already on duty except for Angelina, still at her desk, working. Natalia had sent her to the murder scene again to see if the photograph of Drina registered with anyone living in the vicinity of the killing. No one had come forward so far, and in all likelihood wouldn't, but sometimes confronted with a morgue picture, people were moved to talk.

"What did you get?" Natalia asked.

"Either they didn't want to open their doors, or else they didn't understand why I couldn't spend the afternoon chatting with them, listening to complaints about their neighbors and the government. If it seemed serious, I encouraged them to take their complaint to the *Questura*. But mostly the older ones just wanted company."

"So nothing?" Natalia said.

"There was one." She flipped open her notebook. "A Signora Muraio. The morning Drina was killed she puts a coat on and goes out onto her third floor balcony for a smoke. It overlooks the market. Says two men hurried through the crowd in the plaza right after a young woman rushed by with what looked like an infant in her arms. The child she saw was actually a bundle. She didn't see the woman's face. The men looked up and she says she saw their faces."

"What do you think?" Natalia said.

"The time fits. Though the guys could have been rushing to an appointment, running for a train."

"She credible?" Natalia said.

"I'd say yes."

"Three floors up and what? Fifty meters away? How well could she see what they looked like at that angle and distance, and all those shelter tarps and obstructions in the market interrupting her view?"

"She said one was in his thirties, the other big and older and wearing a hat. They weren't close, so you're right to question her veracity. But something must have made her remember them."

"Damn," Natalia said. "We can't have her standing three stories above a parade of suspects. You think she's telling the truth?"

"About seeing the guys? Yeah. That part's true. But, hell, they could've been joggers for all we know."

"Would she come in and make an ID?"

"Maybe, when we somebody for her to look at."

"How old is she?"

"Recently turned fifty. Claims her eyesight is good. She's never worn glasses a day in her life. But you know how it is. The mind plays tricks. The tall man in the cap turns out to be five feet tall, the bald man has a pony tail."

"She's all we have at this point."

"No disrespect, Captain, but aren't we jumping the gun here? Shouldn't we find the killer or killers before we worry about establishing their guilt?"

"I suppose."

"Excuse me, boss. Are you okay?"

"Yes, why? What's wrong?"

"You're a little distracted. Should I bring you back something?"

"No, thanks. But you're not going for a break, Corporal. You're going home."

"And what about you? You should too, Captain."

"I've got one more stop."

***

"Signor Grazelli?"

He had pale watery eyes, a thick mustache and a full head of grey hair. His charcoal grey pants had seen better days, and the maroon sweater was patched at the elbows.

"Yes, I am he." Drina's music teacher received her with a warm smile.

Natalia held up her ID. "Captain Monte, Carabiniere. May I come in?"

He pulled up a pair of bifocals that hung from a cord around his neck, and used them like a magnifying glass to study her identification. "Captain Monte, come in, come in."

The music teacher lived in a modest flat. A tall bookcase loomed over the living room. A large clock sat on a walnut table. A heavy cabinet, fussy embroidered couch and matching chair filled out the room. Grandfather furniture, as Lola would have called it. Everything a little dusty and cluttered. A cat snoozed on the chair. As Natalia approached, the fluffy white creature stretched and opened its yellow eyes.

A baby grand piano by the window had sheet music stacked neatly on the bench in front of it. The faded Oriental rug beneath must have once been quite elegant.

"May I sit?" Natalia asked.

"Please. Forgive my manners. Would you like coffee, a piece of plum cake? My wife is an excellent baker."

"No, thank you."

"You've come about Drina no doubt."

"I believe she was your student."

"Yes, she was." He looked away. "So hard to say was."

"I'd like to ask you a few questions, if you don't mind."

"Anything if it will help."

"How did you come to be her teacher?"

"Serendipity. I heard her in passing. A churchyard near the port. She was thirteen. No formal training whatsoever and playing an inferior instrument. Extraordinary musicianship."

"How long was she your student?"

"A little over six years. It stopped a few months ago."

"Was there a problem?"

"I had no more to teach her. She'd come at times for advice about a particular piece but not for regular sessions."

"Did she ever talk about her personal life," Natalia said, "problems with family, a boyfriend, that sort of thing?"

"No. Never."

"According to her brother, you didn't charge her for lessons."

He laughed. "The child had no money, no funds from her family for study. Just what she earned on the street, perhaps a bit from her cousin, Mr. Palumbo. I considered myself privileged to teach her. My students are of a high caliber, but Drina, she was so beyond the best of them, on a whole other plane."

"Is it correct that her brother offered to pay for her lessons and you refused?"

"Last year, yes. By then I had imparted all I know. When she did come she played more for my pleasure than to learn. I couldn't take his money. We live modestly, as you can see but I have my pension and several students with means to pay."

"Her brother told me that you had given her a violin as a gift. She boasted that is was a Stradivarius. He assumed she was pulling his leg."

"Not a Strad, no. A Gagliano. Valuable to be sure, but nowhere near a Stradivarius. Though in her hands it didn't much matter."

"Is it valuable enough for someone to kill her for it?"

"The violin is missing?" He looked pained.

"The case was found empty."

"Most people wouldn't have a clue as to its worth."

"Which would be?"

"The last appraisal was some years ago. One hundred ten thousand euros, I believe."

"Would another musician have recognized it and known this?"

"Possibly. Another violinist, probably"

"May I ask how you managed to afford the violin?"

"I had it for many years. It was bequeathed to me by a wealthy music patron when I was her age. My career was long and respectable, my play occasionally inspired, but I was no Biondi. I thought her far more worthy of it."

"You loved her." It sounded like an accusation.

He colored. "Of course. How could you not?"

***

Despite the chilly weather, Augie Forchetta and Lucio Madrone were parked on the white plastic seats in front of Luigi's. Natalia had known the gentlemen since she was a toddler. Up until a couple of years ago they sold an assortment of junk at one of the flea markets. Old postcards and watches, chipped plates stamped with images of Vesuvius, rhinestone clips. As a child Natalia loved searching through the mounds of jewelry, now and then finding a genuine treasure. The two had passed the business on to their grandchildren but still kept an eye on things. Rumor had it their table also laundered small-time sums for the Strombetti clan.

Today, the gentlemen had on several layers of sweaters. Two coffees and a plate of *biscotti* rested on a round table between them.

"*Salve*. Hail, Captain," Augie raised his cane to greet her.

"*Salve*, Augie. Lucio"

"Can we buy you a coffee?" Augie started to get up.

"No thank you, gentlemen" Natalia waved him down. "Sit, please. Another time. Maybe when it's a little bit warmer."

"You make corporal yet?" Lucio teased.

"I'm working on it."

"Don't work too hard, Captain," Augie chimed in. "Pretty girl like you, still with the curly hair." The perennial cigar shifted from one corner of his mouth to the other. "We were just talking about our favorite *Carabiniere*, weren't we Lucio?"

Natalia could just imagine the content of their conversation, and she'd bet a hundred euros it wasn't about how a local girl makes good fighting crime. Like the Roma, the Camorra didn't appreciate one of their own going against the group. Maybe she wasn't so far removed from poor Drina in that regard. The gypsy violinist had challenged the norm. Natalia had done the same. Plus she'd sworn an oath that pitted her against the interests of some of these very people she'd grown up with, these two among them.

She'd loved many, like Maria Napolitano who sold candy from her tiny shop and ran a lucrative numbers racket from her kitchen in the back. And Rico Tramante who dispensed free chocolates along with the pieces of fabric he measured and cut for her mother, and dispensed brutal reprisals just as expertly to those who fell behind in their protection payments.

Did Drina present a similar threat to her community? Natalia had never been shunned by her peers, but as a captain of the Carabinieri she certainly wasn't welcome in certain households anymore. There had been bribe attempts and more than a couple of threats. Ironically, her salvation had often come from the very relationships with people she posed a threat to. In her community, as in the Roma's, loyalty ran deep. So far, Natalia had managed to tread a very fine line in observing that code as she went about her detective work, but it was not always possible to know when she had crossed it in someone's eyes.

Natalia bid the two a good evening and continued on toward home. *Salve*, such an archaic greeting. Then again, in truth her city, despite the modern touches, had an ancient heart – the structures themselves, the layers beneath.

In the tiny *basso* next to the bakery, chairs were stacked upside down on the dining room table as they had been in her house when her mother waited for the floor to dry. The mistress of the house, finished with mopping, was dusting an enormous bottle of wine that occupied pride of place on the sideboard. The young Madonna already had several children under foot. Not much different a life from a thirteen year old Roma mother's.

Natalia calculated her remaining child bearing years as she reached her courtyard door.

Chapter 9

Natalia fell asleep reading and awoke in the morning light, on the musty rose couch her grandmother had given her years ago. She shivered. The ancient flat was drafty. She padded to the kitchen in her robe to make a hot cup of coffee. The aroma of fresh grounds cheered her as she filled the filter, and waited for the water to boil.

Sighing, she yawned and selected her ex-boyfriend's number on her mobile. It rang as she trudged to the doors leading out onto her balcony. Scraps of burlap covered Signora Fontini's large flower pots on the verandah across the way. The smaller plants had been moved out of the weather into the warmth of her apartment.

Gino was expert with string instruments, as well as being a fabulous cellist. He could confirm the value of the violin, she hoped, and that it might have figured in the poor girl's death. Though they hadn't spoken in more than half a year, it was not an unusual gap in their communications. The number rang. Gino's rendering of *Canon* by Pachelbel came on, followed by his automated message. The last time they'd seen one another, he'd announced his impending marriage to Marika, a petite Dutch oboist. They were expecting their first child, he said, giving Natalia a shock, followed by a pang of envy and regret.

Natalia and Gino had had more than their share of problems, chief among them that she was not about to traipse after him from Rome to Sidney, Sidney to Tokyo and on, loyally applauding his concerts, managing his career. She did see herself living in his shadow as the celebrated violinist's wife and helpmeet. Still... Lola and Mariel had to remind her that her nostalgia for this past relationship was just that — nostalgia.

No doubt Gino was confident he had traded up. Marika, a fellow musician, was certainly better suited to the nomadic life of the classical soloist. She never reeked of formaldehyde and was as fastidious as her husband. She looked after his performance attire, his complicated schedule, travel arrangements, and his contracts.

Once, when Natalia was still his girlfriend, they'd attended a dinner for the patrons of the Rome Symphony, held in a magnificent hall overlooking the Quirinale. Unlike the chic slim ladies, dressed in black, Natalia felt out of place in her teal skirt, white sweater, her stocky figure and costume jewelry. The hosts were a nice- enough couple. Skilled at social graces, the lady of the house welcomed her warmly. Later, the husband, a surgeon, peppered her with questions about forensic procedure until his wife gently changed the subject.

No, things had worked out as they were meant to, she supposed. Gino had found his mate in Marika, his progeny was on the way, and she was free to pursue her career.

The message machine beeped. Natalia asked Gino to give her a call when convenient. As she snapped the phone closed, she glanced in the mirror. Was she meant to be alone? Was it a matter of fate – karma, as Pino would have said? Did her future remain open or was she too far along the *longo drum.* Angelina had told her the Roma called it that -- the long road traveled with no return.

Natalia laid out her uniform and took a bag of toiletries and her coffee into the bathroom. When she got out of the shower, she found a recorded message on the answering machine from Dr. Francesca Agari to call her at the lab -- immediately. Natalia punched in the number to the morgue and asked for the Medical Examiner.

"Natalia! Thank God."

"What's going on?"

"I can't get them to leave."

"Who?"

"The gypsies. They're camped in the visitors lounge, dozens of them. It's hard to communicate. They're not all that fluent. One man tried to get into the lab. I had to summon an officer."

"Be right there."

Natalia dressed quickly, checked her uniform in the big mirror and rushed downstairs. She cranked up her motor scooter and hurried over.

A strong odor hit her as soon as she went through the swinging doors into the medical examiner's suite – stale clothes and unwashed bodies. Easily two dozen Roma crowded the hall and visitors area. Men stood in clusters, talking, displaying mustaches and gold teeth. Natalia recognized Drina's mother slumped on the one couch. Gregor stood at her side, decked out in a plaid suit and a large tie made out of pearls. He leaned on a walking stick ornamented with silver bands. It would make a nice weapon, Natalia thought as he gave her a foul look.

The men all had bright scarves wrapped around their necks and most wore a head covering. Drina's mother was in a gown embroidered with gold threads, more appropriate for a gala than a mortuary. Jesus gazed down mournfully at her and the assembled from his simple wooden cross on the wall. He looked like he had been there forever. The crucifix certainly wasn't placed there by the pathologist. "My religion is science," Doctor Agari had stated on more than one occasion while poised over a cadaver with her instruments.

As Natalia greeted Drina's mother, Claudio Palumbo appeared, coming in through the double doors.

"Mr. Palumbo," Natalia said, "I didn't think I would have the pleasure again so soon."

"Captain Monte."

"Can you find out what's going on?" she said.

"I should have warned you. They need to wait for the *mulo* to leave her body. It will most likely happen around dawn."

"*Mulo*?"

"Spirit. The timing is crucial. Otherwise … Excuse me a moment."

He went over to his aunt, knelt in front of her and said something. She started to cry. One of the men handed him a piece of fabric. It looked like several lengths of cloth knotted together.

Natalia texted Doctor Agari to let her know she was there with Claudio Palumbo. He pocketed the fabric and rose to talk with two men standing beside the couch.

"Lashi," Natalia heard one of them greet him. They put their arms around one another and went into a huddle.

The door to the inner sanctum opened and the Dr. Agari came out. She'd traded her brown clogs for a pair of green shantung heels and a green silk scarf. Her pristine lab coat sliced the tangerine skirt beneath.

"Quite odorous isn't it?" she said. "My assistant is threatening to quit. They've been here for hours. Her brother says they have some special ritual they must perform. He's been camped here all night with his sister and is settled in for another. Won't leave her until the *mulo* clears out."

"It's something about her spirit leaving the body," Natalia said. "Around dawn."

"You know?" Francesca Agari said.

"I just heard. If it's not done right, her spirit will probably wander unhappily ever after."

The doctor shook her head. "That poor girl's spirit is long gone, *cara.*"

"We have a similar belief," Natalia pointed out.

"I know. I never got that either."

"If I had your job," Natalia said, "I wouldn't want any unhappy ghosts hanging about."

"Right," Francesca Agari laughed. "Is that why you put a broom in front of your door before you sleep?"

"How do you know that?"

"Please," the Medical Examiner said dismissively, "you are such a Neapolitan."

A murmur went through the assembled Roma as information was passed one to the other. Claudio addressed them in a low voice and the assembled quieted to hear him.

"Attorney Palumbo seems to be talking to them about the situation," Natalia said. "He'll explain your conditions."

"Good," she said.

Her assistant peeked out from a door. "Dottore Agari."

"I'll be there in a moment." She adjusted a silver clip that held her hair in an upsweep as Claudio joined them.

"Sorry about all this," he apologized, "we're not supposed to bathe, even comb our hair until the funeral."

Doctor Agari extended her hand, turning on the smile. "Captain Monte was explaining about this ritual vigil of theirs. "Not to worry," she continued, "we are inured to odors here. Thank you so much for taking the time to come. I tried to explain to them that they can't enter the lab. Unfortunately, they don't speak Italian. Please tell

116

them they are welcome out here, though it's highly unusual for anyone to stay this long. I'd prefer they didn't, but if they must, they must."

She gestured at the group crowded into the visitors room, waiting for the girl's soul to continue on alone.

"I thank you," he said. "You are being very tolerant and accommodating, Doctor. We are grateful."

Claudio held up a length of knotted cloth.

"What's this?" Francesca Agari asked.

"*Mulengi Djili*," he said. "We need another favor. We would never allow an outsider to make the coffin This special cloth is used to measure our dead. That's Drako, he does it." He pointed out a young man in a pork pie hat. "At her burial her brother and his mother will receive the cloth. Any problem they have in the future, they can use it to call on the departed for their help."

"A talisman. I understand," Doctor Agari said, with more enthusiasm than necessary. "However, he can't actually touch the body until I release it. He must comply with that."

"I'll tell him."

"And only one person can come in to be with her if they relieve her brother. He's been there many hours without a break. I've lost track how long."

"Thank you for permitting it."

"I'm almost finished. How much time will it take him to build the casket?"

"A few hours. He works quickly."

"I'll try to finish my part as soon as I can. The group is welcome to stay for the rest of the afternoon. Please encourage them to choose two people to remain out here and the rest to go home for the evening. They can come back as early tomorrow as they like. We never close."

"That might work."

"I'll be right back," she said.

As she returned to the inner sanctum, a man entered wearing a yellow scarf and an expensive black overcoat, the lapels raised around his face. He went directly to Drina's mother, kneeled and touched her cheek. It was such a surprise to see him, it took Natalia a moment to recover.

"That man," Natalia said to Claudio, "the one who's talking to your aunt? What is he doing here?"

"Lenny DePretis? He's a client of mine. We've become friendly over time."

"He knew Drina?"

"They'd met."

"He speaks Romani?"

"A few phrases."

Probably handy in dealing with his gypsy drug traffickers, Natalia thought. Lenny DePretis finished his condolences and approached.

"Claudio, I'm so sorry." They shook hands and embraced.

"Thank you for coming, Lenny. This is Captain Monte, the officer leading the investigation."

"Captain Monte," he said.

"Signor DePretis, we meet again."

It was Claudio Palumbo's turn to be surprised. Lenny DePretis held his lawyer's hand in both of his.

"If there's anything I can do," he offered, "anything."

"Thank you."

Lenny DePretis looked Natalia directly in the eye. "Nice to see you again," he said and retreated toward the exit.

"Excuse me a moment." Claudio Palumbo stepped away and approached the coffin maker. They followed DePretis out.

"All in the line of duty — right?" Francesca said to Natalia. "Is he married?"

"Palumbo or Depretis?"

"The lawyer, Claudio."

"No. Neither one of them is married, as a matter of fact."

A siren announced the mortuary van approaching.

"No rest for the weary." Francesca smoothed her hair as Claudio hurried back.

"I just explained the situation to everyone," he said. "They understand. I'll come back later in the day to take Drina's mother home with me. She hasn't eaten or slept. Perhaps she can get some rest before the dawn ritual. She'll stay with me until the burial."

"Poor woman," Francesca said.

"If you have any more problems," Claudio said, "please don't hesitate to call." He handed Francesca his card.

Was he a practiced heartthrob, a Casanova on the prowl, Natalia wondered, or was he genuinely clueless as to his effect on the female population?

The Medical Examiner reached into her pocket and reciprocated with her card. "And if I can ever be of assistance to you."

Just then the doctor's cellphone chimed. She scanned the text.

"Sorry. I've got to run. An old man on the ferry from Capri. Seagulls are feasting on him," she said, with a winning smile and scurried off.

"Quite a job she has," Claudio said, as they left the assembled Roma and exited the building. "May I walk with you?"

"What did the man call you — the carpenter?" Natalia asked.

"Lashi. My Romani name – 'Wild Goose,' a bird that has left the gaggle but yearns to return. The Roma don't take well to someone quitting the tribe. I tried to explain to them why I needed to go. Not because I don't love my culture. I do, and I'd be lying if I said I don't feel homesick at times. But there's no turning back."

"Very Neapolitan," Natalia said.

"Yes. Still, ours is the more primitive culture," he countered. "Half of the men can't read, almost all of the women."

"Where is she going to be buried?"

"Via Riposo. I had to call in favors to get her in. She'll be laid to rest there if her mother agrees. The community doesn't like it, but I refused to have her interred in what passes for a graveyard at Annunziata."

"I would give that more thought," she said. "Reporters from all over are requesting press credentials. The media will be out in force for the funeral. Satellite broadcast vans. Helicopters. Really a circus."

"I see. Press. Damn. How could I have overlooked that?

"To hold a private ceremony in these circumstances, you'll have to keep the plans under wraps. Share the time and place only within the community and a few close friends. Communicate in your language as much as possible. Warn them all against sharing the information with anyone else."

They parted in front of her motor scooter.

"Thank you, again, Captain. Look, I want to thank you for taking an interest, for making all this easier. I'd like to buy you a drink sometime."

"That isn't necessary, Signor Palumbo."

"Please, call me Claudio. I'm not asking out of a sense of obligation."

Natalia thought a moment. "Perhaps when the investigation has been completed."

She started her motor scooter and pulled away. Glancing in the mirror jutting out from the handlebar, she saw him watch her until she turned at the corner. Natalia's phone pinged as she rode. It was her ex-beau.

"Gino. I'm on my way back to the station. Hang on a sec. I'll pull over."

"Same old hectic schedule, eh Nat?"

"It's been crazy, yes. Thanks for calling back. How are you?"

"Excellent. Busy. You know. This is amazing. You're prescient as usual."

"How's that?" she said.

"I was going to call you today. I'm in town for a few days. The quartet is performing twice at the Opera House. We're staying at the Hotel Imperiale."

"You and Marika are here?"

"No. No, she isn't permitted to fly with the baby aboard. She's withdrawn for a bit, temporarily."

"That's too bad," Natalia said.

"Any chance we can get together?"

"As a matter of fact," Natalia said, "I could use your advice on a case. That's why I called."

"And here I was flattering myself. Just kidding. Sure, I'd be glad to help any way I can."

"Great."

"Nat, I have to run. Any chance we might be free for lunch today? At our old place – twelve o'clock?"

"Perfect. See you at noon."

Natalia spent the rest of the morning checking off her growing to-do list. Then made sure her uniform was lint free and its black leather surfaces – shoes, hat brim, belt, and holster – were buffed and shiny.

***

Gino had put on a few pounds and his hair was shorter. An expensive cut – the tousled look. But aside from a little grey at the temples, he hadn't aged all that much. Gino looked … good, actually. Disturbingly so.

He was at their regular table in the quiet corner toward the rear of the room. He stood to kiss her and hold the seat for her, waiting until she was settled before he resumed his own.

"It's nice to see you. I can't believe how long it's been. Time hurries by, doesn't it?"

"That it does."

"I could swear it's going faster as I get older. How are things with your Pino?"

"We're not together anymore."

"Ah. Sorry to hear it," he said but didn't look like he was.

"It's okay. I'm keeping busy with work."

"Same old Natalia."

"Yeah, well. And the baby?"

"Due in two months. Marika's exhausted. I left the sonogram photo at the hotel. Sorry."

"That's too bad," Natalia said.

"So how's your old gang, Lola and Mariel?"

"Mariel's good. She'd dating a bookseller from Milan. Lola's … Lola."

The waiter brought them menus. Gino signaled him to stay. "You having your usual?"

She nodded. "You?"

"Better not. Since Marika got pregnant, I've put on about ten pounds. What doesn't have any calories?"

"Water and lettuce?"

122

"Still with the sense of humor. I miss it."

"That's not what you said when we were together."

"I didn't appreciate it at the time, true."

Natalia closed her menu. "We'd better order."

"What did you want to talk to me about?" he said. "Is there a problem with Lola?"

"Yeah, but you can't help me with that one. No, it's something else. I don't know if you saw it on the news. A street musician was killed in broad daylight. A young woman. A violinist."

"I know. There are clips of her playing all over the channels. Talented girl and so young. What a tragedy. Your case?"

"Yes it is. Her violin is missing. A Gagliano."

He whistled. "A street musician with a Gagliano."

"She was studying with a Signor Graziella. He gave it to her."

"I know him. First class teacher and a formidable solo violinist himself back in the day. You know, our friend Matteo might be able to help. If someone tried to sell it, he may have heard. I have to bring him my bow for a look-see. You have time after lunch for a visit?"

"That would be great."

"How's your meal?"

"The best clams *oreganato* in Naples. Just like always. Yours?"

They gossiped and joked, comfortable and familiar with one another. Two old shoes, Natalia thought. Gino signaled for the bill as they finished. Natalia reached for her wallet.

"Please," Gino waved her away from the check and plunked down a platinum credit card.

They left their favorite restaurant and she ushered him right over to the Alfa Romeo cruiser.

123

"Is this permitted?" Gino said. "An official vehicle?"

"Get in. This is official business you're helping me with."

Matteo buzzed them into the workshop. Talking on the phone, he lit up when he saw them. The place hadn't changed since Natalia had been there last – the antique wooden chairs for visitors, the small library of violin lore scattered on a table. Bows and tools lay everywhere, and strains of Corelli flooded the air.

A cello lay open on the workbench, its heart exposed -- a sound post not much larger than a wood chip.

"Gino!" Matteo hung up and clasped each of them. "Natalia. What a surprise."

They spent a couple of minutes catching up. Gino filled him in on the approaching baby. Matteo caught them up on his wife and sons. Then Gino took out his bow from a cardboard tube.

"It needs your magic touch," he said.

"I'd be honored. It's been a while."

"Too long," Gino said. "Business is good?"

Matteo shrugged. "So-so. Everyone's watching his pocketbook."

"You'd do well in Milan, Matteo. The place is buzzing. Like Cologne."

"No, thank you. For one, the guild would never allow me to open a shop there. And to be truthful, I prefer to suffer here in Napoli."

The guilds still controlled the market, as they had since Caravaggio's time. Wood, always scarce, was the oil of ancient Naples. Back then, the Church controlled the forests surrounding every city, town and village. They controlled the guilds by doling out the precious wood – a certain amount for the furniture makers, so much for the makers of musical instruments and artists' frames. Profits were kept high by undersupplying. The woodworkers reciprocated for this generosity with lavish tithes.

"Natalia wanted to ask you something."

"Shoot," he said as he worked.

"Anyone talk to you about a Gagliano recently?"

"Are we talking about an Antonio or Nicola?"

"I have no idea."

"Papa Nicola's would be worth more – Antonio's, a close second. But Nicola's are harder to come by than a Del'Gesu."

"How much would the lesser Gagliano be worth?" Natalia asked.

"Around a hundred fifty thousand euros at this point. One go missing?"

"Yes. In a case I'm working on."

"They didn't take the one from Capodimonte. That's a Nicola. A beautiful specimen – maple and ebony."

"No," Natalia assured him. "You may have read about the street violinist."

"She had the Gagliano? I don't think there's even a collector with a Gagliano in Naples."

"Unfortunately it was stolen when she was murdered."

"Yeah, I saw on the news. What a tragedy. The kid had real talent."

"If anyone approaches you," Natalia said, "or you hear anything."

She put her card on the bench in front of him.

"To be sure," Matteo said.

"Give the boys my regards." Gino clapped him on the shoulder. "And Tania."

"Will do. If I can pry my brother out of the house, we'll all see you at your concert."

Gino beamed. "That would be terrific. I'll leave tickets at the door."

Natalia and Gino took their leave and walked out onto the Piazza Dante.

Gino said, "I'd like to see you again while I'm here." He held her hand. "What do you think?"

"It's probably not a good idea."

"Come to the concert, okay? We can grab a drink and some tapas at that Spanish place afterwards. If you're worried, Matteo and Tania can chaperone."

"If I can get away. This case…"

"I imagine there's a lot of pressure, given the publicity."

"Just a bit."

Gino hadn't let go of her hand. Like old times, Natalia thought. A flurry of clouds passed overhead, shadowing the square.

"Have time for a walk?" he said.

She nodded and pulled on her gloves. As they turned onto Porta Alba, a young couple rose from a bench beneath a towering cypress tree and hurried away closely entwined.

"They remind me of us," Gino said. "Remember?"

How could she forget? She and Gino had spent countless hours making out under this very tree.

"It's funny," he said. "For years all I wanted was to get out of Naples, and now…"

Getting involved with Gino was tempting, but she needed to be realistic. That period of her life was over and done with. She was lonely, was all. Gino was safe, though not really. He was about to become a father and was likely scared and feeling overwhelmed. Natalia inhaled the cold air, trying to keep her head clear and her resolve strong.

"My papa was right," Gino said. "You were the one who slipped through my fingers."

"How dramatic."

"No, it's true. I thought I wanted … something else."

"Gino, you're married. You have a child on the way."

"I know, Nat. I'm supposed to be content and happy, but I don't enjoy the thought of it. I'm supposed to but I don't."

Natalia looked at her once-intended. He had improved with age, though some spark was missing.

"The second truth is even harder to confess," he said. "I think you know what it is."

She was tempted. Men hadn't exactly been lining up at her door with any regularity, but an affair with Gino would lead to disaster. Stolen moments would never be enough for him. He wanted admiration and pretty constant attention. She stepped into the street and hailed a cab. It screeched to a halt inches from her.

"Get in," she ordered and he did, expecting she'd follow. She swung the door shut instead.

Gino lowered the window. "What are you doing?"

Natalia gave the driver his hotel address and bid Gino goodbye.

"Will I see you?" he said.

"Not this trip."

Natalia tapped twice on the roof of the cab and it sped off.

***

Natalia's mobile phone buzzed as she got in behind the wheel of the Alfa. Lola was calling.

"I'm reminding you about the party tonight at my place," she said. "You're coming."

"Oh, Lola, I don't--"

"Come on, it'll be fun. Em will be there. Or did you forget?"

"Isn't she in Milan with the bookseller?"

"She's flying in to be with her nearest and dearest for the holidays. It'll be special."

The odds were, various law agencies would note a party at Lola's. They would all be there, ear pieces inserted and cameras mounted with telephoto lenses. It hardly mattered if she changed into civilian clothes. The prudent thing would be not to go, as usual. But Natalia resented the idea of missing another event.

***

A maid Natalia had never seen before took her hat at the door. If she was surprised to find a guest on the doorstep in the full uniform of a Carabinieri captain she didn't show it.

The party was in full swing. A mirrored ball spun on the ceiling casting rainbow shards across the room. The music pumped. Business types huddled together. A tall young black man gyrated to the music, his blue hair shaking. Older types in expensive outfits swayed on the margins. All around, people were busy texting and promoting their gorgeous selves.

Lola swooped over. She had on white jeans and a sheer aqua blouse peeled back to show off a modern turquoise and silver necklace.

"You came!" she said, as they hugged. "I'm so happy you're here. We haven't been together at a party in years. Let me get us some wine."

"Where's Mariel?"

"She's landing right about now and coming straight over."

Lola made for the bar and Natalia stepped into the crowd. Lola was back in a flash, balancing two glasses.

"Cheers!" Natalia took a sip of hers and surveyed the scene.

"Fun crowd — right? I bet you meet someone here tonight." She put her glass on a shelf while she dug something out of her tiny purse.

"It's a young crowd," Natalia said, looking around.

"Young is good. It works for me."

Natalia checked her watch. "I'll meet up with you later."

"No way you're leaving."

"I have some serious cases."

"It's Saturday. Who works on Saturday night?" Lola swayed her hips to the music.

"Me, I work Saturdays," Natalia said.

"You just got here, Nat. You are my guest. Besides, you wanted information from Lenny DePretis. About the gypsy thing."

"DePretis, he's here?"

"Yeah."

"Just walk up to him in my uniform and put it to him?"

"Exactly. The guy's divorced and footloose. We got to talking the other day and he asked if you and I were still friends."

"Why is he asking?"

"Why! He's interested."

"Sure," Natalia said. "He goes for cops." "Must be the uniform. Turns him on. Seriously, the man's got class, Nat. He doesn't want some local bimbo. I tell you, you wouldn't be sorry."

Natalia tossed back the rest of her wine. "I need another drink."

"Or if you want, I can set you up with my trainer. He's adorable."

129

"Tell him you're working out too much. I can see your collarbone."

Lola leaned closer to whisper.

"We can get away with it when we're young, Nat."

"I get the point," Natalia said. "What's this?" Natalia said as Lola handed her a sapphire tube.

"You could use some color."

"Okay, Mama." Natalia opened the tube of coral lipstick and dabbed at her lips. "Better?"

"Better. Here, you got some on your teeth. Wipe." She gave her a tissue.

"Okay." Lola slipped the tube into her bag. "I gotta mingle," she said, and slid away through the crowd, kissing cheeks and making introductions at every turn.

Bianca Strozzi entered, bookended by two male body guards. Except for some cousins, Natalia didn't see many other familiar faces as she ventured into the room. A few people looked surprised by her uniform, but most went on with their conversing and flirting unperturbed.

"You look hungry," Leonardo DePretis startled her. He held out a plate with three butterfly shrimp impaled on a silver pick. The man looked good in a pale linen shirt, black trousers. Great cologne too. All the trappings of the successful *camorrista*, perfectly groomed, perfectly manicured and moisturized.

"There's not much to eat here," he said when she turned down the skewered shrimp. "Would you like to try dinner someplace quieter?"

"That won't be possible. But thank you for the invitation."

Lola, peering across the room, blew a kiss.

"Maybe another time," Natalia said. "I would appreciate a talk, though."

Annalisa Russo and Lola came swooping over. The gallery director had on a dark red cable knit sweater over a red mini skirt and matching boots.

"Is this Natalia?" she said, "I've heard so much about you."

"Nat, Annalisa. Annalisa Natalia." The women shook hands. "Mr DePretis you know."

Annalisa flashed him a smile — "Leonardo, of course." -- and turned her attention to Natalia. "Wonderful to finally meet you. I'm told you're an art expert."

"Hardly."

"Could've fooled me," Annalisa laughed lightly. "You must come by my gallery. I would very much value your opinion of my new artists."

Lola took Annalisa's arm and escorted her away, saying there were people she had to meet. Leonardo DePretis waited until the women were out of earshot.

He stepped in close. "Since you're not interested in dinner, might I invite you to the opera sometime? I have box seats. I gotta say, I never imagined an officer of the *arma* could be so very attractive."

"Can I ask you, in confidence, if you might share what your associates may have reported to you about the events this past Monday at the Montesanto market?"

DePretis gave a startled laugh. "That's certainly direct. I'm beginning to see how you've come by your reputation." He took a sip of his drink. "Your neighbors claim you are a woman of your word. I'll need you to never refer to this conversation if you want your question answered."

"You have my word."

"Two or three men pursued a young woman into the market and lost her. She carried a violin case."

"What did they look like?"

DePretis looked ever more amused and taken with her gall -- asking the enemy for help.

"They looked ... medium, he said. "Medium height, medium build."

She nodded. "Medium hair. Medium eyes."

"You know them," he teased.

"The Medium brothers. Oh, yes. They're well known to us at Casanova station."

"Regrettably, I must be going," he said, and offered his card. "My private numbers. In case you change your mind about an evening out."

She took it and extended hers. "In case your conscience ever requires it."

Depretis accepted graciously and made for the door.

How ironic. Natalia had not been interested in anyone since Pino. Now there were two. Leonardo DePretis wasn't young and handsome like Claudio, but he did have a rough charm. Sexy, without a doubt. Though she could never confide that to Lola.

Mariel came through the front door and came straight toward her. As usual, her friend set the fashion bar high in her navy suit, creamy blouse – hair in a French braid, and a long strand of dark garnets and beaded gold that had once belonged to her mother.

"Em, happy holidays." The friends kissed.

"Thank God you're here," Mariel said. A couple gyrated by, the girl in pink spandex leggings and orange hair. "I feel a bit fish-out-of-water. Why didn't we ever dress like that?"

"We had too much sense."

"Who was the hunky guy you were talking to?"

"Mr. DePretis. We had some business."

"Didn't look businessy to me," Mariel teased. "Reminded me of those guys Lola fixed us up with when we were thirteen."

"My God, I'd forgotten that."

"Your parents had the neighbors looking for us and we were at the docks making out with those junior hoods."

"They were sixteen and eighteen and already in the family business."

The maid approached and invited them into the living quarters in the north wing of the huge flat. Mariel and Natalia followed until they heard Giovanna's teenaged shriek coming from the family rec room. She was just hanging up as they entered.

Mariel and Natalia shared guardianship of both of Lola's surviving children. Her brother's discipline problems had dissipated and he seemed to be doing well at a military boarding school. Mariel and she had been particularly concerned about his sister. After her father and oldest brother were killed, she had become angry and rebellious, flirting with full-body tattoos and unspeakable piercings to strike terror into her mother's heart, and skipping school whenever possible. To the horror of her teachers, she cut her short and colored it a bright orange. Mercifully all that passed.

"How's our favorite freshman?" Natalia said, as she and Mariel embraced the girl. She had her father's thick lustrous hair and dreamy eyes and her mother's lips, and looked all grown up in her plum colored sheath. She wrapped her arms around them both the way she did when she was small.

"You look spectacular," Mariel said. "Some dress."

Giovanna stepped back, showing it off.

"You really like it? Fausto says it brings out my eyes."

"He's right," Natalia said. "Where is the handsome fellow?"

"He wanted to come but he's cramming for a calculus exam."

"So this is where you're hiding out," Lola said, cradling a large bottle of champagne. The maid followed with glasses.

"Merry Christmas," Natalia said, raising her glass when she'd finished pouring.

"Merry Christmas," Lola and Mariel chimed in.

"To my favorite godparents," Giovanna offered.

They clinked, and sipped.

"Yesterday we were Giovanna's age," Lola said, "and now here we are."

"Don't tell me you're going all sentimental on us, Signora Nuovaletta," Natalia said.

"She's crying," Mariel said.

"Hand me a tissue, Giovanna."

"Must be the change of life," Natalia teased.

"Shut up." Lola blotted her eyes.

"You okay mom?"

"I'm fine, kitten." She dug in her clutch. "Where's my mascara?"

While Lola re-applied, Giovanna excused herself to call her boyfriend.

"She's a beauty, isn't she?" Lola said, composing herself.

"That she is," Mariel agreed. "She has her mother's looks and her smarts, as well."

"Let's hope she's smarter than me. By the by," Lola took a sip of champagne, "did I tell you, Em, that Nat is interested in a guy?"

"What! I go away for five minutes and …"

"We just met," Natalia said. "He's a lawyer, does some criminal work."

"Claudio Palumbo," Lola announced.

"I don't know where it's going but…"

"About time," Lola said.

She had to get back to her guests. Mariel and Natalia followed her, made themselves plates from a buffet and retreated to the kitchen to hide out and talk.

After a while the party quieted down. Mariel yawned. "It's been a long day."

Natalia drove her home and returned the Alfa to the station's motor pool. The night was cold, the streets silent as she walked. All the shops were closed and shuttered along the way until she came to Lucia's Bakery. A stick propped open the door to vent heat from the ovens. The aroma of fresh bread wafted out. A short woman with red tufted hair slid the newly baked items off a tray onto a countertop covered with parchment paper.

"My child," Lucia exclaimed, greeting her warmly and bagged some sweet buns for Natalia as she had since her childhood. When she was a youngster, Natalia and her mother enjoyed the ritual together. Errand completed, they'd stop to buy sweet buns for breakfast and then stop for hot chocolate and a cream cake at a café nearby. It was time Natalia treasured.

As she passed their café, her mother's face came to her in the dark window – the delicate grey eyes, the olive unlined skin. Her mother kept her hair short, like Natalia. Unlike Natalia's unruly tangle, her sleek locks were always soft and meticulously styled. Natalia missed her, a humble woman always happy to listen, to offer comfort. She never complained even after she fell so terribly ill.

When you were young you never realized time traveled ever forward, that there would be no turning it back.

Chapter 10

She arrived at the station the following morning, anxious to get her information into the system. Bumping into Angelina at the coffee urn, she informed her she'd attended a function the previous evening where she learned of men chasing the gypsy girl into the Montesanto Market the day she was murdered.

"Any descriptions?" she asked.

"No. Not working for anyone local or my informant would never have told me."

"Who was that?"

"I can't say."

"Got it. Captain Villari is still trying to figure how you identified the person who confessed to Monsignor Montalba the morning the Segli went missing."

"They should be grateful they have someone who can get them such information."

At her desk Natalia quickly entered DePretis' private cell phone and home number into the Carabinieri data base before she even took off her coat. Colonel Donati called at the stroke of eight as she finished.

"Natalia, can I see you for a moment?" he said.

"Trouble, sir?"

"Probably."

Natalia shed her coat and checked to make sure her uniform was in good order, her hat insignia shiny, and took the elevator.

Waiting with her boss was a young lieutenant.

"Captain Monte, this is Lieutenant Marco. He works for the Disciplinary and Ethics Committee."

He stood and they shook hands. Donati wore a serious expression.

"Lieutenant Marco needs to clarify something. Lieutenant?"

Marco smiled. "I understand you were at a gathering at the home of a known member of the Camorra."

"Yes, last evening."

"You don't deny this?"

"No.

"And were you aware that operatives from several criminal families were in attendance, including the *madrina* of a powerful clan?"

"Bianca Strozzi?" Natalia answered.

"You have dealings with her?"

"We were in the same confirmation class."

Lieutenant Marco looked to Colonel Donati for guidance.

"You went to the gathering in uniform?" Colonel Donati said. He seemed startled.

"Yes, sir."

"I see."

Lieutenant Marco seemed genuinely mystified. "Why in heavens would you do that, Captain?"

"I was pursuing information about a homicide. In the course of seeking it out, I also obtained private phone numbers that I just this morning entered into our data base."

"Ah," the colonel brightened, realizing where she was heading.

"Conducting interviews at a convention of hoodlums," the lieutenant said, skeptically.

"Conversing at a Christmas party," Natalia said. "I hope you're not suggesting I and all the prominent citizens who attended are criminals. Four senators, the water commissioner, lawyers from--"

"Who provided you with this ... valuable information?" The lieutenant's hand was poised over a notebook.

"I don't reveal sources, lieutenant."

"Let's leave that for the moment. You are aware, Captain, of the rules regarding fraternization with undesirable elements?"

"I am aware of regulations forbidding marriage to certain ... elements."

"Is it true you're a guardian of Signora Nuovaletta's daughter?"

"I am."

The lieutenant looked peeved. "What I am saying is that Central Command frowns on officers socializing with known gangsters, ethically speaking."

"Perhaps it's different in your area, Lieutenant. I work in criminal detection, which involves familiarity with criminals. It takes me to places and people you may consider unsavory and immoral, and prefer to avoid."

"I think Captain Monte has a point." The colonel steepled his fingers and regarded his visitor. "I'm sure too, the information she's gathered will prove useful in our investigations, as has been true so often in the past."

"Very well." Lieutenant Marco consulted his watch and donned his hat. "Good morning, sir. Captain."

Natalia rose too. When she saluted, the lieutenant had no choice but to return the courtesy, as much as it displeased him. Natalia's boss waited until the visitor's footsteps receded.

"Captain," he smiled ruefully, "you never fail to surprise."

Natalia took off her hat. "I'm being spied on."

"It appears you may be. Be cautious, Natalia. Loyalty is commendable. Do be careful it doesn't exact too high a price."

"Will that be all?"

"Yes. How is Signora Nuovaletta?"

"Lola is good."

"And Leonardo DePretis?"

There had been an informant among the guests.

The question was a warning.

"DePretis seemed well enough," she said. "*Madrina* Bianca seemed older than when I last saw her."

"What prompted DePretis to give you his private numbers?"

"He wanted me to call if I was ever interested in joining him in his box at the opera. He also invited me out to dinner."

The colonel's eyebrows lifted. "Natalia, Natalia. My grey hairs are multiplying as we speak. Be careful, please – for your sake and mine. I would hate to lose you."

She returned to her office with heart pounding, and asked if Angelina would like to have a coffee.

"I would. But not the stuff here. Let's go to the Arab's."

As they exited the station, a woman approached them to say a man in the park didn't seem to be breathing. She pointed to a grizzled black figure lying on a bench and wrapped in dark plastic bags. Urine had collected below him. Angelina put on latex gloves and laid a hand on his chest.

"He's breathing," she assured Natalia.

Nearby a very pregnant woman in a filthy jacket scratched her arms. An equally neglected child played at her feet.

"*Amaro chi ha bisono,*" Angelina recited. The unfortunate condition of those in need.

The old Calabrian saying spoke to the feeling of helplessness in the face of the growing number of poor. Natalia was herself getting tired of putting in calls to social workers only to be told they didn't have the funds to take in any more from the streets. Their roving van circulated much less often, its hours cut back.

The church on the corner had taken up the slack and provided a meal every day at noon. It took a 'guest' to die before an ambulance was dispatched.

Two birds dove onto the pavement. Black wings extended like weapons, they pummeled and pecked one another, competing for a wedge of pizza.

"*Kaulo Chiriclo,*" Angelina said.

"What's that?"

"What the Roma call a Blackbird."

"Your gypsy friend teach you that too?"

"Mmm. One spring we found a nest in the playground. The boys saw us talking and threatened to beat the shit out of us."

"Charming."

"That they were," Angelina said. "Ten years old – half of them already ran errands for the Mafia. They were so bad off – My friend told me they sometimes ate road kill – hedgehogs they collected from the side of the road."

Natalia made a face. "That is gross."

"I wonder what happened to him. He was a sweet boy. Invited me to his house once. A real shithole. No plumbing.

Just a shack. Seeing me, his mother started screaming before I got in the door -- *Mahrine! Mahrine!"*

"Dirty," Natalia translated. "Nice."

"My mother wasn't much better. She honestly believed gypsies were plotting to steal Sicilian babies. As if they didn't have enough mouths to feed. Me and the gypsy boy," Angelina continued, "we were both outcasts. As young as we were, we sensed it, knew it like you do when you're a kid, though we never said it."

They got their coffee and proceeded to a tiny table.

"I didn't have many friends," Angelina went on. "Never wanted to do the girly things. Never told him or any boy I was gay. Though I was already in love with a girl who worked in the bakery. Wrote her secret love letters I kept under my pillow. Mother couldn't figure out why I'd always volunteer to go get the bread. My crush still works in the bakery. Married the owner's son, had babies, got chubby."

"Your first love."

"Yeah. You know how that is. You think your soul is broken, that you'll be unhappy forever."

"Do you know you're wearing one earring?" Natalia said.

"Yeah." Angelina touched her ear. "A present from Giuletta. She wanted to get me the same pair again. I said no. Like the old Sicilian saying goes: *You fly with one wing and someone else flies with the other."*

"What would they have done – the boys -- if they knew you were sweet on a gypsy?" Natalia asked.

"Rearranged my face, probably. Most of them had already been in and out of jail by the time I graduated high school." She took a sip of her latte "The coffee here is really good. Why can't we get decent coffee at Casanova?"

"Because we'd be hanging out in the canteen all day instead of working?"

Angelina laughed, then turned serious. "I've been looking through the videos. Can't find any from Turin. They're being dated, courtesy of Captain Villari's lieutenant."

"Sapetto?"

"Yeah."

"Good work. Anything else happening?"

"Someone offed an old man at the Galleria."

"Anyone we know? Camorra?"

"Nah, just some innocent home for the holidays. Probably walking around with too much shopping money."

"'Tis the season," Natalia said.

"Speaking of which," Angelina said, "what are you wearing to the colonel's party?"

"Probably the same thing I always wear. A long black skirt I've had forever and a gold lame top, courtesy of Mariel."

"Nice. I don't even own a skirt. Giuletta thinks we should go shopping."

"I wouldn't bother. Wear whatever's comfortable," Natalia said. "A nice pair of slacks, a sweater. The Donatis don't operate with a dress code, trust me. Last year a guest showed up in spandex shorts and orange platform shoes. Nobody batted an eye."

"Now I know you're having me on."

"Seriously, God's truth. He had skulls tattooed on his biceps and neck. Elisabetta has a thing for artists."

***

That evening Natalia stepped onto her balcony in boots and just a t-shirt and pajama bottoms. Holiday lights twinkled in a window across the courtyard. Somewhere nearby, an old vinyl record player played scratchy Christmas songs. Memories of holidays past flooded her. Mama mixing batter for her special cake studded with citron, and soaked in rum. Every season relatives arrived at the train station, shy cousins pushed forward by their parents. Strangers again for the first half hour, they were best friends by day's end. The boys hung out in the alley, the girls in a bedroom where they combed each other's hair. How innocent they'd been.

Years had passed since the Monte families had enjoyed a holiday together. The custom stopped the year after her mother's death, which was followed over a short span by the deaths of the majority of her aunts and uncles. Natalia, caught up in her career, had neither the time nor the inclination to orchestrate the reunions. No one else stepped forward either. Now her cousins were grown up, busy with their own lives and not eager to travel or revisit the past. All of them had married except Natalia. She was the only cousin who didn't have a child.

"You're lucky you're not saddled," Cousin Luisa had said when they'd last bumped into each other. "I'd give anything for your exciting life."

Exciting. Not exactly. It wasn't that she wanted Luisa's life, or her three rowdy teenagers and alcoholic husband. She just wasn't sure she wanted hers anymore either.

A firecracker-bomb boomed somewhere nearby, rattling the windows and setting off a car alarm. Damn kids. Every Christmas. Shivering, she stepped back inside, closing the balcony doors behind her. The evening news was on and yet again carrying stories of right wing violence against a gypsy community, this time in Rome. Natalia watched the footage of an encampment burning. A horrific scene, with onlookers jeering and giving the fascist salute.

Ironically, the first positive publicity the Roma had received in a long while was the amateur video of Drina playing her violin. Inevitably, in a few days the attention would fade, the press decamp, the flowers at her shrines wilt.

Natalia turned off the television and laid out appropriate clothes for the next day. No uniform. A black dress with long sleeves, tights, shoes, a black ribbon to hold back her hair -- and her weapon, in case.

Chapter 11

A long black hearse with glass side windows rolled out of the morgue's loading area led by two police motorcycle outriders and followed by a black limousine and a gleaming black Volkswagen pickup truck jammed with wreaths and flowers. An escort of two Carabinieri vehicles brought up the rear. Crowds were gathered along the curb as they passed. A few crossed themselves; many were weeping.

The funeral service was to be conducted in the open air at Via Riposa Cemetery, where a grave had been dug on the farthest outside perimeter of gravestones, allowing for hundreds of chairs to be set up. The far side of the cemetery road was taken up by satellite TV trucks, their corkscrew antennas extended into the air. Television reporters and cameramen milled about, warming themselves with soup from thermos bottles. Coffee urns were propped up on truck fenders.

Large white rectangles painted on the tarmac, indicated where the limousines delivering the immediate family would arrive. Reporters were already staking out positions, some erecting tripods or unfolding ladders to stand on for better shooting angles, still others sat cross legged on the grassy apron down front. The service was two and half hours off. Mobile calls chimed and rang all up and down the line, reporting the departure from the morgue of the hearse bearing the coffin.

As the hearse turned toward the highway, SUVs and autos of paparazzi fell in behind, some of them darting up beside it to get shots of the casket through the side windows. The coffin was golden, covered with white flowers woven together. It took nearly an hour for it to arrive.

Stopping as close as possible to the gravesite, the coffin was lifted from the hearse and carried to the graveside by attendants and there placed upon the hydraulic lift above the grave. The reporters checked their watches. Ninety minutes remained until the internment.

***

As soon as Dr. Agari noted that the 'vultures' had gone from the mortuary – which is how she often referred to the crowd of paparazzi and news people who had lain siege to her workplace -- a small pine box was loaded into a van. With a lone motorcycle following, Drina started her journey to Ponticello.

Francesca alerted Natalia by phone and Natalia left Casanova station for the Piazza Garibaldi and her rendezvous, passing on the way, through a crowd of students at a church gathered to commemorate the young woman. Many held placards with her image or single flowers. A few held lighted candles. Several raised their fists in solidarity– the letter 'Z' printed on their knuckles – the tattoo the gypsies were forced to wear in Auschwitz.

At the edge of the student gathering, a newscaster with 'RAI' emblazoned on her microphone faced her cameraman. An assistant ran a comb through her hair as she prepped for her stand-up.

Claudio Palumbo's Ferrari idled in front of the Garibaldi statue. He hopped out to open the door for her and she slid into the passenger seat. The lawyer had on dark sunglasses and Natalia wondered if he'd been crying. He thanked her for coming, and announced they had one stop to make before their journey to Drina's resting place.

At the side door of a church in the San Lorenzo quarter he picked up a young priest, Father Fontano, dressed in a brown sweater and gabardine trousers. Natalia had been surprised earlier to learn that a Catholic priest would preside, but Claudio had explained that gypsies' fear of death transcended their usual strictures concerning the *gadje*. The presence of a cooperative Catholic priest was desirable. It was common, he said, to include a priest in their more public ceremonies.

"Father Fontano helped me persuade Zorka that Ponticello was the right place for Drina's burial. This is where her father and brother are buried."

Of course, Natalia thought, the camp burned by neo fascists where her sibling and parent died.

Claudio informed her that all of Drina's possessions — her clothing, personal affects, even utensils and the plates she had eaten from, had been given away or destroyed. Luckily, the violin was not among them, he said. The mourning period would be one year, after which time Drina would be released from the shackles of their survivors' grief.

"How are we doing for time?" Natalia asked.

"We're right on schedule," Claudio said, glancing at his watch. "The van left the Medical Examiner's twenty minutes after the hearse with the white coffin and the police escort departed. It should be at Riposa and Drina should be well ahead of us on the way to Ponticello."

Nearing their destination, they caught up to dozens of rusted and rickety automobiles, including several Cadillacs from the '40s and a powder blue Lincoln Continental. Leaving the highway, they stopped for a red traffic light. Natalia asked what the passengers in the other cars were scattering and why. Kernels of corn, the priest explained, to mislead evil spirits.

"Why are they scattering the corn here?" she wanted to know.

"The cross created by the intersection," Claudio said. "It's a significant mystical form in our culture too."

A boy leaned out of a car window in front of them and clanged two metal lids together while an old man in the back seat blew a big brass horn.

"Here's the turnoff."

As they arrived at a narrow point in the roadway, Claudio pulled up and waited in line for the rest of his aunt's relatives and neighbors to make their way into the camp. The Roma youth standing guard pushed back his black fedora and said something to Claudio in Romani as he waved them forward. Claudio put the car in gear and rolled on. A large tent stood in a field on the far side of the hovels. All were ringed by small mountains of trash. Like Annunziata, the camp sat next to another municipal garbage dump where no Italian would have dreamed of settling, much less being buried.

"Will there be many non-Roma at the service?" she said.

"Just you and Father Fontano."

Natalia felt sorry for the girl's boyfriend and her music teacher not to have this opportunity to mourn with so many who loved her. Perhaps it would be uncomfortable for them, two *gadje* males. Especially for her lover if their affair had been a cause of her problems with her people. He might have found himself more than unwelcome.

Claudio found a space at the far end of the lot. Natalia waited until he and the monsignor went ahead and joined the throng of mourners easing forward. Natalia wrapped the black shawl around her face and exited the car. She joined a group of women in long skirts and walked slowly, all of them wailing a haunting dirge. A crow watched from atop a large tent, its sides rolled up and open. A horse drawn wagon, the canvas appliquéd with yellow flowers rolled toward them across the field. Dozens of men followed behind it, playing violins. The people gathering stopped and stood in place as it passed and halted by the main entrance of the tent. Eight men removed the casket and brought it inside under the canvas. The hearse waited. The tent filled. To the side stood a lone violinist and two guitarists, played traditional gypsy music. A fourth man joined in on a mandolin.

The coffin was lifted onto a low platform and leaned against a metal stand at an angle so that Drina was raised and visible to the assembly. Natalia recognized Drina's mother and Nuzi's wife among the circle of women who ringed her daughter who lay in the open casket. Glimmers of silver thread ran through her black shroud. The women wailed and beat their breasts. Some ripped their hair. Men tore buttons from their clothes and threw them on the ground. Nuzi chanted as he rocked back and forth. Claudio put an arm across his shoulders to comfort him.

The priest appeared by the casket wearing his gold vestments and took his place by a makeshift altar atop the rough wooden platform. White candles were affixed to a metal stand that curved around the bier. Their flames made a halo around the casket.

A crone shoved a candle into Natalia's hands and urged her to go forward. She joined the small group standing to one side of the body. Drina's dark hair framed her face and lay along her shoulders. Her face was deathly pale, though a touch of rose colored her cheeks and her lips. A fringed shawl of crimson silk draped her shoulders and golden flowers adorned her long red skirt. Gold shoes protruded from under its hem.

The hand crossed over her heart held a broad white ribbon; the other, a comb, a small mirror and a sewing kit. For use in the afterlife, Natalia guessed, and glanced at Gregor. She doubted he would recognize her out of uniform, distracted as he was by his grief. He was dressed as other males, in a grey suit and black shirt, a fedora on his head. Unlike them, his shoes were purple and his neck draped with gold chains.

Young girls, with headscarves pushed back and candles in each hand, came to stand behind the female mourners. They looked no more than fifteen but gold coins strung around their necks indicated they were already wives. And probably mothers too, Natalia thought.

She stepped a little to the side. Claudio spoke to the priest and said a few words to the crowd in Romani. Immediately the wailing stopped and the women moved away from the casket.

The priest spoke, Claudio translated, and the mourners sobbed. Then, Father Fontano put on a white surplice and held aloft a silver chalice filled with holy water, Natalia thought. Intoning a prayer in Latin, he sprinkled it around the body. It was wine.

Drina's mother screamed and swooned. Claudio and Gregor caught and held her upright while four young men placed the lid onto the coffin and nailed it shut. Zorka looked stricken. Two more men joined them and together they carried the coffin back out and placed it again on the wagon.

Natalia slipped outside and waited. The winter's sun cast its cold light. A sorry looking horse grazed in the meager grass where several boys huddled together for warmth. They were barefoot in the cold, dressed in tattered pants and their father's oversized shirts. A pint bottle passed between them.

The wagon rolled forward and the crowd flowed from the tent, trailing after it. Natalia followed across the stubby field until the group stopped in front of some plain structures that looked like concrete playhouses. Tombs, Natalia realized.

The mourners formed a circle around the family and the casket, Claudio held his aunt close as if she might faint again. No sign of Father Fontano. Looking back, Natalia saw him standing well to the rear.

With Claudio and Nuzi leading, a few of the men slid the coffin into the open crypt and stepped to the side. Gregor and another man took up shovels and sealed the opening with clumps of fresh mortar until it was smooth.

Behind them, back in the middle of the field, some men approached a traditional barrel-shaped gypsy house wagon and touched it off with a torch. It burst into flames, shooting sparks high into the evening sky.

"An old tradition," Claudio said, standing near her briefly. "Burning the caravan and the person's remaining possessions."

The crowd walked toward the bonfire. Some took up a Romany song and the violins joined in.

Natalia asked Claudio what they were playing.

"A Roma favorite of Drina's." He listened a moment and translated for her: "A gypsy urges his girl to come with him to another land. Says he'll steal a little horse and make their fortunes."

Women's voices answered: "Not so my little gypsy boy, for then you'd swing on high."

"It has a wonderful melody," she said.

"Yes, it does." Claudio wiped his eyes. "I'm taking Father Fontano to the station," he said.

"I should go too," she said.

"Stay, please, for the Pomona, the wake. It would be a great comfort to me."

"Claudio, listen. I think we might be pushing our luck." Natalia resisted the impulse to touch his arm.

A helicopter thumped closer and closer.

Claudio looked up as it thudded by overhead and circled back around. "Police?"

"No, not police. We only have one unmarked car here that's come to fetch me," Natalia said. "Up there, that's press."

"They've found us."

"Too late this time," Natalia said.

"May I call you later?" he asked.

His question took her by surprise.

"Yes," she answered before she'd acknowledged what that implied.

***

Shedding her clothes, she fell across her bed and slept. At some point the phone buzzed.

"Am I calling too late?"

"Claudio?" Natalia tried to focus. "How did it go?" she said, squinting to see the time on the bedside clock. Midnight.

"It's still going," he said. "It will go on till morning. Ah, listen … I'm downstairs."

"Downstairs?"

"Yes. May I come up? Hello?"

"I'm here." Professional duty clashed with her feelings. "All right," she said, her head still swimming. "Come."

Natalia threw on her one lacy nightgown and her robe and headed to the door. She opened it at the first knock and a shadow moved past her in the dark. Claudio embraced her, burying his head against her shoulder and hair. He smelled of alcohol as he pressed her against the wall and kissed her.

"I've wanted to do that since we went to see Zorka," he said, and kissed her again.

She led him back to her room and sat him down on the bed, then knelt to untie and remove his shoes, his coat, his jacket, his shirt, pausing now and again to gently kiss his face, his hands, his eyes.

Chapter 12

He shifted in his sleep, his arm sliding across her waist. She hadn't dreamt it. He was there, next to her, naked: Claudio Palumbo, sleeping.

She liked having him in her bed, in her flat, perhaps her life. Whatever happened, she'd never forget the phone call, her invitation.

She collected her robe from the floor and snuck off to the bathroom and turned on the taps in the tub. It filled quickly, steaming up the mirror on the old medicine chest and warming up the large square tiles. Shedding the robe, she slipped in and lay back.

What a sweet place, he'd said sometime in the night.

"Thank you," she'd answered. "Not to your standard though, I'm sure."

"No, that's not true. Yours is a real place. Mine is more of a decorator's show piece. You'll see," he said and kissed her.

You'll see. She liked that. Closing her eyes, she dozed off briefly in the water. Washing quickly, she got out, toweled dry, and wiped the steam from the mirror to see if the night of passion was visible on her face. One cheek was red. There were marks at her throat and breast too. Her curls were wilder than usual and sprang from her head in all directions.

Creases around her eyes and mouth gave her pause. She pulled her cheeks taut and whatever she'd seen vanished only to return the moment she released them.

When she was young, she couldn't wait for adolescence, and woke each day anxious to see if her flat chest had sprouted breasts yet. Though never glamorous like Lola or a beauty like Mariel, she had been cute. Neither she nor her two young friends had really needed make-up. Their skin was smooth as a willow. No more. Time had done its work.

Many Neapolitan ladies had taken to having plastic surgery. But the idea seemed totally alien. She didn't possess the vanity required either. Certainly no one in her family and the neighbors she grew up around would have ever considered it. Sofia's beauty salon on the eve of christenings, weddings and anniversaries was the extent they'd go.

She should get dressed and prepare for the day. But not yet. She padded quietly back to bed, tossed aside her towel and got in.

"Bella," he said, half asleep. "You came back. Always come back."

***

As she crossed Via Librai, the morning bells of San Domenico started to peel. Others answered. No matter how long she'd lived in Naples, the sound never failed to thrill. A strong gust blew from the sea carrying the sound all over her city. Natalia tucked her hands into her pockets and trekked on, grateful for her warm woolen uniform.

Sky and clouds reflected in the tall panes of an elegant *palazzo* constructed atop a crumbling wall where Queen Ann's lace and spindly vines spouted. Schoolchildren jostled, a vendor hacked open a pumpkin and the seeds spilled onto the market table in a golden hue. Curled in a wedge of pale sunlight, an amber cat lifted her head and fixed Natalia with turquoise eyes. Everything looked beautiful this morning in the dull winter light.

Nuns never retired. It was the norm at all the Catholic schools in the city. Terribly paid, they had no place to go and, as brides of Christ, they were married to the Church anyway. The majority of sisters, in fact, continued their service at the same schools where they first began, faithfully imparting wisdom and catechism lessons for many years until they were carried away on a stretcher.

A cluster of girls sat on the wooden bench in the entrance foyer, arms draped around one another's shoulders. Natalia caught the flash of glittery nail polish. Things had definitely changed since she, Lola and Mariel had been at school. They would have been sent to the office immediately, nail polish removed, then off to say Hail Mary's until hoarse.

A Roma student would have been unusual enough surely for one of the good sisters at Drina's old school to remember her.

"Of course," said the headmistress, "our lovely Romany girl."

Forsaking a habit, she had on a sensible navy suit and black orthopedic shoes. Below a cap of starch white hair, her pale face was worn and spare. A philodendron sat in a pot on her oversized school desk looking forlorn. There were two hard backed chairs. Quite a contrast from Father Montalba's lavish quarters.

"A wonderfully musical child," the headmistress recalled. "I often wondered what became of her. It's hard to keep track as you can imagine. Is it bad news?"

"I'm afraid it is. Drina is deceased."

"May God have mercy on her soul," The older woman stared out her window. "And it wasn't from natural causes, I assume." She turned toward Natalia. "How can I help you?"

"What do you remember about her?"

She thought for a moment before answering. "Drina was a fine student. Really outstanding. But in her second year of gymnasium her grades suddenly went down. A couple of her teachers came to me about it. I called her in, asked if there was something she wanted to tell me. She said a *gadje* wouldn't understand. You know this Romani word?"

"Yes."

"I called her cousin, a lawyer who had been instrumental in getting her enrolled. He told me everything seemed fine with her. He hadn't been aware of any problem. We rang off. I wondered if she'd gotten pregnant and looked for signs. They do that, you know, adolescent girls. Sorry if that's too blunt. To judge others is such a terrible impulse, isn't it?"

"It can be," Natalia said.

"Mine certainly was," said the headmistress. "What had happened? One of our more privileged girls had a fifty euro note pinched while at soccer practice. She rallied all her friends and accused her locker mate, Drina, who denied all knowledge. The girl persisted in hounding Drina and lobbying successfully to have her shunned, first by the team, then the whole student body. Ostracized."

"And Drina never complained to a teacher or you, never sought help?"

"Not a whimper."

"Girls can be so mean."

"They called her a smelly gypsy, and worse. A day later, the girl's missing money turned up. She had stuck the large note in a book and forgotten. Finally the faculty was made aware and she and I had our conversation. The next day she was gone."

"You mentioned Attorney Palumbo, her cousin. You got in touch with him?"

"A lovely young man. He'd made something of himself and wanted the same for her. She hadn't really attended grade school and we were reluctant at first to have her. But we needn't have worried. With some tutoring she caught up quickly. A couple of years later she was performing well beyond her grade. Such a shame she gave it up. Claudio Palumbo had such hopes for her." She gazed into the middle distance. "He must be heartbroken. Such a lovely child. I will pray for her."

"Did anyone else from her family ever visit the school?"

"Not that I recall. Only her sponsor, Mr. Palumbo. He came to discuss her progress every term."

A bell sounded in the corridor. Doors slammed open and the halls erupted with the swell of voices and shuffling feet. Once upon a time she and Lola and Mariel shared just such a setting.

"Do you have a television, sister?"

"No, we are quite cloistered when we're not in our classrooms teaching. Why?"

"It's not important."

"So young. What a shame. We try to influence our girls, help them to choose the right path at least, a decent life. We have them for too short a time. So often I find God has a different plan. We can't really shield them from the world's evil. At some point, I suppose, we all encounter it. Though I'm sure I don't need to tell you that, Captain, do I."

***

Natalia headed back to Casanova through the familiar neighborhoods. Despite the chill, vendors were out in full force, filling the streets with a swirl of colors and languages. People streamed by, some coming from the train station. Many were new immigrants who would cram into squalid rooms nearby and take whatever work they could. Some arrived by ship, many from North Africa. The sputtering economy stoked peoples' prejudices and fears. Newcomers were accused of polluting the society, taking scarce jobs, bringing disease.

Best tolerated were the Chinese. Africans were looked down upon but their hard work respected. Reviled were the Roma who worked as little as possible, spoke little or no Italian. They inhabited vile slums and did their best to ignore the mores of the larger society.

Antonio Da Fenzattta stood outside his younger brother's butcher shop. He and his relatives were fixtures in the district. Antonio's hair was neatly combed, as always, and he wore a tidy blue jacket, yellow shirt and baggy brown cargo pants. Whenever he started to rave, his brother would appear from his shop in his blood-stained apron and quiet him. If he was busy with a customer, someone from the social club next door would come out and calm him. It was touching, Natalia thought, the way the tough guys pitched in, often setting Antonio up with coffee and a *cornetto* at Francy's Cafe.

"Loredana," Natalia said to a serious young woman pushing a stroller past Lucio Da Fenzatta's shop. "Loredana Massa."

Once upon a time, Loredana had been the wildest of their bunch with the foulest mouth imaginable. She roared around town on a bright red Piaggio, hair flying. To the

159

envy of the neighborhood girls, she'd dated Gianfranco Todi, the cutest and most dangerous boy in the neighborhood. Loredana brightened, recognizing Natalia and the two caught up.

So this was how fires burned out, Natalia thought. Gone was the Botticelli hair and dimpled smile. Growing up was inevitable, she supposed. You sacrificed the joy and uncertainty of youth for hard won knowledge. That's how you survived, while life took a toll and marked your passage.

The baby kicked her legs. Natalia leaned into the carriage. A chubby infant with a halo of blond ringlets. So, Loredana hadn't married Gianfranco after all. Mother had shopping to complete before her older ones came home for lunch. The baby started to wail. The women kissed and they held each other's hands for a moment before parting.

As Natalia approached Piazza Maggiore, the sweet sea-smell of beer wafted up from the cobblestones. Empty bottles from the night's revelries lay about. It seemed a life time ago she'd been among the revelers, flirting, testing her sexual powers. Pigeons rustled on the ground and took up positions on San Domenico's stone shoulders. A rumpled looking couple drifted into the plaza, wrapped in last night's passion. As they turned onto Vico Severino, a monk in a long saffron robe and overcoat hurried past them.

As Natalia crossed the street, she recognized Lorenzo Mira, a hit man for the Torrino crew, sitting on a bench with a male friend. She had never seen him without his wrap-around sunglasses – rain or shine. When he was thirteen, he'd been shot in the face while doing an errand for Nicki Torrino. For years afterwards, he'd gone around scaring people with it until he made enough money to get a new one. He nodded as she passed and they both said, "*Buon Giorno.*" The Torrinos were Cervino's headache.

Considered bottom feeders because they did business with Palermo, he was welcome to them.

Arriving at her office, Natalia found Angelina consulting her monitor and busily printing something out.

"Morning, Captain. How was the funeral?"

"Exotic," Natalia said, while reattaching the heel to her shoe by banging it loudly on her desk. "What've you got there?"

"The list from Rome that you wanted when we first caught the art theft at Sant'Angelo. These are all the art thefts in Europe going back seven years."

"Great." Natalia picked up a stack of call slips to leaf through. "Now they send it."

"What do you want me to do with it?" Angelina rose and stretched.

"Nothing. I'll see if Captain Villari can use it."

"Yes, ma'am. Oh, the colonel would like a word when you have a moment."

Natalia made her way upstairs to Colonel Donati's office. He waved her in as he finished a phone conversation. She stood a moment, waiting. He directed her to a chair and hung up.

"Captain Villari sends his regards," Donati said.

"Is he making any progress on the theft of the Segli?"

"No, not really. He is up at Capodimonte for the next few days."

"Investigating?"

"Consulting. They requested his expertise in evaluating the museum's new security systems."

"Does he need me to assist, sir?"

"No, no. That's not what I wanted to talk to you about." Donati rose and went to close the door, then he returned to his desk.

"Anything wrong, sir?" she said.

"I thought you should know Tommaso Cervino is making noise again."

"About my friends?"

"Your one friend primarily. He's threatening to go over my head to someone he knows in Rome at Carabinieri Command."

"Thank you for the warning, Colonel, but I'm not sure what I can do about it."

"Perhaps you could be more ... circumspect, shall we say? At least until Lieutenant Marco finishes his inquiry."

"I don't have any plans to marry into the Camorra, sir. But I don't plan to give up lifelong friends either."

Donati sighed. "Loyalty is a wonderful virtue, Natalia, but perception is a factor in this. Be careful, Captain. Please."

"Yes, sir."

Colonel Donati sighed. "I feel responsible for your dilemma, Natalia, and I don't know how to rectify my mistake."

Natalia's boss had waived the restriction on officers serving their home territory until eight years of service had been completed. The reasons were twofold: one, the colonel was determined to offer a posting to one of the first females admitted to the force. And beyond that, he understood that her relationships with locals of dubious reputation could well reap benefits for their unit. It had.

"Sir, it was of great benefit to me being assigned to Naples, a gift, and you have my heartfelt thanks for it."

"No, please Natalia. It has complicated your life."

"I'll be fine, sir. I am fine. It's not anything I can't handle."

Donati took a deep breath and exhaled. "I pray so, Captain. I surely do."

***

Virginia Woolf jumped off Mariel's desk and retreated to her basket in the sunny front of the bookshop as Natalia and Lola entered, announced by the old bell hanging over the door.

"The cat's getting fat, Em." Lola sat down and dumped her bag on the desk. "Hey, Chubby, I'm gonna put you on a diet! No wonder she's fat, all she does is sleep."

"You busy?" Natalia said.

"Not very." Mariel was on a step ladder in the back, shelving a new arrival of books. "Let me finish this and I'll be right with you."

"Take your time," said Natalia and slid into the comfortable armchair by Mariel's desk, tipped her head back and closed her eyes.

Lola smoothed her little dog's braids, freshly shampooed and banded with tiny jeweled clips. She kissed its pointy nose and put it down on the floor, then went to peruse the art books. Miniature diamond chandelier earrings twinkled through strands of her lacquered blond bouffant. Her purple leather mini-skirt perfectly matched the five inch stilettos on her feet.

"Who is this guy Titian?" she asked, tugging at the black lacy bustier peeking from her low cut red silk top.

"Since when are you interested in Renaissance art?" said Natalia.

"Hey, I want to have conversations – you know – about art. Like you and Mariel are always having."

"Renaissance art? That's a huge topic," Mariel said, from up on the ladder. "What is it you're after in particular?"

163

"I just bought and sold a Guttuso. The buyer was impressed I knew so much about him. Courtesy of Nat here, and Lenny DePretis who's been giving me tips."

Natalia's eyes opened. "You're trading in art?"

"Dabbling." Lola reached into her bag and pulled out a piece of paper. "Certified check. One hour of bullshit and I made more than moving a whole load of --."

"Lola," Natalia interrupted, making a face. "Please!"

"Just teasing, Nat."

The bell tinkled. An elderly lady in a brocade suit and a mink stole appeared, followed by a woman in a maid's uniform.

"Signora Bizetti." Mariel descended the ladder to welcome her.

"We were doing some errands in the neighborhood," the woman said, "and I thought I'd pick up my new selections. You look wonderful as always, my dear."

Mariel picked up a shopping bag by the register and put it on the counter. "Your books."

"You're a dear. I wish more shopkeepers were as thoughtful. It's not like the old days. People had respect. Oh, I love your scarf." She turned and fixed her rheumy eyes on Lola's dog. "How adorable. May I?"

"Of course," Lola said, walking over to pick it up for her to touch and see better.

Signora Bizetti stroked its head with gnarled fingers. "Doesn't she remind you of Dahlia?" she said to her maid. "I had that darling for eleven years. Broke my heart when we had to put her to sleep last August."

"I am so sorry," Lola said. "You must have a puppy immediately."

"I'm too old for another pet."

"Not a bit, Signora," Lola insisted.

"Aren't you sweet? One thing about getting old," Signora Bizetti smiled, "people humor you." She turned to Mariel. "It must be near to lunch time. Is there a moment for me to browse? Or should I come back another day? I can see you're having a nice visit with your friends."

"She's not closing yet," Lola said. "We just came by to bother her."

"We went to school together," Natalia explained.

"Lovely," the old lady smiled. "And you are?"

"Natalia Monte and this is Lola Nuovaletta."

Lola stuck out her hand. "Pleasure."

"Nice to meet you both. Such an interesting world. I try to tell my husband that he needs to get out more. But he has his routine, his café, his social club. I ask him, 'Don't you get tired of seeing the same faces day after day?" Madame Nuovaletta," Signora Bizetti added. "Have we met before?"

"Nah," Lola replied.

"No? Such a charming girl. Can I ask how you manage our cobblestones in those shoes?"

"Been doing it since I was a kid."

"I'm glad to see you're more sensible, Mariel. Now, we will collect our books and leave you to your reunion."

Mariel saw the women out and put the closed sign in the window. Coming back, she said, "I have some personal news."

"Yeah?" Lola dropped her dog onto a chair.

"What?" Natalia asked.

"Cesare called last night. He wants me to move to Milan."

"He wants you to live with him?" Natalia said, suddenly queasy.

"He wants us to get married."

"Over the phone?" Lola said. "He proposed over the phone? How romantic. That'll be the day you get married – right?"

"I said I'd think about it."

"God," Natalia said, unable to imagine what would it would be like if her Mariel wed the bookseller and moved away.

"So you're supposed to give up your life and move there?" Lola huffed.

"His children are there. His mother."

"The guy is that hot?" Lola said. "All this time you've been holding out on us?"

"Who'd run the store?" Natalia said. "Lola, talk to her."

"Hey, Em. Dominick's been on his knees like five times already, pleading. You don't see me running to the priest to get hitched."

"Dominick proposed?" Mariel said.

Lola made a face. "You think I'm wasting sleep over it? Marriage ain't happening. No way."

"Anybody else hungry?" Mariel said. "We should go."

With the shop dark and locked, they headed off to Porta Alba. Perhaps it was juvenile, but the thought of Mariel deserting them for a husband was more than Natalia could bear.

Growing up, Natalia had wheeled her dolls around as faithfully as all the other little girls in the neighborhood. She'd held off on serious romantic involvements until she had finished university. When her first real boyfriend broached the subject of marriage and family, she said she wasn't ready. He didn't wait around. When she joined the Carabinieri, her training and police work consumed her to the exclusion of most everything else. Like Mariel, she hadn't ever pictured herself as a mother, much less married.

"Natalia!" Lola snapped. "In or out?"

"What?" They'd arrived.

All the outside tables were unoccupied except one. There was no evidence of gas heaters.

"Inside," Mariel, shivering, answered for her.

"God, yes," said Natalia, clutching herself. "Inside by all means."

Raffaele, busy with the register, waved them to the table closest to the back door.

"Since when did they put in the television?" Mariel said.

The huge screen sat mounted on the wall at the end of the bar. A soccer game was just beginning.

"This is shocking." Natalia sighed and pulled out a chair facing toward the front and the door. "Is nothing sacred?"

Bruno plopped down a bread basket and handed them a couple of menus.

"Bruno, when did you get the TV?"

"Couple of days ago."

"Business must be good." Natalia opened her menu.

"So so. I'll be right back. I got a customer upstairs."

"Where's Pietro?"

"Ah…taking a day off."

"He never takes a day off," Natalia said to her friends. "What's up with that?"

"Ask him." Bruno indicated to Raffaele, the owner, going through receipts at the bar.

"Rafe, where are you hiding our favorite waiter?" Natalia asked across the room.

Raffaele walked over "He's taking some time off. A vacation."

"He okay?" Mariel asked. "He's not sick."

"Yeah, he's fine. Bruno will take care of you."

"When is he coming back?" Natalia said.

"Depends."

"On what?"

"*Tavola tre.*" Table three Raffaele said to Bruno, returning from upstairs. "See if the love birds outside need anything besides each other. Then take care of these ladies."

"What's that brush off mean?" Mariel whispered to Natalia.

"Nothing good for Pietro."

Lola put down her menu. "Bruno ain't gonna say with the boss around."

As always, Raffaele sat on his high stool by the register, all the better to keep his eye on his employees and customers.

Mariel said, "The only time Pietro ever leaves Naples is to visit his mother in Potenza."

"Yeah, he's like my *zia,*" Natalia said. "When Aunt Antonietta has a doctor's appointment away from the neighborhood, you'd carry on like she was going on an ocean voyage."

Mariel laughed.

Natalia said, "You remember when I took my mother to Florence on a holiday, Em?"

"Of course. She packed for a year."

"Right," Natalia said. "She couldn't understand paying to stay in a hotel. 'Why do you want to waste your money?' 'Mom, relax,' I said. 'It's supposed to be fun.' She was so fascinated by the rowers gliding up the Arno, we missed a private viewing at the Uffizi. I got her a lovely scarf to remember the trip. She kept it wrapped in tissues at the bottom of a drawer. Wore it once just to placate me."

Lola studied her menu. "Sweet Pietro. Jesus, I hope he's okay."

"How old do you think he is?" Mariel asked.

Natalia took a bread stick. "Hard to tell. Sixty? If he's lost his job, he won't get a pension until he's sixty-five. How's he going to live in the meantime?"

"Some reward," Lola scoffed "For a life of honesty and hard work, he gets the boot. He'd have done better working for me. At least he'd be taken care of in his old age."

"Ladies, are you ready to order?" Bruno stood over them, pen poised.

Lola ordered penne, Mariel the minestrone and half order of pasta, Natalia the same. The haunting strains of *Ave Maria* suddenly filled the air. The restaurant fell silent. On the large television screen Drina played her violin in another video. The setting seemed familiar. The hymn soared through the church of Sant'Angelo a Nilo, the hand-held camera slowly circling her twice. Her dark hair flew over her shoulders as she played. Many in her audience were documenting the performance with their phones, a few with video cameras. A close-up of the musician highlighted her soulful face. Natalia got up and walked closer to the screen as an announcer reported on the clandestine funeral.

Natalia leaned against the bar, thoughts racing. It had only been visible in the video for a second, over and behind Drina's shoulder – Segli's *Ascension* hanging in its niche.

Natalia returned to the table and picked up her bag as Bruno appeared with their food.

"Where the hell you going?" Lola said.

"Something's come up." Natalia pulled some euros from her bag and held them toward Lola.

"Put that away," Lola said. "You didn't even eat."

"Everything okay?" Mariel whispered as Natalia leaned over to kiss her.

"Yeah. I'll call you later."

She left her pals and hurried back to the station.

Chapter 13

In the time she was gone, someone had dragged the old holiday tree out of a closet. A strand of multi-colored lights blinked frenetically as "Oh, Holy Night" played at a speeded up tempo. A few synthetic branches had gone missing since last year.

"You think we could take up a collection for a new tree?" Natalia asked as she signed in.

The security desk officer looked away from the monitor. "What's wrong with this one?"

"Never mind," Natalia said. "What did I miss?"

"Somebody hijacked a truckload of *mozzarella* on the way to the airport."

"Seriously?"

"God's truth."

"Do you know where Captain Villari and his art crew are?"

He consulted a sheet. "Still at Capodimonte. Oh, and your Corporal Cavatelli said to tell you she's taking a long lunch -- Christmas shopping. Said she'd be back as soon as she could."

"Thanks."

"You have any plans for the holidays, Captain?"

"Work," Natalia said "I have duty Christmas Day. You?"

"The annual trip to Bari. Three hours in traffic, all the way to the Adriatic, one side of Italy to the other. Ten years and her mother still hasn't warmed up to me."

"I find that hard to believe, a charmer like you?"

"Trust me."

Natalia scanned the staircase to make sure Cervino wasn't lying in wait before she started up. Bypassing her office, she walked to the end of the corridor to the evidence room and asked the clerk on duty for the empty frame brought in from the Sant'Angelo robbery and the violin case from her gypsy girl's murder. The clerk went to consult his records. Industrial sized paper bags on top of tall shelves held the larger items. The shelf just below held marked vials of ash debris from mob car bombings.

Natalia sneezed. Pausing to retrieve the maroon handkerchief Claudio Palumbo had left behind the night they'd spent together, she recalled his tender words and wished she were with him languishing in her bed. The clerk returned with the case but no frame. Captain Villari hadn't turned it in. It was still in their mobile laboratory, the clerk said, being tested.

Back at her desk, she took up the Art Registry files, hundreds of collated sheets Angelina had bound together, a catalog of art robberies as thick as a book. Natalia glanced over the first couple of pages. Six months ago someone had removed *The Coronation of the Virgin* from the Szepmouveszti Museum in Budapest. A Duccio. No request for ransom received. A big ticket item. The next page listed a pair of silver candelabras taken from a church in Reggio Calabria. The right venue but wrong item. She checked to see if anything else was stolen there. Nothing. A month ago a ruby necklace disappeared from a catacomb exhibit in Perugia. That didn't fit at all, nor did anything else. A local kid had been caught trying to pry a gold cross off a wall from a church in Umbria. He spent a night in the town jail.

"Sorry, Boss. The crowds," Angelina said as she deposited a shopping bag by her desk. "You got my message?"

"I did," Natalia said. "How'd you make out shopping for presents?"

"Okay. My mother and Giuletta are no problem, but my nieces? I don't know what to get teenagers nowadays?"

"How about one of Giuletta's kittens?

"You serious?" Angelina took off her jacket. "Those girls can barely take care of themselves."

"Make-up?"

"Of course. That's perfect, thanks. What did I miss here?"

"I've been looking through these robberies," Natalia said, tapping the huge inventory list as Angelina hung up her coat.

"Find anything?"

"Not yet."

"What are we looking for?"

"Heists of a certain type. Anywhere that thieves simply went in and grabbed a painting — slashed it out of the frame. No finesse, no care. Small canvases, low or no security."

"Like with the Segli?"

"Exactly."

"We're on the case again?"

"Unofficially. You busy?"

"Not at the moment."

"Good. Listen, I know it's a bother, but we need to check these records further."

"Sure," Angelina jotted a note. "Physically small paintings easily snatched by amateurish means and spirited away under a coat, that sort of thing. How small?"

"Fifty by fifty centimeters, fifty by sixty. On that order."

"Any other criteria?"

"Yes."

"What might that be?" her partner smiled. "Only paintings with angels?"

"No. Those valued between half a million and maybe three million euros. I'll be right back. I've got to run to the powder room."

Angelina booted up her computer. "Our poor plant could use a drink."

Natalia snatched up the ivy and took it with her to water. Returning, she found Angelina on her feet, waiting.

"I've got something," Angelina announced.

"That was fast."

"Modern technology. I went to the online edition of the Registry and entered the parameters you gave me in the advanced search function."

"What did you turn up?" Natalia placed the ivy on the windowsill.

"Ten months ago a Caceri was taken from Saint Agata's in Turin."

"I know Saint Agata's. Caceri? Never heard of him."

"Somebody has," Angelina said. "It's appraised at eight hundred thousand."

"Good work," Natalia said. "Good start."

"Start?"

"I need you to go back another two years. See if there any more robberies that fit."

"Just in Italy?"

"Start with Italy. I'm going out to Capodimonte to see Captain Villari."

"What's up with this line of inquiry?" Angelina said.

"I just saw a video of Drina being broadcast over Channel 3. She's playing in Sant'Angelo...in front of the Segli."

"You think she might have witnessed something?"

"I don't know. It feels like too much of a coincidence her being murdered eight hours after the Segli vanishes."

Natalia threw on her uniform jacket and hat. "I've gotta go see Captain Villari."

Via Toledo was the main artery connecting the waterfront to the hills of Naples. It was also the one and only direct road to Capodimonte. Traffic was heavy but Natalia navigated through using her flashing lights to disperse cars out of her way. Using her dashboard phone, she reached Father Montalba in his office and asked if he was aware of the young murder victim prominent in the news. Had she ever performed within his church? She had. He had regularly allowed her playing liturgical pieces in the sanctuary during the past year.

A twenty minute drive and Natalia turned onto the vast grounds of the Museo di Capodimonte. The long driveway wound through small hills dotted with benches. She cruised up to the building slowly and parked near the entrance beneath a majestic chestnut tree. Someone had carved a heart into the trunk with two names inside. On a branch above, a bird trilled a five-note melody. A nightingale. Her father had taught her their many vocal patterns. Natalia recognized the song.

The museum was closed to the public. A handful of staff vehicles occupied the parking spaces by the entrance. Its enormous stone columns and arches opened onto a courtyard larger than several city blocks.

She knew the layout well from her days at university and had spent many wonderful afternoons on the tree lined lawn behind the museum. Its observation point looked out over the city and the harbor. From there she'd watched the ferries and freighters plying the Mediterranean, the colorful fishing boats in Porto Santa Lucia.

Doctor Levi was waiting for her by the reception desk, beautifully groomed as always and wearing a black velvet suit, striking in contrast to his mane of white hair. Sixty or thereabouts, lean with just the beginnings of a belly, he was a favorite with the women and twinkled whenever they crossed his path. Natalia had personally experienced it in the course of her art investigations.

"We're all in my office," he informed her as they shook hands and crossed the lobby to ascend the wide staircase. Their footsteps echoed on the marble steps.

"The museum looks amazing as always," Natalia said, glancing down the long corridors. "Such a wonderful space."

"Yes it is," he agreed.

But change was coming, he informed her. The board was agitating for more portable video guides and recorded lectures transmitted to rented headsets. Electronic recordings instead of having visitors interact with live docents.

"I'm fighting it," Dr. Levi said. "I mean, what is the point of looking at a screen instead of the original and talking with a knowledgeable human? As it is, visitors wander through the museum with those ridiculous machines. They might as well be at a shopping mall. They hardly look at the art. The young ones are texting. I know," he laughed. "I sound like an old fossil – that's what my granddaughter says. I *am* an old fossil!" he laughed, "that's the problem."

"Hardly, Dottore Levi," Natalia reassured him.

"A young person with remarkable intelligence, obviously," he teased and ushered her in. "Come, come."

Doctor Levi's office overlooked the garden behind the museum. His office was a grand space, with pristine walls and a massive carved desk in front of huge windows hung with sea foam brocade curtains. Natalia recognized a Tiepolo on the wall facing his desk.

Angelina had managed to get their office painted a less-depressing shade of grey. She'd even commandeered a few pieces of functional furniture. But their faded poster of Madam Matisse didn't quite match up.

"Captain." Villari stood to greet her. His lieutenant followed suit and saluted as his boss introduced him again. Lieutenant Sapetto had the pink cheeks of youth and the fair complexion of a northerner.

Doctor Monica Miglacci, the curator of Renaissance art, sat alongside the director in a sixteenth century walnut chair in a perfect blue wool suit that set off her pale skin and sleek jet hair.

"Natalia!" she beamed, and rose to greet her.

Natalia and the curator had been in the same class at university, only Monica Miglacci had completed her graduate work and gone on to a doctorate.

Captain Villari said, "The curators of the city's major art collections are nervous. We've been called upon to check the security system updates at Capodimonte. Everything looks sound so far. We're just about to run another motion test. Why don't you come along?" he invited Natalia.

A guard picked up a carrying case sitting by the door, and everyone was startled by a ferocious yowl.

"Dottore Levi was kind enough to donate Marmalata to the cause," Villari said. "I suggested we needed a trained rat, but that was unacceptable. We're testing the integrity of several major exhibits today."

The group proceeded to the third floor where they trooped the long hallway toward *The Flagellation*, a route Natalia knew well. Major was no exaggeration. The piece was a Caravaggio. It instantly made her recall seeing his Seven Works of Mercy for the first time, as a child. Natalia had been dragged through the *palazzo* then ordered to close her eyes when her grandmother realized she was staring at an old man suckling the milky breast of a comely woman in a corner of the canvas, a typically shocking subject of Caravaggio's. Too late. Natalia was delighted to report her findings to Mariel, whose sophisticated parents were much amused.

"Such a marvelous collection you have here," Captain Villari said. "I must say, Naples absolutely rivals Rome in some respects."

The northern attitude, Natalia recognized – subtle and patronizing. She and Monica exchanged glances while Doctor Levi beamed.

"Yes, and there's word around that a work of his lost during the war has resurfaced. Who knows, we might be adding soon."

The Flagellation of Christ occupied Gallery 78, a solitary niche where the public could admire Caravaggio's luminous creation without the distraction of other pieces.

"Are the motion sensors on?" Captain Villari asked as they approached it.

Monica pointed to a dark glass disk mounted on the wall. "That green light means it is."

"You can release the test pilot," Levi instructed. The guard put down the carrying case and lifted open a door. Dr. Levi's large orange cat crept out cautiously, surveyed the bipeds gathered and made a dash for freedom. She charged through the space, all eight pounds of her, and instantly a high pitched beep commenced thirty feet from the painting and sped up the closer the cat bounded until it was a single painful screech that Lieutenant Sapetto cut off.

"Good," Villari said to his lieutenant. "Retrieve the kitty before she gets into the furniture collection and set the sensor again. We'll try a smaller intruder."

"That's quite a security device," Natalia said.

Doctor Levi said, "It has to be. *The Flagellation* has been insured by an American carrier for three hundred and twenty-five million U.S. Dollars. That's two hundred million British pounds."

With the electronic vigilance reactivated, Villari took a ping pong ball from his pocket and bounced it across the floor. Again the beeping alarm sounded and grew in intensity and frequency the closer the ball came to the painting.

"Excellent," Captain Villari said. "Modern technology. Soon it will make us redundant, I'm afraid. Your night security is in fine working order, Doctor."

"I'd best be off," the Director said. "If you'll excuse me. Feel free to use my office as needed. I won't be in it the rest of the day. I have two meetings and a reception in Gallery Twelve. Another amenity our illustrious board members expect — the museum as their living room. A pleasure to see you all."

"I'd better get back to work as well," Monica said,. "Let's have lunch one of these days," she invited.

""I'd love that. *Ciao*, Monica."

"What brings you here?" Captain Villari said to Natalia as the curator left.

"You, actually. Do you have a few minutes?"

"Of course. What is it?"

"I was wondering if there's anything new on the Segli theft."

"Absolutely nothing. No attempted sale, no ransom. *Niente.* My guess is they're sitting on it, waiting for any fuss to die down."

"We've come across some other art thefts," Natalia informed him. "They may be connected. Also, a murder investigation of ours might be linked to the Segli as well."

"A murder? Really?"

"A young gypsy violinist. She was killed in the middle of the day in Montesanto market. It happened hours after the Segli went missing. Now there's evidence she played a number of times in the chapel alcove where it hung."

"You think she might have witnessed something she shouldn't have?"

"That would be one possibility." Natalia's phone vibrated. "Excuse me."

"Captain." It was Angelina.

"What do you have?"

Angelina listed several Italian artists whose work had been stolen in the last three years: among them – Lionello Spada, Giovanni Baglione, Giovan Battista Recco, Jusepe de Ribera, Battistello Caracciolo, and Artemisia Gentileschi. All of them respectable second rank talents and better. Gentileschi was probably the most valuable of the group. All of them, seventeenth century painters like Segli. The paintings had been cut from their frames and removed from churches.

"Good catch," Natalia said. "Well done."

"I'm just about to run through more data and go through the rest of the European Union countries."

"Excellent, Corporal. Let me know what you find." Natalia rang off and turned to Captain Villari to report what she'd learned.

"Well, well," he said, "this minor robbery at Sant'Angelo is getting interesting. We have to rethink everything." Villari tapped his lip, pondering.

"Perhaps these thieves aren't such amateurs," Natalia said. "Maybe they just prefer targeting lower risk exhibits and abducting modest works that attract little attention from the press or insurance investigators."

"Or us, for that matter," Villari said. "We've got twenty thousand art and antiquities robberies a year to contend with. There's only so much effort we can allocate to investigating and recovering them."

"Captain," Natalia said, "I've also come to ask if I might borrow the Segli frame."

"Certainly. It's in the safe in our mobile lab. I'll have Lieutenant Sapetto get it to you immediately."

"Thank you."

"If you could keep me posted on whatever else you find, I'd much appreciate it, Captain Monte."

"You'll be the first call."

When Natalia got back to her office, Angelina closed the door behind her.

"Natalia," she said, somber faced.

"What's going on?"

"I just had a visit from Sergeant Bonicci in Narcotics. Besides some flirtatious small talk, he very casually mentioned that they're working a stake-out at Tania's."

Tania's was a club three blocks from the waterfront. It had been in business for a dozen years – its proximity to the docks perfect for moving drugs. Dons partied on the ground floor and visited prostitutes on the second. Attempts to close it down had always failed.

"So?" Natalia asked impatiently.

"He's convinced they're going to get them this time."

"Angelina …"

"There are some new players, Captain, Lola Nuovaletta among them."

"He was just here?"

"Twenty minutes ago."

"Hitting on you?"

"Hardly. I know he knows I'm gay. No, this was a message."

Like Natalia, Sergeant Bonicci was also a native Neapolitan from a tough quarter. Unlike her, he had left his old life far in the past. She was the only remaining connection he allowed himself, and only because she was a *Carabiniere* like him. She was surprised that he would risk himself passing such information.

"Okay. Thanks, Angelina. Isn't it time for you to go home? You've put in a full day while I was off gallivanting."

"I want to check out a few more of these theft reports or my buzzing head will keep me up all night. I'll let you know if anything more turns up."

Natalia thanked her and headed out. She tried to remain calm, but her insides were roiling. In minutes she was at Lola's door.

The dog trotted to her, decked out in a red and green sweater with *Buon Natale, Merry Christmas* stitched in red and green along the sides.

"What a nice surprise!" Lola said as she kissed her cheeks. "Come. Sit."

Natalia complied as Lola plunked down beside her. Natalia closed her eyes. Lola in pigtails flashed in her imagination. Never exactly the innocent but more so then for sure.

Lola picked up the dog and turned him to Natalia. "No kiss for Micu? Auntie Nat is having a bad day, sweetheart. Mama loves you, baby." She kissed the dog's mouth, hugged him and put him down. "Look what I got for your god daughter." She opened a box and dangled a topaz and pearl necklace worth a year's salary.

"Pretty," Natalia said.

"What's wrong? It can't be that bad."

"It may be, Lola."

Isabella appeared, sporting a blond crew cut, sports bra and black stretch pants advertising her muscles. If she was armed, the weapon was well hidden.

"Is there a difficulty?" she said.

"No." Lola waved her away. "Everything's okay. Do me a favor, though. Call Simone and tell her I'm running late. We need a few minutes here."

Natalia waited until the bodyguard retreated.

"Narcotics has Tina's under surveillance," she said.

"So? What does that have to do with me?"

"Why are you doing this?" Natalia said. "Your kids are down to one parent now, and you get into trafficking?"

"Oh, Nat."

"Bianca Strozzi treats you good, no? You're earning in a major way," Natalia said, arms spread, taking in the huge living space.

Lola shook her head.

"Bianca? Yeah, maybe," she said. "But the money's not flowing so good lately and her daughters wouldn't mind if I had an accident sometime. Don't worry – I'd never cross her or freelance on her."

"Shit, Lola!"

Micu barked.

"Keep your voice down," Lola said. "You're upsetting Micu."

"When are you gonna wake up? You keep on like this and..."

"You're not going to lecture, are you?" Lola moaned. "Do I really postpone Micu's pedicure because you heard something?"

"I'm trying to help you, for God's sake."

"You can help me by backing off, okay? I appreciate your concern, *cara,* I really do. It's sweet."

"Drugs, Lola? You said you'd never go there."

"You have to move with the times. We're careful. We don't sell shit. You're coming to midnight mass, right? And don't you dare tell me you're going to Antonietta's."

"She doesn't have anyone else."

"She doesn't have anyone else because she's a royal pain in the ass. Besides, you promised."

"We'll see." Natalia's phone vibrated.

"Angelina?"

"I've got it."

Natalia rushed back to Casanova. The empty Segli frame was on her desk.

She pulled on a pair of latex gloves and broke the log seal. The frame was a work of art in itself, she thought, as she removed it from the evidence bag and the protective wrapping, carefully freeing its ornate carvings of cherubs and blossoms.

Angelina whistled at the sight of it, saying, "Wow. That's gotta be worth a small fortune."

Retrieving her magnification loop from a drawer, Natalia scanned the edges of the canvas protruding from beneath the wooden interior border that had held the canvas in place. A few bits of fabric that had come loose during the hurried surgery clung to the frame. The incised edge affirmed what she had already ascertained: the thief used an especially sharp knife. Whoever had taken the painting from the church had worked fast. Either they had no respect

183

for the very treasure they were stealing, or else were in too great a hurry to care. It was daring, also reckless.

"Talk about cut and run," Angelina said, watching closely.

Putting the glass down, Natalia ran a bamboo stick along the frayed canvas edge. Tiny flakes of gold and blue paint crumbled onto the table, debris that was further evidence of the painting's dissolution. Luckily there were skilled restorers who regularly performed miracles. Several experts had workshops here in Naples and might be able to minimize the damage if the painting was ever recovered.

She took up her jeweler's loop and peered at something along the edge of the hemp canvas. It didn't look like paint.

"Corporal, I need to take it to Dr. Agari's, and I can't drive holding this thing."

***

The waiting room was empty and scented only by formaldehyde. The 'perfume of the dead,' the Medical Examiner sometimes jokingly called it. The pert young receptionist informed Natalia that Doctor Agari was in the middle of an autopsy and encouraged her to have a seat while she went to tell her boss Captain Monte wished to see her. Natalia balanced the frame against the couch and took a seat beside it. The violin case too, safely processed as evidence in transit, rested at her feet in a large, sealed paper bag.

The sound of a running brook came over the sound system. She didn't remember ever hearing it before. Closing her eyes for a moment, she thought about Claudio Palumbo. She wondered if the lawyer would call her again, or if it had just been a momentary need fueled by grief, an assertion of life over death.

The door opened and Dottore Agari strode into the reception area still wearing her soiled scrubs and rubber apron. "Did I forget a meeting?" she asked, glancing up at the wall clock as she pulled off her sterile head covering.

"No. Sorry, I couldn't reach you," Natalia said, and explained why she was there.

"Give me a second." Dottore Agari threw her apron into a special hamper. "I'll have my assistant put everything back in our guest and zip up. Why don't you wait in my office?"

The receptionist buzzed them in. Dottore Agari preceded Natalia, who deposited the frame and violin case by Francesca's desk. On the wall opposite loomed a new art poster – Turner's *Road to Orvieto*. Natalia thought it an early painting of his. The sepia tones of the road and surrounding woods were subdued, washed in pale sunlight. The Medical Examiner had chosen a soothing image for her lifeless workplace.

Not for the first time, Natalia wondered how her colleague coped. She'd never seen her ruffled. The pathologist never broke down, even when hardened officers did in processing the corpse of an infant or child.

Natalia's encounters with death were not pleasant. Murder victims gored with knife wounds or disfigured by bullet holes were never pretty. Sometimes there were bloody caverns where eyes had been, oozing stumps, a pulpy mess instead of a head. Over the years, she had grown somewhat inured to scenes of such carnage, had trained herself to maintain a professional distance and not react. It helped that a good number of her murder victims were not innocents. Many had more than earned their deaths. But she never got over young lives cut short, like Drina's. Fortunately, her exposure was always limited. She didn't have to linger over the dead like Francesca Agari, slicing flesh from bone, lifting out organs one by one to weigh and study.

"Coffee?" Doctor Agari offered.

"No, thank you."

"Make yourself comfortable. I'll be right back."

Minutes later, she returned, scrubs replaced by an elegant grey pleated skirt, matching pumps and gauzy white blouse.

"So," the Medical Examiner said, picking up a crystal atomizer and spraying a cloud of perfume, "the Segli. I thought the art squad from Rome was handling it."

"They are. They're still here working on it, actually. I'm just checking on something. I'm interested in getting a forensic report on the frame. Their mobile lab can't handle that."

"Forensic analysis of evidence from an art robbery? Interesting. I would have thought the art squad's lab would have discovered any present. But sure, okay, I'll run some tests. Do you have any idea of what you're after?"

"Yes," Natalia said. "Would you have a moment to look at something on the frame?"

"Sure."

Doctor Agari cleared her desktop of its few papers and moved a vase of pink tulips to one side before spreading a plastic sheet across it. Natalia slipped the frame out of its layers of preservation and laid it carefully down.

"I wouldn't mind having one of these," Doctor Agari said, admiring the carvings.

"Pretty, isn't it?" Natalia agreed.

"Magnificent."

Doctor Agari slipped on a pair of glasses with orange and black striped frames. Trust Francesca to make a fashion statement out of eyeglasses, Natalia thought, wondering not for the first time how she herself had managed to avoid a fashion sense while studying art at university.

"Since when do you wear reading glasses?" she asked.

"Since the letters started going fuzzy."

Natalia drew her attention to the inside edge of the frame where the canvas had been sliced. "What do you make of these?"

The Medical examiner peered closely. "These tiny stains? Some kind of pigment or resin I would guess. It's permeated the fibers."

"Can you run some tests on them?" Natalia asked, "Focus on this area?"

"Of course. What are you thinking we'll find."

"I'd rather you told me."

"How mysterious. Now what would the art squad officers not have looked for? When do you need it?"

"Yesterday."

"If I find something and can't reach you, do you want me to text Angelina? I assume you still don't text."

"That would be ideal."

"Anything on the gypsy girl's murder?"

"You tell me," Natalia said, indicating the frame.

"Everywhere you turn they're selling bootleg CDs of her street performances," Dr. Agari announced. "I bought one. She's quite marvelous. Such a waste. How's her dreamy cousin?" she asked. "He must be terribly sad."

"He is."

"Between us, I was thinking of inviting him for coffee. What do you think? Too soon?"

Natalia was tempted to say yes but said, "I don't think so." She pulled off her latex gloves and dropped them into the trash bin. "Listen, thanks. I've got to run."

"Right," Francesca said. "There's no rest from this, is there?"

"No. Ah. Can you spare another favor?

"What?"

"This is Drina's empty violin case retrieved near the murder scene. You tested it for blood, of course, but would you mind checking it for fibers and particulates."

"You want a different angle on the examination of evidence from the murder and a forensics exam of evidence from the robbery?"

"Yes. And especially of the sheet music compartment in the lid of the violin case."

"We looked in there but there were no signs of spillage. There wasn't much of it at the crime scene, anyway. Quite a neat job as murders go."

"I know."

Dr. Agari eyed her closely for a moment. "You're up to something. I take it, I may find out for myself."

Natalia thanked Francesca, knotted her scarf and hurried out. Her thoughts tumbled as she breathed deeply, inhaling the cool air. She had no claim on Claudio Palumbo. In fact, anything more than a casual relationship between them could only complicate matters at this point in her life. What did she care if Francesca invited him out? Then she remembered the taste of his lips, and that he was due at her place in an hour. A taxi approached and she hailed it.

Claudio rang her bell promptly at seven and came up. God he was handsome. His dark eyes and lustrous hair. He looked elegant as ever in his camel hair coat and paisley scarf. He carried a pot of purple orchids and a bottle of wine.

"No one's ever brought me so beautiful a flower," she said. "Such a gorgeous orchid."

"It reminded me of you. I would have brought you a bouquet from the florist except we don't cut living

188

flowers." He touched her cheek. "I'm so glad you finally called back. I've left messages with your office."

"It's been out most of the day," Natalia said.

"Good. I was afraid I'd disappointed you somehow."

"Not at all," Natalia said, feeling awkward. "On the contrary."

She took the plant and the wine and set them down.

"Come in."

She fussed with the locks, closing them, and turned to him.

"I missed you," he said, leaned her gently against the wall and kissed her, and began undressing her one article at a time, their clothing abandoned on the way to the bedroom, where they fell onto the bed. He undid her bra and stroked her breast.

"My *gadje* lover," he said. "You are forbidden to me, did you know? This is forbidden," he said, touching her. "And this."

***

It was so early even Luigina's canaries were silent as Natalia's neighbors slept peacefully. She envied them their dreams and wished for nothing more than slumber. Toward dawn, Claudio had asked her, "Which is greater — an oak tree or a dandelion?

"Trick question." She'd burrowed into his chest. "Obviously a dandelion? No, wait. An oak."

"Whichever realizes the truthfulness of its own nature."

Clever and other worldly, she'd thought, reminiscent of Pino. Was she attracted to abstruse men? Vaguely worried, she drifted toward sleep. What was the truthfulness of her nature, she wondered.

On waking, she remembered the question and pushed it away. She would have liked nothing better than to abandon her duty, take a rest from seeking Drina's killer, and spend the day in bed with him. But this is the life you wanted, she reminded herself as she unlocked her motor scooter and rolled it into the street, leaving him in bed. The motor refused to turn over. Damn. She rolled it back into the courtyard, leaned it against a tangled clump of vines covering the wall and walked away.

Even on foot, Natalia made it to the office early, put down her things and called Doctor Agari.

"I see I'm not the only early bird," Francesca said. "How can I help you, Captain?"

"I wondered if you'd had a chance to test the tiny stains on the remnant of Segli canvas left in the frame, not that I'm pressuring you, you understand."

"You think we're wizards? This is a science lab not an alchemist's den." Francesca teased. "I have it."

"You've been there all night" Natalia said, "haven't you?"

"Affirmative. I decided to let you sleep. I was just getting ready to text your corporal and go home to collapse when you called."

"What did you find?"

"Blood. The stains are blood. Not enough for a proper DNA test. We're removing the canvas border to see if there's more."

"Not centuries old?" Natalia said.

"Not at all. More like days. I went back through my autopsy notes. There was evidence of a small recent cut on Drina's left hand, in the crook between her thumb and index finger. She had sustained it hours before the killing. It had nothing to do with her demise so I didn't mention it. It seems more pertinent now that we found the blood drops on the Segli frame last night. The test results are going to Angelina right now. You need to come over while I'm still here and awake."

Natalia told her she'd be there as soon as she took care of some pressing business at Casanova. She rang off and phoned to request a meeting with Captain Villari in Colonel Donati's office. She got confirmation as Angelina arrived.

Jumping up, she soothed her hair and started out.

"What's up?" her partner seemed surprised.

"I'll fill you in later, Natalia said, and hurried upstairs.

They convened around Donati's conference table. Natalia informed them that the murder case she was working on and the theft of the Segli seemed to be dovetailing. She told them she was considering the possibility that the theft was capably organized by a group of professionals, and not a lone amateurish robbery. She formally requested that Captain Villari and she combine their investigations: his of the Segli theft; hers of the murder of the gypsy violinist in the Montesanto street market.

"You believe the victim's death is related to the Segli theft," Villari said, "that she may have been murdered because of it?"

"Yes. I think she's implicated in the theft."

Colonel Donati's eyebrows rose. "Really?"

"Forensics examined trace evidence left on the fibers of the slashed Segli canvas remnant stuck in the frame," Natalia informed them. "The presence of centuries old resins and pigments were no surprise. Fresh blood was. There's not enough for a DNA test, but it's A positive -- Drina's blood type."

"How do you think that's possible?" Colonel Donati said.

"A recent small cut on her left hand was noted during the autopsy, unrelated to the cause of death."

"You're suggesting she might have nicked herself in removing the painting from its frame?" he asked.

"It could well be. Yes, sir."

"If it's agreeable to the Colonel," Villari said, "I'd like to join Captain Monte in requesting your approval of combining investigations."

"You have it," Colonel Donati said.

Natalia left them and headed to the morgue. Passersby strolled through the streets gaily, holding aloft wrapped cakes and carting presents. She'd almost forgotten how close the Christmas holiday was. At the Medical Examiner's, two men unloaded a body bag and rolled it into the building on a gurney. Natalia followed them and walked to Dr. Agari's office.

Francesca Agari was on the phone. She held up a finger, indicating she'd be off in a minute. Natalia took a seat. The violin case lay on the desk looking more worn than she remembered it. The handle was chipped, its reinforced leather frayed.

"Sorry." Francesca put down the phone. "*La Repubblica* wanted a quote about the declining murder rate. News to me, I told them."

She opened the case. What had become of the cloth Drina used to rest the instrument under her chin? Natalia wondered. Doctor Agari drew her attention to the compartment in the lid where sheet music would have been kept.

"We found this in there," she said, and held up a glass tube. "These are minute flakes we vacuumed from within the violin case."

Natalia squinted but couldn't make them out at all. Francesca flipped open a file and brought out color photos of the trace evidence magnified.

"Bits of resin," she said, pointing, "and paint — blue and gold. Several centuries old."

Francesca Agari slid another color photograph across the desk toward Natalia.

"The traces from the violin case exactly match the fragments taken from the canvas remnant in the frame."

Natalia clapped her hands together and interlocked them, excited at this news.

"There's a bit more," Francesca said, and out came several more macro close-ups: wine red, green, pale yellow.

"What are these?" Natalia picked up a photograph and brought it closer to her eyes.

"More paint fragments we vacuumed from the violin case. Four centuries old too, like the blue and the gold chips. Except this paint, it's not from the Segli."

***

"She wasn't interested in art?" Natalia said.

Drina's boyfriend made a face. "Not at first. I took her to a few galleries. Drina didn't like the modern stuff. Then we went to Capodimonte. She took to the Baroque painters, wanted to know everything about them. It was like she was making up for lost time. We must have visited a dozen small museums and churches looking for more."

"You knew about her pilgrimage in France?"

"I did," Santini said. "I went along to a couple of the places. Beautiful spots, beautiful old towns."

A key clicked in the door and a girl let herself in. Turquoise streaks highlighted her tufted hair. The canvas bag that hung over one shoulder had large paint brushes sticking out. Her blue jeans and jacket were studded with paint stains. Startled, she looked to Santini for help.

So life went on, Natalia thought.

"It's okay," he reassured the girl, "Captain Monte is here about Drina. This is Lila, a friend from school."

Lila frowned, unhappy about competing with a dead girl, especially one so exotic looking and talented. The unfinished love story was proving compelling. Drina would never grow old, her lustrous hair never fade. Neither would Drina's bright gaze dull or her legend diminish in Santini's eyes. Natalia felt bad for Lila, but it wasn't her problem.

Chapter 14

Villari and Natalia assembled their small group in a windowed conference room that looked down onto Casanova Street. Angelina reported that more videoed performances were being posted on the internet and started off the meeting with a voice tape.

"Sorrowful Years," Drina's voice announced, as she accompanied herself on violin. The melody was haunting. Voice and instrument joined together in a dirge, the music transcendent, her voice croaky. All but one stanza was in Romani.

"Beautiful," Lieutenant Sapetto said as it concluded.

Natalia clapped her hands together once – "Okay." -- and got them started on reviewing the data.

Angelina said, "The robbery in Turin in February." She consulted her notes. "Methodology similar to the Segli snatch. Similar sized painting, of comparable market value. And then in the three previous years we found more."

Seven robberies of the same variety. Relatively modest value, relatively modest canvases by known Italian talents. All seven perpetrated in Italian churches. On average, a little better than two such thefts a year for three years running. Some handled regionally by police, some by Carabinieri.

"In addition," Angelina said, "we found three slash and run art thefts conducted in a two month period – a much tighter window. All three of these were in France this past summer. All three paintings by French artists of the 1700s. Wrong nationality, wrong time frame, wrong century. Not the Italian pattern except in the simple audacity of the robbery method — sliced and taken. Similar yet seemingly unrelated — except, two locations appear in the internet videos of Drina performing."

"She played in France?" Villari said.

"Yes. We're checking to see if there's video of her at the sites of the three robberies. The three thefts appear to coincide with some kind of spiritual journey that Drina undertook, to play in historic places of worship. So far we have videos and still images confirming that she visited nine churches and a grotto. Her boyfriend confirmed her presence there and at the other two. She performed in each location."

Captain Villari said, "Lieutenant Sapetto is working on an exact time line and looking for more pictorial evidence."

"Why the change in the pattern," Lieutenant Sappeto said, "from widely spaced Italian thefts, separated by many months, to three in nine weeks in France? A lapse of four months and then the last one in Naples at a small but pretty prominent church."

"We don't know," said Natalia. "Not yet."

"The question remains too," Captain Villari said, "why steal Italian Baroque paintings and eighteenth century French works? All of them of relatively modest in interest and value. The thieves passed up much better known artists and far more lucrative canvases: a Massacio, a Duccio, the Monetti next to the Segli."

"Neophytes," Angelina suggested, "they may have targeted the lesser work to avoid security systems and then trying to fence highly publicized heists – recognizable pieces."

Lieutenant Sapetto looked troubled. "Do you think these thieves have it in for the Church? All these involve religious art swiped from Church property."

"More likely they picked on churches because of the lax security," Captain Villari said, "and because the Church keeps publicity about such thefts to the minimum. If they do acknowledge a theft, they report the value of their stolen art as being much less than it actually is. I suppose to keep coverage and criticism sparse, and so as not to discourage donors."

Natalia informed Sapetto and Angelina that they needed them to check with both Italian and French journalists who filed stories on Drina, and with the radio and televisions stations that broadcast videos of her performances. They should also seek contact information for people they interviewed on the air and those who made the impromptu recordings of Drina. They were to get in touch and see what they noticed, or if they remember anything unusual surrounding the gypsy girl.

"Yes, ma'am," Sapetto responded, as he scribbled notes. "And we're to look too for more online posts of such material and, if at all possible, identify the churches in the videos."

"Correct," Villari said.

"Meanwhile," Natalia added, "we'll contact the parish priests in charge of the looted churches and find out if they remember her passing through, playing on the grounds or in the sanctuary."

"What are we waiting for?" Villari said. "Let's get to work."

***

Natalia dialed her old art teacher. The number rang repeatedly and the message machine came on. As soon as Natalia announced herself, Cesa picked up.

"Natalia! It is you."

Professor Cesa Cherubini was in her fifties when Natalia studied with her. An unconventional academic, Cesa was known for her edgy theories on feminist art and for being the only female on the venerated art faculty. Rumors also had her as gay and never promoted to full professor because of it. The males particularly complained of her flashy lectures drawing gullible students to her classes, jammed full each semester. After retiring, she'd rented herself out as a consultant to insurance companies and groups of art investors.

"How have you been, Cesa?"

"Good, but you're not calling to inquire about my health."

Natalia laughed. "All right. Here's my ulterior motive. I've been investigating an art theft, one of Segli's smaller canvases, *The Ascension*."

"Ripped from its frame. Yes, I heard. Odd choice," Cesa said. "Not very ambitious crooks, taking a minor work like that. There are so many more valuable treasures in our city, and some at Sant'Angelo for that matter."

"In the course of our investigation, we discovered six other Italian artists whose lesser work had been stolen in the past three years."

"That's interesting," Cesa said.

"Yes it is. We believe the same people are also behind these thefts. They're spaced one every half year or so. All at smaller Italian towns. Then an anomaly – three thefts in much less time -- two months. Not in Italy. All stolen from French churches."

"What are the other paintings, specifically?"

Natalia rattled off the Italian artists and the titles of the pieces. Cesa pondered for a few moments.

"All are moderately okay works," she said, "not terribly valuable. Nor very inspired. And you're saying an additional three went missing from churches in France?"

"Two, yes. The third from a hall beside a church. These were committed last summer."

"I see. You interested in scuttlebutt?"

"Exactly. Do you mind?"

"Of course not. Tell me – have any been fenced or ransomed?"

"None that we know yet."

"Huh, well I can tell you one of the French canvases was recently sold in Paris to a collector for not terribly much money. I'll run it down for you. You're sure it's the same thief in both countries."

"Fairly certain. Thank you, Cesa. I appreciate the help."

"So you're putting your art education to work. Tell me, Natalia, are you enjoying life as a Carabiniere?"

"Most of the time, yes."

"I confess. I do get vicarious pleasure reading about you in the news, Captain Monte. I imagine investigating is quite demanding."

"It can be."

"Dangerous too."

"At times, yes."

"Academic life would have been easier, though boring by comparison."

"I never had the impression your life was boring," Natalia said.

"That it wasn't. But being a rebel made things harder. Not that I had much choice. Just being female and gay stamped you as a radical intruder in the eyes of the Old

Boys in the department. It can't be easy being a female in the Carabinieri either."

"It's had its challenges."

"I bet. Well, there's one fabulous aspect of aging. You are no longer seen as a threatening figure. You can come and go and do as you please. I pick up some fascinating information – kind of a fly on the wall."

"Sounds good," Natalia laughed. "Talk to you soon."

***

No street noise disturbed Regina Tibaldi's tranquil apartment. Natalia noted the floor to ceiling double-paned glass. She'd called ahead and the musicologist said she'd be happy to speak with her. She was tiny, less than five feet, with dark lanky hair held away from her face by a garnet clip. They sat across from one another on matching bentwood chairs.

"It's heartbreaking to speak of her in the past tense." Signora Tibaldi looked at her hands. "Every life is important, of course, but she was so young and alive, so gifted."

"That she was."

"Have you any idea who did this terrible thing to her?"

"Not as yet."

"What an unusual talent," the musicologist said. "Such range. Drina could play the most demanding Bach and Paganini pieces with as much command as her own music. So unusual, that child. There are a good many gifted musicians. Most stay within the confines of their skill and understanding. She always ventured further. Such a brave spirit. If you ever heard her play, you didn't forget it."

"I know what you mean," Natalia said. "She played in our churchyards and streets for years. I heard her several times."

"Marvelous, no? I have a tape we made here in our little studio. She's singing in Romani. The words are poetry, but even without them, her music, it's … ethereal."

"You are fluent in Romani?"

"No, not at all," Tibaldi said. "She translated it for me."

"How did you meet her?" Natalia asked.

"Drina just showed up one day. Said she knew of my work. I enjoyed her company. She was much younger, but I was someone with whom she could share her ambitions. She had many."

"She owned a terribly expensive book on Stradivarius violins," Natalia said. "It catalogues all the known Strads - - what collections they are in, where they are, who owns them. I suppose those wealthy enough to afford a Strad could afford a couple of hundred euros for a high end picture book. But I was surprised she had it."

"I'm not," Signora Tibaldi laughed. "She was well on her way to being a virtuoso and fantasized playing a Strad one day. I tried to warn her not to set her sights too high. She found the suggestion amusing. Said she would play the finest violin in the finest halls before she was twenty-five. Good as she was, there are other superb violinists. The competition is daunting. Still, I didn't want to discourage her. What are we, after all, without our dreams? And who knows? She had the talent, the drive. In time she might very well have performed on the stage of the San Carlo."

Natalia paused over her notes. "Was there anything about her goals that you particularly recall?"

"She especially wanted to change people's perception of Roma and thought she might through her music. She wanted the larger world to appreciate her people's mysticism. She would go on pilgrimages to places of worship, open hearts with her violin. She traveled to the shrine of the Black Virgin in Biella and played there, as a test of sorts. She was very pleased with the results."

"In Sicily?" Natalia asked.

"That's correct. You know about her trip to France?"

"Yes, we do."

"She felt an affinity for Avignon in particular. She knew the story -- how they broke away from the church to worship Mary. I got cards from Paris, Avignon, Troyes. She wanted to be heard in as many churches as she could. A colleague made this video of Drina for me in my home studio. The visual quality isn't the best but the sound track is excellent and you can get a real sense of her."

Natalia asked if she could have a disc copy of the recording and borrow the postcards.

"Absolutely. You know, I had the feeling she was planning a change. She said she'd gone as far as she could playing street venues and houses of worship. It wasn't satisfying to her any more. Poor child. Let me give you an extra disc. I would appreciate it if you could pass it to her family."

***

Natalia made a stop at Lola's before returning to Casanova.

"Friends?" Lola said and held Micu toward her. The dog licked Natalia's mouth.

"Eeww!" Natalia wiped her lips with the back of her hand. "Of course we're friends, but not if you keep sticking that creature in my face."

"Good. Sit. I was just going to take refreshment. What can I get you?"

"Nothing, thanks. I can't stay."

"So why are you here?"

"I needed to know we were okay."

"We'll always be okay, *cara mia*."

"What smells so ... pungent?" Natalia said.

"Bergamot and rose. Each room has a different scent. Perfumes for the house. The bathroom is mint."

"Sounds like your decorator at work."

"How did you guess?"

Back in her office, Natalia found a note stuck to her lamp shade. It was from Angelina and said she was upstairs, meeting again with Captain Valleri and his Lieutenant Sapetto. Natalia joined them in the conference room they were using as their office. When she got there the three were reviewing the theft at a church in Peronne, a small historic hilltop town in France high above the Somme River. Villari explained that a not particularly distinguished *Madonna and Child* by Simon Vouet had disappeared after being cut from its frame last summer. It was chronologically the second French theft. Beloved by the townspeople, the local gendarmerie did everything in their power to intercept the thieves and get the iconic painting back, including quickly throwing up road blocks. The constabulary checked the buses, the nearest train station in the valley below, and all private vehicles leaving the area by way of the few winding roads leading off the peak. Nothing. The picture had vanished, the thieves with it.

"Drina played there," Villari said. "I spoke to the priest. He even gave her a bed in the parish house the day before the robbery. The next morning his housekeeper made her breakfast and he tucked a few euros into her bag as the beautiful young musician made ready to leave. It was chaos, with everyone chasing around, searching for the criminals. The priest drove her through the road blocks and some distance before she got out and proceeded to hitch hike."

The same template applied to all three French thefts as the seven Italian, with one small deviation. A Black Madonna in Provence was snatched from a church building. Not normally used for art exhibitions, the three hundred year old refurbished rectory had no video monitors and no security to speak of, just a lone night watchman.

"I did a rough tally of all the stolen pieces," Lieutenant Sapetto said. "On average they're valued at two million euros. Just under twenty two million for the lot. But of course they would only get a fraction of that from a fence. Maybe a third if they were lucky. Six or seven million. Not a huge return for more than three years work but certainly enough if they're just starting their careers as art thieves."

Valleri said, "Still no ransom demands for any of them, no attempted sales we're aware of except the French one Cesa Cherubrini alerted us to. None of the other paintings have re-surfaced in any way."

Angelina passed around a series of stills made from the video supplied by Signora Tibaldi. In one, Drina is in a black shawl and long white dress decorated with sunflowers, her face pressed against her violin, her eyes closed. In another she wears a red dress, violin clenched against her chin. There were several dozen photographs taken at different street and church locations. Two showed the same young man lurking in the background. In his early twenties, dark hair, a captivated look on his face. Drina had another admirer. He seemed familiar but Natalia couldn't quite place him – and then she did.

"That tall man. He was with the gypsies camped out at the Medical Examiner's. He's the carpenter who measured her for her coffin. His name is Drako."

"Maybe he went along to hear her play," Angelina said.

"No," Natalia said. "No. He's in one of the videos also."

"Too much coincidence?" Villari said.

"I think so," Natalia said

"I agree," Villari said.

Natalia suggested they go to work and reconvene later in the afternoon. She went back downstairs to her office with Angelina to read the latest update from France.

"Angelina," she said, pausing over the papers. "Get on to the intelligence people. We need records on all the Roma in Annunziata. Arrests, indictments, convictions, suspicions — the works. Start with Drako."

"Coming right up."

Fifty eight minutes later Angelina re-appeared with a complete run down. Drako had been charged with misdemeanors and received reduced penalties three times for admitting his guilt in each case – petty thefts, loitering. He had no serious felonies. There were no surprises involving Drako. The group reconvened and Natalia shared what they'd found.

Captain Villari focused on the same thing about Drako that had caught her notice as well.

"It says this Drako has been associated with fences in Manchester and London, where he lived for a while, and with fences here in Naples."

Natalia said, "I see where he's much more a fine woodworker than a carpenter. And," – she looked up from her papers – "he's known to make and repair string instruments. I think we need to make a surprise visit. Take along an expert on string instruments and drop in on Drako with a search authorization, quick."

Natalia called Matteo on her mobile. The good news was Matteo was excited and happy to participate --

immediately. The less good news was that Cervino was on standby to lead the rapid response intervention squad. Given that Carabinieri would be going into the alien territory of a gypsy community, there was no negotiating the thing down to a lesser operation, like a simple search.

"You're saddled with a crowd," Villari said. "The lieutenant and I will stay back and hold down the fort." He wished her luck.

Natalia was scanning yet another crime projection report when Cervino and his partner burst in, both in body armor, black combat fatigues and helmets.

"You ready, Captain?" said Cervino.

"I'm just waiting for the expert who's accompanying us. Should be within half an hour."

"We'll be downstairs by the vehicle," he said as they left

"Right," she said and went to change into black fatigues herself, and gather up her gear before joining Cervino, the other Carabiniere in the street. At the last second, she put back her helmet and rifle and kept her holstered sidearm and beret. Angelina followed suit.

Cervino had everyone else in helmets strapped tight to their chins.

"We're not going to a riot," Natalia said, and donned her beret as they joined the group downstairs. Cervino made no reply.

Matteo arrived. He'd brought his 35 millimeter digital camera. Angelina strapped him into body armor and put him in a red helmet to specially distinguish him. She didn't reveal that it was what prisoners wore on their way to and from prison and court.

The only officer in the group, Natalia, took the front passenger seat in the SUV as Cervino slid behind the wheel. The five Carabinieri in the back two rows of seats carried assault rifles. Marshal Cervino had signed out a Franchi shotgun from the armorer and had it propped vertically in the holding stand between them. Only Matteo was unarmed, wedged in a corner in the rear.

Cervino ran through procedures on the drive to Annunziata. Finally, they bumped along the access road leading into the Roma settlement. Natalia urged them to use restraint and pointed out that Roma were not known to be violent. She emphasized that a public relations nightmare would ensue if anyone got roughed up, especially in the light of the recent murder of the young gypsy musician.

"I'm running this operation, Captain," Cervino reminded her sharply. "Before this little raiding party of yours came up, we were about to go there in pursuit of a stable of little Bulgarian kids someone is running downtown. They're here somewhere. When they're not robbing people, they're kept in a container truck. Nice people, your gypsies. If the kids don't obey, they're beaten. If and when force is to be used, I'll let you know, thank you. You just look after your civilian."

Great, Natalia thought. So much for damage control.

Cervino ignored the man who tried to stop them at the bottleneck entrance to the camp and drove on through. Smoke from cooking fires spiraled in the air mixing with garbage burning in the dump nearby. Cervino parked near what they hoped was Drako's workshop and he and his men held their weapons at the ready as they advanced. It seemed to Natalia, excessive, but it wasn't her call.

He quickly led the way down a makeshift street, weapon raised. Children stood gaping alongside old women and men who had paused in their labors to take in the sight of armed Carabinieri apparently raiding the settlement. An old woman in a lace shawl cooked over an open charcoal fire. Babies wailed somewhere as the officers trudged forward in small fast steps, as if dancing with weapons at their shoulders. Matteo and she followed, striding normally. A growing group of Roma strolled after them at a safe distance.

Cervino marched in and out of hovels. Where they found a man on the premises, they pulled him outside and checked to see if the photo of Drako matched. One man had the temerity to spit and Cervino shoved him roughly. The trailing group gasped. Angelina rushed over to help the man up.

"Fucking leeches," Cervino hissed, and pressed past them.

"You may be commanding," Natalia said, loudly after him, "but I will report any abuse I witness. You'll get nowhere by frightening people, Marshal."

There, she'd done her duty. Cervino was free to dig his own grave. Be my guest, she thought.

They turned down an alley near the end of the dwellings. A chemical smell wafted from a lean-to where half a dozen men plated tin. A huge fire blazed in the center of the room. Their faces were black from smoke. Natalia waited while Cervino approached them. All were too old or too short to be Drako. Cervino signaled for them to troop forward. The passage narrowed.

The alley came to a dead end. Someone was using a handsaw. The door to a ramshackle building stood open. She followed Cervino and stepped inside into sawdust. Drako stood bent over his work. Cervino quickly wrapped him up and cuffed him. The young man looked startled but not terribly intimidated as Cervino and two of his men led him away. The rest remained on guard outside.

The shop was a poor man's version of Matteo's. A great many mandolins and violins hung by their necks on the walls. Two violas as well. Violin making and woodcraft were a Roma tradition, passed down generation to generation. She doubted Drako had any formal training, like Matteo, yet the instruments were obviously beautifully crafted. One lay open on the work table, being repaired. A young apprentice stood by it, trembling.

"Repair?" she said, pointing. He nodded.

"You make them as well?" She pointed to the wall.

"Yes."

She motioned him out and the youth darted off like a released bird. Matteo circled the shop, taking in everything.

"If you see any needle-like tools," she said, "let me know."

Matteo removed one of a dozen tools wedged into a can and stuck it into the countertop. "There's a bunch of these awls and fine chisels over here."

The small crowd gathering outside grew louder.

Matteo studied the pieces of the violin on the repair bench, its neck gripped in a cushioned vise.

"Maple and spruce," he told her. "Magnificent workmanship to go with the magnificent wood, beautifully seasoned and treated."

"Matteo, we haven't much time," Natalia urged. "There are the makings of a mob out there. Is there any sign of her violin?"

"The Gagliano. Oh most definitely," he said, as if it were obvious. "Right here."

She saw no violin. "Where?"

He pointed to the dismantled instrument being repaired.

"Is it broken?" she said. "Why is it in pieces?"

"It's perfectly all right. It's just being taken apart."

Chapter 15

"Like stripping a car for the parts, correct," Matteo said, on the way back to Casanova. "It's like what a

chop shop would do to a stolen car in dismantling it to put its parts into other cars."

Captain Villari looked back toward Drako in the last row, riding between two Carabinieri and listening to Matteo.

Matteo told them the gypsy was making a knock-off out of the parts, creating a rarer looking, more valuable instrument built from the pieces of the Gagliano. Most likely replicating a Nicola. It was a lucrative business. He knew for a fact, last year, Interpol had broken up a ring that stole and took apart antique violins to transform them into copies of famous ones. They took beautiful and ancient wood from lesser violins and combined it with pieces of exceptional instruments. They were skillful, he admitted – you couldn't tell the forgery from the original. They'd caught the forgers, but the profits remained hidden.

Where was this gang? Angelina wanted to know.

"England," Matteo told her. "A gang of Romanian gypsies."

Natalia led Villari to Interview Room 2 and entered. Drako sat at the table uncuffed; beside him, his state appointed attorney. Drako rubbed his wrists as Natalia audibly identified those present and had the prisoner identify himself for the recording.

"I am Drako."

"In accordance with the law, we must provide you an attorney within twenty-four hours of your detention if you haven't one. This is Counselor Armand Pellograno."

"You can't keep me here. I want my own attorney."

"Who would be?"

"Claudio Palumbo."

"That won't be possible, Drako."

"You can't deny me my lawyer."

"Mr. Palumbo already represents someone involved in this case. He can't represent you too. Mr. Pellograno can fill in until you've retained someone you prefer."

"You aren't allowed to keep me like this."

"Actually, Sir, in cases involving organized crime we can. Up to five days. Ask your attorney."

Drako slumped in his chair and fell silent.

"Your associate claims you were repairing this," Natalia said, and presented him with color photos of the Gagliano violin being dissected on his work bench. She noted the rest of the Gagliano pieces, and listed the assigned evidence coding of each as the tape ran.

"When am I getting out of here?"

"Answer the question, please."

He sat with hands folded, silently fuming.

"In that case..." Natalia said, and began gathering up the images.

"What do you want?" Drako growled.

"Answers." She tapped the photographs. "How did you come into possession of this violin?"

"Found it in the street."

"Which street?"

"Don't recall."

"When?"

"A couple of days ago."

"Beginning of the week perhaps?"

He nodded. Natalia spoke into the microphone.

"Drako indicated affirmation. Was it Sunday, sir?"

"No."

"Monday?"

"Yes."

"Do you know an individual named Drina?"

"Yeah."

"Did you murder her this past Monday with something like this?"

Natalia produced another photo. She flipped it down like a playing card and held the others back. He colored slightly and shifted in his seat. The man was nervous, Natalia realized. Perfect. A nervous suspect often spilled the beans.

"It's from your shop, sir. An awl. You must have half a dozen. Anyone of them could have been used to murder Drina. Where were you Monday from noon to three?"

"In my shop."

"We have a witness who saw you from a balcony overlooking the Montesanto market where the body was found. You were seen by this witness in the company of another man. Would you identify that person?"

"Don't know what you're talking about."

Possibly true, she thought, since she was bluffing him.

"Did you find this violin — the victim's violin -- before or after she expired?"

"I don't know anything about anybody expiring. When are you letting me go? What's the charge?"

"We're still going through the possible choices," Natalia said. "There are many. We can charge you as an uncooperative witness. For harboring stolen property. For stealing said property. For tampering with evidence – removing it from a major crime scene. Or we can consider you as an accomplice in that crime. Maybe we should just get on with it and lay charges for capital murder."

Drako was formally notified that he was a suspected person and processed as being charged with possession of misappropriated evidence valued in excess of one hundred fifty thousand euros.

***

Natalia's mobile chimed. She checked the screen. Claudio.

"Do you mind?" she said to Angelina, "I'll be right back," and slipped outside.

"Claudio, you okay?"

"Good, good. I had this wonderful dream I spent the night with a beautiful Neapolitan with shiny black curls and the body of a goddess."

"You did, did you?"

"Yeah. I'd like to dream it again. Meantime, I have to see my latest client – Drako."

"Drako? He's still at the station. We found Drina's violin in his workshop."

"I know. He's sent word asking me to represent him. I'll be there in an hour."

"Claudio, you can't take him as a client.

"Why? What do you mean?"

Natalia reminded the lawyer that he already represented the victim's sibling – that, plus the fact that Drako was most likely present at Drina's murder and may have even participated – made his involvement inappropriate, not to mention, illegal. She informed him she had not yet laid the more serious charges, as she was trying to get him to cooperate with them.

"Yes, I see your point. I'll refer him to another lawyer he might accept." Claudio sounded depressed. "I can't believe he had anything to do with Drina's murder. He and Drina have been friends since childhood. Do you think you'll get anything more out of him?"

"Most definitely, Claudio. It's just a question of time before he gives it up."

"I'm sure you're right, *bella*. I wish you weren't. *Ciao*."

"*Ciao*, Sweetness."

***

Elisabetta Donati and Natalia touched cheeks. Mozart played softly in the background.

"Your corporal was asking where you were," Elisabetta said. "We were beginning to worry."

"Sorry. Something came up at work."

"No apologies necessary," said the colonel's wife. "I'll get you a drink. Go. Mingle."

The apartment had been in his wife's family for years. Nothing ostentatious, just tastefully furnished in a blend of traditional pieces interspersed with Elisabetta's more contemporary selections. It worked. Spend as she might, Lola would never match it. Unlike her pal, the Donatis didn't have to prove their good taste.

Colonel Fabio waved a greeting from across the room. An elegant adult party. People were actually having conversations. Captain Villari stood in front of the fireplace. Beside him, Doctor Agari was having a talk with Villari's lieutenant, who appeared very much smitten with the glamorous pathologist. Natalia approached and she and the doctor wished one another happy holidays as they brushed cheeks.

"Francesca," Natalia said, "nice to see you away from your patients."

"Isn't it? Let me pay my respects to our hosts. Back in a minute."

The lieutenant looked sorry to see her go.

"Nice party." Captain Villari said upon greeting Natalia. "You're so lucky. Our commander in Rome would never invite us into his home to fraternize with his august self, nor would we ever be permitted to use his first name under any circumstances."

"The colonel is unusual," Natalia acknowledged. "Can I have word, privately?"

"Of course." He suggested his lieutenant circulate and turned his attention to Natalia.

"We're so glad to have you with us," she said.

"Thank you." Villari bowed ever so slightly. "Very much mutual, I assure you. Though I can't say for how much longer we will be here. My superior wants to know why we haven't found the Segli. He's under pressure to get me back, but you can't say no to the Vatican. You know how that goes."

"Maybe we'll get something useful out of Drako," Natalia said. "I'll let him stew a while before he's interviewed again."

Holding up his empty glass, Villari offered to bring her a drink. Natalia declined and he headed for the bar. Natalia spotted Angelina and her partner in a corner. Giuletta was resplendent in a purple sari edged in silver. Angelina wore navy pants and a white shirt under a maroon sweater. The peacock and the hen, Natalia thought as she made her way toward them.

"Angelina, glad you could make it. Giuletta, you look amazing."

"Doesn't she?"

Giuletta seemed tense. Natalia wondered if she'd interrupted something.

"Speaking of amazing," Giuletta said, "I had no idea Angie's boss lived in such a fancy place."

"Nice, isn't it," Natalia agreed.

"Very. I'm just going to grab another delicious shrimp puff before they disappear."

"Everything okay?" Natalia asked, as Giuletta made her way across the room through the crowd.

"Not really," Angelina said. "She's making noises again about wanting babies. What's the sense of having a kid so someone else can bring it up?"

"I assume Giuletta does better financially than a Carabiniere corporal," Natalia said. "Couldn't you two manage on her salary for a while and you look after a baby?"

"You trying to get rid of me?"

"On the contrary. Just being sensitive to the needs of my partner."

"Thanks, boss. I appreciate it – but being stuck home with a *bambino* is not my idea of a good time."

"Maybe Giuletta could take a long maternity leave and see if that satisfied her baby lust. Colonel Donati is lobbying for a promotion for you, by the way."

"He is?"

"Mmmm. You might be able to manage with her not working for a while, if it comes through."

"That would wonderful."

"Yeah. Not for public broadcast, though."

"Got it," Angelina said.

"I'll be right back," Natalia said.

On her way to the buffet, she encountered Cervino talking on his cell phone. When he saw her, he snapped it shut.

"My sister--" He grimaced, slightly inebriated. "Wants to know when I'll be home. She was invited. Must have tried on a dozen outfits. None of them satisfactory. Truth is, my sister is a painfully shy person. You alone too?"

"I am," Natalia said.

"Signora Nuovaletta was busy?"

She tried to get by him. "Excuse me."

Cervino blocked her. "Sorry. I didn't mean anything."

"Quite alright." Natalia pushed by.

"We need to talk." Cervino said.

"No. We don't."

"I'm old fashioned, Captain. Having women on the force doesn't please me."

"Tell me something new."

"You think I hate you – want to see you taken down. Would it surprise you to know that's not true?"

"It certainly would. What's your point, Marshal?"

"I take my oath seriously. You go against it and put us all in jeopardy -- everybody at Casanova. If you keep your ties with your Camorra pals, you can't continue as a Carabiniere. Simple as that."

"My private life isn't your concern."

"It is, Captain. We're soldiers, same as your friends in the Camorra."

"Natalia?" Elisabetta called from the living room.

"I grew up Forcella," he continued. "Did you know that? Teodoro Grappi was my best friend. I played football with him and his brothers. The girl I proposed to when we were six married one of the Gallos."

"Why are you telling me this?"

"Divided loyalties. I've been there. Colonel Donati did you a disservice when he arranged for your early posting to Naples. He should've followed the rules."

"Natalia," Elisabetta called again, waving.

Cervino stepped away so she could pass.

"Merry Christmas." He held out his hand. "Truce?"

"You reached out to some old boy at Carabinieri Command in Rome to tell him I had a loyalty problem? Now you want to make nice? I don't think so," Natalia said.

"Have it your way then."

"Bastard," she said under her breath. She gathered her things from a back bedroom quietly and slipped out the back door to the emergency staircase leading down. As soon as she got to the street, she phoned Claudio. He met her on Via Sapienza and drove her to his apartment. The doorman dozed beside a giant potted palm. He woke yawning. No doubt Claudio arriving home late accompanied by female visitors was commonplace.

The lobby and hallways were marble. Not too shabby, as Lola would have said. The elevator opened directly into his apartment. The man lived well. Soaring ceilings. A brocade couch with matching love seat. Leather club chairs. Wine colored drapes. Books lined one wall. Artwork tastefully displayed everywhere. Sounds from the street didn't penetrate the double-glazed windows. The dark marble floor in the living room was covered with a huge Persian carpet. Everything was well chosen, everything neatly ordered. Someone had a good eye, Natalia thought. Had a girlfriend done it or had he professional help? She preferred thinking the latter.

"What a fabulous place," Natalia said.

"You like it? I'm glad."

"Hungry?"

"Not very," Natalia said as he embraced her.

"I have a marvelous Barolo."

"Perfect," she said and hugged him back.

While he retrieved the wine, Natalia perused the bookshelves. Old law books with embossed spines filled a large section. On a side table were two photographs in leather frames: the snapshot she had seen of Drina and Claudio at his graduation, and a sepia print, quite faded, of a boy and a girl. Teenagers. She in a long skirt, he in a suit. Both wearing starched ruffled shirts.

"My grandparents," Claudio said, putting the wine on a green mosaic table and coming up beside her. He pressed his lips lightly against her neck. "Their wedding day. She was twelve. He just turned thirteen."

"So young."

"Our life expectancy isn't too good."

"What did they do?"

"Worked as migrant farmers, mostly. If the landowner was decent, he'd assign them a piece of land to grow themselves a garden. If not, they went hungry a lot of summers."

"A hard life."

"Yes, it was. I spent a few summers with them. I remember picking apricots, digging up potatoes. Cristina was a weaver. She made me a basket I still have. My grandfather made a guitar from scraps of wood. They could have been artisans," he returned the photograph to the small table, "if they hadn't the bad fortune to be born gypsies. I'm glad you're here." He put his arms around her. "I haven't been this happy for a long time. Strange, right?"

"What?"

"So much sorrow … to be happy at the same time."

Natalia didn't say anything.

"You're sure there isn't a boyfriend lurking in the wings?"

"Negative, Counselor."

"I find it hard to believe, a woman as attractive as you."

"And you?" Natalia said. "Have you ever been married?"

"No. No wife, no fiancée, not ever. Building my career ... there wasn't much time for a personal life. And truthfully, I never met anyone I felt this strongly about."

Natalia flushed. Lovely words, yet wasn't it too soon for such declarations? She exhaled. Her angel argued not to overthink each situation. Her devil jeered. Had she become so jaded, she questioned someone saying he was falling for her?

Of her girlfriends – Mariel was the most cautious. She took relationships very slowly – the few she engaged in. Her Milanese bookseller was the most serious suitor Natalia could recall. Ironically, it was tough girl Lola who had played it the safest with her choice of a man. Dominick wasn't exactly handsome but he obviously worshipped her.

"Natalia," Claudio reached for her hands.

"I'll just wash up," she said and stood.

"Of course." He led her down a long hallway. Its textured wallpaper reminded Natalia of bamboo, if bamboo were flecked with precious metals. Several large paintings, complete with brass light fixtures, were mounted there. Natalia recognized a Trunchette a nineteenth century sentimentalist who painted idyllic scenes of his home town. Pricey. Claudio's practice must be doing very well. Lenny DePretis kept him on a handsome retainer -- DePretis and who knew what other lovely entrepreneurs in the crime business? Perhaps she'd be smart to look into Attorney Palumbo's roster of clients before she got even more deeply involved.

"Voila!" He opened a mirrored door and flicked on the light in the bathroom. "I await your return."

The bathroom was larger than Natalia's oversized kitchen. A bouquet of periwinkle blue hyacinth sat on an onyx table. Fluffy beige towels filled the racks. She glanced at herself in the mirror. Her face was flushed. She opened the medicine cabinet, snooping. No evidence of female products. No evidence of anything. Empty. She closed it quietly and washed her hands with a bar of lemon scented soap, dried her hands and padded back to the living room. Claudio handed her a goblet as she sat down beside him.

"To us." He touched her glass with his and held her gaze.

Such beautiful eyes, she thought, grey with black flecks.

"To us."

Us? Natalia wasn't used to such declarations. She'd never experienced much success in the love department. What made her think her luck had changed? Did she and Claudio Palumbo really have a chance at a future, or was she simply another female in a long list of women he got involved with and abandoned when the thrill wore off?

"I wanted to tell you how sorry I am that we didn't meet under other circumstances," Claudio took her hand. "Since Drina's death I haven't functioned all that well. It's been hard just to get myself out of bed in the morning."

"It's natural after such a terrible shock."

"Would you like some music?"

"No. I like the quiet," she said.

"I wanted to thank you again for your help with Drina's brother."

"How's he doing?"

Claudio shook his head. "Not great. None of us are. I don't think Zorka will recover any time soon either, if ever."

"Poor woman."

He stroked her cheek, his forehead against hers.

"You never told me how it is that you're not in Annunziata."

"Luck. A teacher came to the settlement looking for children to attend school. She convinced my parents I should go. For her kindness, the Roma men set her car on fire."

"That's horrible."

"The first time I left our encampment and went into town alone I was nine. I'd saved money to buy cherries for my mother. A group of boys chased me into an alley. They beat me until an old lady called them off. They said it was a warning. If I came back they'd break my arms — or worse. 'Filthy *zingari*!' they called me. I remember thinking, how can a mosquito be dirty. It's so small."

"Tell me more," Natalia said.

"About what?"

"The Roma – polytheistic, right?"

"You've been studying up."

"Our teachers said nasty things about gypsies when I was in school. I decided to find out for myself. You have no churches, no bibles printed in your language."

"You need a literate population for that, and there aren't even Romani words for read or write. We're outcasts even in our own myths – and those of others. The Christians believe that gypsies forged the nails that crucified Christ – like the Jews drank the blood of Christian children. We declared we wouldn't have anything to do with the rest of mankind and kept moving. In hundreds of years none of that has changed much."

A line of Baudelaire's popped into her head and she quoted it to Claudio: "'*Life is so short, hope is so violent.*'"

"I'll have to think on that."

"Is Claudio Palumbo your name really? It sounds so Italian."

He swirled his wine. "My secret name is Culvato."

"Not Lashi?"

"No."

"Why is it all so secret?"

"What's the point of secrets if they're not secret?" He kissed her more passionately.

"Why tell me if it's all secret?"

"Because I don't like having secrets from you. You're not like them. I want to tell you everything. I want you to know my heart."

"Them?"

"The *gadje*."

"Lenny DePretis. How long have you been his lawyer?"

"More questions." He drew away.

"How long?"

"About five years. Why?"

"You were just starting out. No insult intended, but why did he choose you?"

Claudio retrieved his glass.

"I had a few write-ups when I started out. He read one of the articles. I guess he saw me as a kindred spirit."

"How so?"

"We're both outcasts. Me more than him. But he's from Bari – not the same as a homegrown Naples' boy."

"Did he and your cousin ever have a romantic relationship?"

"What?" He choked and put the goblet down.

"He came to the morgue when Drina was there."

"Everyone came to pay their respects ... to me, to Drina's mother."

"Did your cousin ever talk about her music teacher, complain that he was bothering her in any way?"

"The old man?"

Natalia nodded.

"No. Just about the *bashadi.*"

"Pardon?"

"The violin."

"What did he want in exchange?"

"Nothing. For her to accept it. The truth is she didn't trust anyone – couldn't imagine a gift without a price."

"And was there a price?"

"Absolutely not. Just that she take care of it, play it well, which she did."

"Are you sure? Such an extravagant gift. Perhaps he expected something in exchange?"

"He admired her talent. That's all there was, and she was appreciative. Anyone who believed in her – took an interest. She was fiercely loyal. No. He never laid a hand on her. I will swear to that. I don't think her teacher and his wife ever had children of their own – so in a way she was his legacy, a talent he helped nurture."

"Your cousin was a dedicated musician."

"She was."

"Did she have other interests?"

"Not that I knew of. Her life was her music – her violin and her bow. Performing, practice – it didn't leave time for much else."

"Were you and your cousin ever involved?"

"Romantically? Drina and I?"

"Yes."

"This is …. unthinkable." He moved away from her.

"I know in Roma culture it's not forbidden for cousins to marry," Natalia said. "Things happen. They're not meant to, they just do sometimes. We're not always in control of our emotions."

"I could never see Drina in that way," he said, gently. "I knew her when she was no bigger than a kitten. For me it would be like incest. Impossible. You're wasting time with this, Natalia."

"Maybe. Regardless, I have to look at everything in her life, Claudio. You understand – there maybe something hidden in the corners. Your cousin was murdered – a violent senseless act. I need to find answers."

"Very well," he said, growing serious. "Go on."

"The headmistress at her school once told me that she stopped attending suddenly. You knew about that of course."

"I did."

"Did you know she'd been bullied by some of the students in her second year in high school?"

"Not until later. Drina didn't ask for help. She never displayed weakness. It's a Roma trait. The world reviles us and we learn to take care of ourselves – no outside help. If we suffer, no one must know it – even those closest to us. Drina handled her problems by herself."

"Apparently the bullying had gone on for a time," Natalia said. "And then one day she left abruptly. Did you ever try to persuade her to go back?

"I tried. I tried to reason with her," Claudio said, "tell her that school was her chance. She said it was clear she would never belong in the *gadje* world. My cousin saw the world in black and white – no shades, no nuance. Her classmates treated her like shit, and she was gone. If she'd had any second thoughts – which I seriously doubt – those gypsy girls at Torregaveta finished them."

Natalia knew the story of the two little girls. Eight and nine years old, they'd traveled from their squalid settlement in Scampia to the beach on the Bay of Naples. Their objective was to escape the brutal heat and maybe sell some trinkets to families enjoying a day by the sea. The youngest sister climbed onto some rocks and fell into dangerous waters where the current was treacherous. The older sister leapt in to save her. They both drowned. Their bodies were hauled out and laid on the beach where sunbathers continued to picnic. A group of teenagers tossed a Frisbee back and forth across their corpses. A picture of it hit the papers. For the first time the attitudes toward gypsies became a public issue debated in parliament and the press.

Claudio seemed about to weep again.

"She never went back to school." Claudio hunched forward, face in his hands. "Is that what you wanted to talk about?"

"The headmistress suggested she might have gotten pregnant."

Claudio looked startled.

"It's not uncommon," Natalia said, "girls want to be free, trying sex for the first time, not knowing about precautions. In your culture they are women at a very young age. And Drina was what — fifteen, sixteen when she left school?"

He stared into his hands.

"I don't mean to upset you, Claudio, believe me. I'm so sorry. I heard her play," Natalia said, trying to cheer him. "She had an amazing talent."

"You saw her perform?" He seemed surprised. "Where?"

"The last time was in the courtyard at San Domenico. Maybe a month ago."

"I gave her an allowance so she wouldn't beg coins from tourists. I hated it and told her it embarrassed me."

"It's hardly begging," Natalia said. "People appreciated her talent, as you've seen from the tapes. Where Drina wasn't welcome was in the Roma community. You've explained some of the reasons, but could there have been others as well — a transgression you were unaware of?"

Claudio shifted. "I can't imagine."

"There is some kind of tribunal system within the Roma community, yes?"

"The Rom Baro it's called. It settles small disputes."

"What about bigger ones? Serious disputes?"

"They go before the Kris Romani, a tribunal the elders convene. I used to eavesdrop when I was small and could get away with it. Probably the reason I became a lawyer."

"Were Roma ever condemned to death?"

"I've never heard of them ruling on a capital crime, no. The most severe judgment was exile. For us being ostracized means oblivion. It's unthinkable, unimaginable."

"Claudio, you live your life as a *gadje*, yet you identify as Roma."

"How I live is one thing. Who I am, is quite another."

"In spite of her self-sufficiency — would Drina have confided in you if she was in serious trouble?"

"Probably not."

"Did she seem at all different recently?"

"Other than concern about her audition for the competition in Rome, she was her usual bubbly self. God, it's unreal. Some nights she comes in dreams. I wake up mornings and I expect to see her." He tossed back the last of his wine.

"Her murder was brazen but not random," Natalia said. "Whoever did it was an experienced killer." "It couldn't have been a Romany."

"Claudio, you've participated in murder trials. You know ninety percent of the time the victim knows the killer. Drako was there. Maybe involved. Why not a Roma?"

"No."

"There are plenty of gypsies trafficking narcotics nowadays," she continued. "They are not unacquainted with violence."

He ran a hand through his hair. He looked miserable. "How did we get on this?"

She reached for him. "Let's not talk about it anymore. My fault."

She put her arms around him, but he shook her off.

"Do you want me to leave?" she said.

"No," he mumbled. "I'm too tired to talk anymore. Let's go to bed."

He fell asleep immediately, before she'd even finished undressing. Natalia lay awake, berating herself for ruining their evening. Why couldn't she leave the case alone?

Claudio's cousin had started her climb out of Annunziata with his help and her magnificent talent. Why would she turn to crime, risk a bright future, acclaim -- her very life? What would have been worth such a risk?

Chapter 16

Natalia slipped out before Claudio woke up. She took the stairs. Not a sound came from behind the sleek mahogany doors on the way down. On the ground floor, next to a table of orchids, the doorman shook himself awake as she approached. Pulling on his cap, he unlocked the wrought iron gate that guarded the entrance to the building and let her out.

Claudio Palumbo's Ferrari wasn't the only fancy car in the courtyard. A sleek red Mercedes, with tinted windows, was parked beside a cobalt-blue Miatta. Its uniformed chauffeur buffed the hood.

She cut across Via Toledo and proceeded toward her flat. The narrow streets were quiet. In front of the fish market a skinny black cat gnawed a spiny carcass. As she passed the pink *palazzo* on the corner of her block, an old woman peered at her from behind lace curtains. With her cap of white hair, black scarf and weathered face she could have stepped out of an old painting. She was old world, like *Zia* Antonietta. Between work and her new romance, Natalia had neglected her father's sister and reminded herself to check on her soon.

She thought about her again as she passed Luigina's door on the way to her own. Luigina's canaries were singing loudly, while their mistress prepared for early

229

mass, surely to be followed by coffee with her pals at the Café Partenope.

Luigina's husband was long gone, her children busy with their own lives. She and Natalia's other neighbors were mostly well on the far side of passion and its heartaches. In some way it must be a relief, she thought, although sometimes she imagined it must be lonely. The night with her new lover hadn't gone well at all and she wondered how long it might be before she bought a songbird for herself.

Natalia took a quick shower. As she dried off, she examined her face in the mirror and pulled at the skin starting to sag under the eyes, and the pillow of flesh under her chin. She and Mariel had sworn they'd never resort to plastic surgery, but that had been when they were young and immortal. Mariel, with her slim features, and elegant bone structure, had no need for it. Natalia was another story. But she didn't possess the vanity required. And certainly she hadn't the funds. The idea of cosmetic surgery seemed totally alien, Lola's forays notwithstanding.

No one else in the neighborhood would ever have considered it. The beauty parlor was one thing, but surgery? Even her mother and grandmother made the trip to Sofia's salon on the eve of christenings and weddings. It was a tradition as well to go the afternoon before Christmas, to beautify oneself in time for midnight mass.

Natalia was ten when she'd been initiated, accompanied by her mother and grandmother. Fussed over by Sofia, subjected to the torture of the curling iron, she emerged with a lacquered crown and a new sense of possibilities. They'd stopped in various shops along the route home to show her off. *Nonna* bought her a package of satin hair ribbons. The baker slipped a handful of fresh *biscotti* into her bag. She could see how beauty might work for a girl.

Among the neighborhood, women temporary fix-ups were fine, even celebrated. To alter the face God gave you wasn't. That was like a sacrilege. You lived with the face you were born with, for better or worse. It was an unspoken covenant -- to accept the appearance God provided. The work of undertakers was exempt.

The *madrinas* and other Camorra ladies who'd risen to power, Lola among them, had revolted against such strictures. They'd consolidated their power with guile and merciless force, and had grown comfortable with the concept of altering fate — their own and that of others. The mobster godmothers tended religiously to their physical well-being and youthful appearance. That included wearing whatever face they could buy. The exception was one Camorra lady who'd risen to fame while Natalia was growing up. She was called *Masculona* -- Tomboy. Early in her career she'd been shot in the jaw and proudly wore the damage as a testament to her strength and disregard for brutality.

Women had to be wilier than men, Natalia thought, make choices that served them, no matter the consequences. It was the only way to survive.

"Claudio, Claudio," she said out loud. She was falling hard — yet why did she continue to doubt his feelings for her?

***

Outside the pet store on Via Foria bird cages sat covered and sitting in patches of sun.

"Good thing Giuletta isn't here," Angelina said. "She'd probably go inside and complain the birds were freezing.

231

Last week she brought home a baby swift. The cats went crazy. We locked it in the bathroom. It's a wild creature, right? It'll probably die."

"Maybe not," Natalia said. "It might recover." She took a pastry out of the Lucia's Bakery bag and offered it to Angelina.

"No thanks. I was ten pounds lighter when I started at Casanova."

A group of girls was taping a poster to the wall of San Pascual. It was another enlarged still from a video: Drina playing in front of San Domenico Maggiore. The girls wore tight jeans and heels though they couldn't have been more than fifteen. There were youngsters putting up such posters of Drina all over town, on kiosks, buildings, clinics, and the many permanent street shrines that were a Neapolitan tradition. Most of the tourists ignored them as they moved beneath the fluttering palms, in the cold bright sun. Several stopped and posed for photographs in front of the palace, others stepped into the courtyard where stone busts and marble cherubs surrounded the fountain.

Natalia was familiar with the Church of San Pascual. When Lola had been pregnant with Giovanna, she'd insisted Natalia and Mariel accompany her there to the preserved body of Blessed Egideo, the two-hundred-year old saint – protector of pregnant women.

Natalia recalled Lola dressed in white – "for purity," she'd declared, her stomach straining against her dress. A white hat, complete with veil, completed the outfit.

Natalia and Mariel thought the preserved body was creepy. They'd never known Lola to believe in prayer as a method to get what she wanted, but apparently she'd had a dream with evil portent. She was determined to protect her unborn baby in the final weeks before she came into the world.

232

"You see, what'd I tell you?" Lola said when Natalia and Mariel visited her in the hospital after she gave birth to a healthy ten-pound girl.

Lola's round young face came back to her. Devoid of make-up, without a wrinkle, she could have been a schoolgirl. Never an innocent, nonetheless, there was something of the Madonna that evening, as she held her newest in her arms. The sun was going down and Naples was bathed in a ruby light. Mariel and Natalia had deposited their bouquet of roses, and left mother and daughter sleeping.

As Natalia and Angelina approached the Angevin Castle, street merchants dumped their wares into blankets and hurried away. That was odd. Police usually left them alone. It seemed strange they'd flee. After the Piazza Garibaldi, this was the most popular spot for the Africans to sell their wares, the bright colors and modern designs of their Gucci and Versace knock offs making a striking contrast to the ancient stone.

A skinny policeman in wraparound sunglasses lounged against one of the sculptured lions. He ground out his cigarette as the officers approached.

"Is there something going on?" Angelina asked.

"They're making a special," he indicated to a man and woman setting up a large video camera on its tripod. "The Africans don't want to be on camera."

"They have a permit?" Natalia asked.

"Yeah."

"RAI TV?"

"Al Jazeera." The cop looked completely bored. "Soon as they're out of here, we get to leave."

"Lucky you," Angelina said.

"What's going on?" A young woman accompanied by two Chihuahuas addressed the officer. Despite the chill, her white jacket was open to a revealing pink t-shirt with black sequins and plenty of cleavage. They left him to deal with her and made their way back toward the station.

"Any news on the promotion?" Angelina asked.

"Soon," Natalia said. Though privately she wasn't so sure. Unless the economy improved, there wouldn't be the fund to implement any promotions. Colonel Donati had recently confided that if he didn't retire a *Generale di Brigade*, he'd made peace with it.

"Any progress on the baby negotiation?" Natalia asked, changing the subject.

"Not really. Every time we talk about it we get into an argument. Promotion or no -- a kid with two moms? Maybe in Rome. Here? Less likely. We'd always have to be antsy and careful. You?"

"Me what"?

"Are you contemplating having kids."

"Probably isn't going to happen."

"Sorry. Didn't mean to intrude."

"That's okay."

"No. No it isn't."

"Yes it is. Really."

Nico Ortuna was up on a ladder stringing lights above the door of his café, overseen by a pair of elderly cigar smokers.

"It's almost Christmas," Angelina said.

"Doing anything special?"

"Dinner at my aunt's in the Vomero. She's an amazing cook. Otherwise we're just taking it easy, catching up on sleep."

"Sounds nice."

"It should be if we can manage to avoid bickering. You?"

"Dinner with Lola. Pay a visit to my father's sister. Midnight Mass. Pray we don't get a call-out. I'm watch commander Christmas Day."

"How'd you get stuck with that?" Angelina looked at her sympathetically.

"How does a quick bite at Manny's sound?"

"Good. But I'll have to take a rain check. I promised Giuletta. It's our anniversary."

"How many years?" Natalia asked.

"Five."

"Impressive," Natalia said. "*Brava.*"

"Thanks."

Natalia's mobile buzzed. Lola.

"Mario Tortou is dead. Thought you'd be interested."

"You're sure he's dead?"

"He's dead."

Tortou. That was interesting. Killed days after the hit of the young gypsy girl.

"Thanks, Lola."

She told Natalia where he'd been found.

"Who is he working for these days?" Natalia asked.

"The Fabricantis mainly – odd jobs for a bunch of others."

"Like who?"

"I can't go there."

"Can't or won't?"

***

"I have to check out a body," Natalia said.

"Where?" Angelina asked.

Natalia told her. "But I'll handle it. Have lunch with your love. I'll call if I need you."

"You sure? Why doesn't the Angevin precinct handle it?"

"Because it's Mario Tortou."

A cool winter light angled across the plaza. The Africans had made themselves scarce once again. Several pigeons, unconcerned with the commotion, waddled, scavenging for crumbs. A police officer ushered Natalia to the victim. They'd taken him out of the dumpster and laid him out. A crew from RAI was setting up. Natalia informed them it was a crime scene and they weren't permitted to film. They retreated to the perimeter, and began interviewing people in the crowd, which included a few horrified tourists. Natalia didn't like it, but there was nothing she could do.

A bullet shot from close range had ripped open his chest. The man was soaked in blood. Natalia slipped on her plastic booties and gloves before she bent down. Tortou's face was untouched save a stipple of blood clotted around the lips. They'd sewn his mouth shut. Before or after he was killed? she wondered.

Sewing of the lips was done by the Camorra when someone had snitched – a lesson for anyone else who might be tempted. But Tortou's reputation rested on the fact that he never ever talked.

"It wasn't a robbery," the young officer said, handing her an evidence bag. "Several hundred euros."

A girl in white jeans and a polka dot blouse leaned in and snapped a picture with her cell phone.

"I'll take that," Natalia reached for it. "You can pick it up at Casanova Station tomorrow."

"Fucking Bitch," the girl said as she stomped off.

Natalia assigned the officer to crowd control and crouched back down to look at the victim. If he had known he was going to die that day, might he have bothered to shave? A sociopath for sure, Natalia thought, responsible for untold brutal deaths over the course of his long career – but in the face of death his eyes had frozen with fear.

She slipped felt for a weapon. Nothing. Tortou would never step outside his house without one, so whoever did the job had helped themselves.

Had Tortou killed the gypsy girl? But who had killed him? Someone who knew the game, but not that well. Which implied an outsider. Someone from elsewhere – or someone not of the culture.

The mortuary van rolled into the plaza and stopped. Dottore Agari emerged clad in white overalls and booties. She waved away a reporter and hurried toward Natalia.

"What do we have here?" she asked as she snapped on her gloves.

Natalia explained.

"Pretty," she said. "Who'd he piss off?"

"Not sure," Natalia said. "Can you manage here without me?"

"*Certo.* I'm a trained professional," she smiled. "I'll let you know if we find anything interesting. Raffi!"

The forensic photographer emerged from the van, cameras dangling, cell phone pressed to his ear.

***

Tortou lived not far from Natalia on Vicaria Vecchia above a cheese store. The *palazzo* was elegant, as the nineteenth century buildings tended to be – but its mustard-colored shutters hadn't been painted in a while – nor the dark stone cleaned. An enormous white lace tablecloth hung from a line suspended between Tortou's and the building across the street. That and a child's tricycle.

The smell of mozzarella assailed Natalia as she rang the caretaker's door. They climbed the stairs to the dead man's apartment.

"I knew his mother and father. There's never been any trouble," *Signor* Panza said, "why did they do that to him?"

He informed Natalia she was the first person to visit the deceased man's apartment. That was no surprise. A good hit man kept his personal life a shadow. Natalia asked him how long *Signor* Tortou had lived there.

"Since he was a boy," he said, "over thirty years."

So Tortou inherited his apartment and had chosen to remain. A humble address – surely he could have afforded more lavish quarters. But he was loyal to his roots.

Signor Panza admitted her and left her to do her job.

A gloomy space – even after she opened the heavy drapes. Natalia did a quick inventory: a shabby green couch – a copy of last week's *Il Messagero* lay on the floor. One beige chair with springs sticking out of the upholstery – a plastic TV tray set up beside it. Other than the newspaper, there was no sign of reading material. Natalia wondered how far Tortou had gone in school.

A half-empty cup of coffee was on the kitchen table next to a piece of *pane nero*. He'd managed only a few bites of the black bread before he'd rushed out. Once upon a time, Tortou had felt optimistic enough to purchase a plant. He'd put it on a sunny window ledge above the sink. Its brown leaves were twisted and crumbled. The linoleum floor was worn to the wood below.

Natalia opened the refrigerator to a package of moldy cheese, a box of pasta, one shriveled tomato. She could have been looking into her own she thought, as she closed the door and proceeded to the bedroom.

There was the requisite wooden carving of Christ bowing his crown of thorns above Tortou's narrow bed.

Otherwise, the dingy walls were bare. It looked like they hadn't been painted in decades. The closet contained three pairs of trousers and half a dozen shirts – everything was either brown or black. A hit man did not own a light-colored wardrobe, for obvious reasons. The one suit looked custom made – but the collar of the jacket was frayed.

In the top drawer, his underwear was neatly folded – the middle drawer neat where he kept his tools.

He was organized – an important trait in his line of work. Tortou did his jobs close up and quick. He didn't have the need for fancy equipment – the stiletto and the Glock had served him just fine. The stiletto was too large for the wound inflicted on Drina. If it was Tortou, he'd gotten rid of the murder weapon. There was something taped to the side of the drawer – a plain envelope. Inside was a thick needle, used for stitching canvas or leather. She put it into the evidence bag.

The room reminded her of a monk's quarters – no relics of a private life, no memorabilia – and no photos save one – a black and white snapshot of a plump middle-aged couple smiling into the camera. They were posed on a sunny balcony with the sea and dramatic cliffs of Capri behind them. She imagined that the dutiful son treated his parents to a nice vacation when he realized his first real profit.

Tortou certainly hadn't spent much on himself. His one indulgence was a large flat screen TV on the wall opposite his bed.

Nothing in the apartment had been updated – the bathroom had the original black and white tiles. A worn toothbrush and a flattened tube of paste. An electric razor and a comb. A bottle of stomach medicine. No aftershave, no cologne, but there wouldn't be – scents can trigger a bystander's memory.

Tortou was a man who'd lived and died, leaving almost no trace – like a snail, she thought, making its careful way across its small world – albeit a snail that moved silently from rivers of blood.

He'd kept his parents' bedroom as it must have been when they were alive – the *camera di letto,* the large mahogany matrimonial bed, its lilac quilt preserved under a sheet of plastic. Another photograph of the happy couple in white aprons outside the cheese shop. Natalia wondered if they'd been unhappy that the son hadn't wanted to follow in their footsteps. Had they realized their dutiful son was a cold-blooded murderer?

She returned to the living room. Tortou had been a solitary man – his life was his work, much like hers.

He'd taken an oath as had she. He knew the dangers of his profession. There was always the possibility that he would be sacrificed in the pursuit of crime, as she in the pursuit of justice.

Had he been lonely? Had he survived on memories of his parents? In his profession, it was dangerous to have friends, even if he had been so-disposed. It went with the territory – same as for her. But she had Mariel and Lola she reminded herself, and Antonietta, plus a boyfriend now and then. Certainly, she wasn't in the same category as this man – was she?

She descended to the ground floor and returned the key to the porter. Across the courtyard, a young woman was mopping. Canaries sang, flaunting blue and yellow wings.

***

Dr. Agari called to confirm that Mario Tortou had died of gun trauma and added that the thin, sharp tool recovered at the deceased's apartment had been recently soaked in bleach, destroying all possible trace of contamination. Between Drako's awls and Tortou's needle, she now had an assortment of possible weapons, none of which she could definitively assign as the instrument of Drina's death.

Natalia asked Angelina to pull everything they had on Tortou. Angelina shortly reported that a note in the Camorra database indicated it was a large file going back many years and hadn't yet been digitized.

"Want me to put in a request for the hard copy?" Angelina asked.

"Please," Natalia said. "We need it soonest."

His full original file, four inches thick, arrived from central records by motorcycle courier half an hour later. Angelina glanced through and summed up the contents for her boss: "Not a nice guy. Two convictions earlier on for violent felonies. Served a year in Filanghieri before the Gracci's lawyer saw to it that he got out. Accused of killings on three dozen occasions after that. Implicated in homicides in Palermo and Marseille. No murder convictions. Not so much as an assault charge."

"Yes," Natalia said. "Witnesses had a way of disappearing each time."

"Most recently suspected in a double murder. The Bandini twins, four years ago."

"The mad twins," Natalia said, mind drifting, remembering Mario when he was the sullen, silent kid in elementary school.

"Correct," Angelina said. "Each brother was stabbed once in the throat ... with a shoemaker's awl. A serious killer, from the look of him."

"Yes, he is -- was. And reasonably priced. Someone wanted her seriously dead if he hired Mario Tortou to do it."

"So much for a crime of passion," Angelina said.

241

Chapter 17

Drako still refused to talk. Natalia sent him back to his cell, still concerned for his safety. Jails were easy enough to reach into if someone wanted his silence assured. She ordered him segregated.

"He's scared." Angelina took off her cap and smoothed her hair. My instincts say Drako's not a killer. Forgery, yeah okay. Murder...?"

"How did you come to that?" Natalia asked.

"His eyes."

"Eyes?"

"Yes. They don't look like a killer's eyes."

"And what do a killer's eyes look like?"

"I don't know. Cold. Like when they look at you they don't see anything."

"If he helped Drina with the thefts," Natalia suggested, "the violin could have been a payment. Or she may have simply given it to him before she made her getaway."

"Or maybe he just picked it up from the street as she lay dying," Angelina said, "after he helped kill her. Before I forget, I put together a summary for your signature of where we are in the case. It can go on top of the report."

"Looks terrific." Natalia slipped it into her bag. "But add Captain Villari's name to mine and get his signature too before you send Colonel Donati a copy."

"Will do." The radiator clanked. Angelina said, "I put in a requisition for a new one. We might get it by next winter. Oh, this is for you too." She slipped a sheet of paper across the desk. "I organized the information on the art thefts chronologically -- location, artwork stolen, its dimensions and approximate value. Villari's guy helped me."

"Excellent," Natalia said. "Do add him to the distribution on this. How did I ever manage without you?"

"You didn't?" she grinned.

Natalia's phone buzzed. Cesa. She informed Natalia she'd taken it upon herself to look into the sale of one of the French canvases stolen last summer. It had been quietly sold to a collector. She contacted him, and explained about the theft. He seemed shocked, clearly worried, but he wouldn't give her any information except to say he had privately purchased it from a dealer. Her guess was that it had been fenced and given or sold to a dealer to act as intermediary.

***

As Natalia approached the Sanzari Funeral Parlor, Dora sloshed a bucket of dirty water into the street.

"Sorry, Natalia," she apologized.

"It's okay. You didn't get me."

The caretaker had a face like one of Gepetto's creations. Tidy always, she made do with cast-off clothing and the occasional coffee at Francy's, accompanied by a sandwich if the benefactor was feeling generous. She had a room behind the embalming studio where she spent her nights, her only protection being a *cornetto* on a piece of string tied around her neck.

"Has Tortou's wake been held?" Natalia asked her. Dora knew each death in the quarter – cause of death, behavior of next of kin.

"Has it ever. Old man Fabricanti laid out a feast. I went. Took home a shopping bag of food. Not that many people there, if you know what I mean. What could he do now, I told them? He's dead."

Natalia rummaged in her purse and found a ten *euro* note. She slipped the bill into Dora's apron pocket. "*Buon Natale*, Dora."

"Bless you." Dora kissed her hand. "You're an angel."

Hardly an angel, Natalia thought. Only too human. And humans need groceries if they want to eat, she reminded herself, as she stepped into Sergio's grocery store to peruse the cheese and *antipasti* in the cold case. None of it appealed. The Sicilian tomatoes, on the other hand, were lush and red. She bagged a half dozen and grabbed a box of fresh penne pasta on her way to the cash register.

Sergio added a bottle of his homemade Chianti and resumed his seat outside, impervious to the cool evening. Sergio had dreamt of becoming a singer but that hadn't panned out. Every year around the holidays, he brewed a vat of wine in the back of his shop and gave it out to his neighbors. The wine was closer to battery fluid than ambrosia, but it would've been insulting to refuse. Natalia thanked him for her bottle and promised to stop by soon for a chat.

As she approached her building her cellphone chimed and vibrated. Claudio.

"You slipped out and left me sleeping," he said.

"You looked like you could use it."

"Actually," Claudio said, "I'm calling to apologize."

"Don't." Natalia entered her building and started the climb to her flat. "I understand."

"I need to tell you something. I think I'm falling in love, Natalia."

"Oh, Claudio." She didn't know what to say. "I can't talk right now."

"Maybe when this is over--" He sounded hurt. "I miss you."

"I miss you too," Natalia said. She didn't add what she was thinking: more than you can imagine.

"I want to help you find Drina's killer."

"Please, it's not your job to find Drina's killer," Natalia said. "It's mine. You need to leave it to me."

"I still want to see you, *Cara.* I'll expect you Friday."

Distracted by the phone call, Natalia almost didn't notice her door mat was pushed to the side. Luigina Recchio scrubbed the hallways almost daily, being obsessively tidy. She would have left the mat exactly as she found it.

Sweat beading her neck, Natalia drew her gun, worked the key in the lock, and pushed the door open. She moved quickly through the rooms. *Il Messagero* was strewn on the couch where she'd left it. Likewise the pile of mail dumped on the coffee table. She was sure she'd left her coffee cup on the side table in the living room, yet there it was in the kitchen sink. Was she misremembering?

Mariel and Lola had keys, as well as Luigina and the porter. But they would never have entered her apartment without her knowledge. A break-in would have been the more obvious way to intimidate. This was a clumsy but surreptitious visit. Had that weasel from Rome gone over the colonel's head and planted a bug somewhere? Maybe a microphone was already in place and they had removed it so there would be no evidence they'd used illegal means to entrap her? Was it there that first night with Claudio? Upsetting thoughts all.

The front door lock was an antique. The lieutenant would have had no trouble gaining access. Shit. She put her groceries down, unlatched the balcony door and stepped outside for some air. A cat shot through the shadows down below. The temperature was dropping. Natalia shivered. She went back in, threw a few overnight things into a bag and let herself out.

***

Virginia Woolf made a beeline for Natalia's lap, while Mariel, elegant in a caftan and matching slippers, retrieved two glasses and a bottle of brandy she rarely opened. Her hair fell loose to her shoulders. Natalia noticed the first hints of gray.

A crystal vase with a spray of yellow and rust red chrysanthemums graced a low wooden table. Such a lovely and peaceful place, Natalia thought as she eased a thick down pillow behind her back. Virginia Woolf purred with contentment.

"Boyfriend trouble?" Mariel inquired after they'd taken sips.

"That too, yes. But it's the job, actually."

"If it's any consolation, Cesare and I are no longer an item."

"Seriously?"

Mariel tucked a strand of silky hair behind her ear. "Don't sound so happy. Yes, seriously."

"What happened?"

"He gave me an ultimatum. Move to Milan by the New Year or else he needs to explore 'other options,' as he put it. He was quite stern."

"I hope you're not suffering," Natalia said, "because, yes, I admit it. Thank God you're not moving away, dear friend."

"I have to admit I'm relieved on some level," Mariel said. "I'm so used to doing things my way: going where I please, when I please without consulting my lord and master, which is about how he presented himself. So what's happening with your dreamy lawyer? The dew is off the rose?"

"It isn't," Natalia said. "That's the problem."

"That doesn't sound like a problem."

"Trust me, it is."

"Men," Mariel said. "And we thought it was going to be so easy. Sort of automatic."

"Like the fairy tales," Natalia laughed.

"That's why they're called fairy tales," Mariel said. "Are you hungry?"

"Actually, I am."

"Good. I was just going to indulge in some mozzarella and some bread from Lucia's."

"Perfect." Natalia produced the tomatoes from Sergio's.

Mariel shifted a candle and a stack of magazines on the low wooden table. "Let's have it here, it's more relaxing than at table."

"Can I help?" Natalia started to get up.

"Sit. Keep the old girl company."

Natalia lay back. Virginia Woolf stretched, pushed her back paws against Natalia's stomach before curling into a ball once again. She could hear Mariel slicing on the wooden cutting board in the kitchen.

"Lola said to remind you about Christmas Eve," Mariel called out and brought back a basket of bread and a platter artfully arranged with layers of cheese and tomato.

"I wouldn't miss it," Natalia said. Midnight Christmas mass at the Duomo was a ritual of theirs going back to their childhoods. "This looks delicious."

"You want to talk about whatever is getting to you?"

"Not particularly. It's *complichisce,*" Natalia said. "When I figure it out you'll be the first to know."

Mariel offered her more *mozzarella.* "It's nice having you here," she said.

"I appreciate your letting me hide out."

"For as long as you like. You couldn't be more welcome," she said and raised a glass.

***

Refreshed after her night at Mariel's, Natalia arrived at Casanova ready to tackle the day's work. She looked over the report and summary Angelina had prepared, and took a copy along to Captain Villari's office in the second floor conference room for him to co-sign.

He greeted her warmly and asked her to sit. She indicated the report in her hand.

"You better look and see if you want anything changed since your name is going on it as well."

"Speaking of names, I've been going over the list of artists and paintings." He passed her a copy. "The six earlier canvases and the Segli are all from the Baroque period. All are by Italians – males except for Artemisia Gentileschi."

Natalia was familiar with Gentileschi, one of her favorite painters. Artemesia left Rome for Naples to be closer to her idol – Michelangelo Merisi da Caravaggio. She opened a studio on Via Troya, painted portraits and lived for the rest of her life in her adopted city. Villari noted that Carraciolo and Spada were Neapolitan by birth.

248

Recco as well. Recco, known as the fish painter, worked in his family's studio churning out still-life paintings of fish. Copies of the thickly rendered sea creatures dotted the walls of many *trattorias* until this day. Spada and Carraciolo had spent considerable time in Caravaggio's studio. As had the others.

From what Natalia recalled from art history classes – Spada was particularly close to *Signor* Merisi. As was Segli, she mused, and wondered if they'd been rivals for Carvaggio's affections.

Villari peered at her over his reading glasses.

"All were like their leader, either Neapolitans or hiding out in Naples, or both, where they kept company with Caravaggio and the other *caravaggistas*," she said.

"Yes. Caravaggio's posse," Villari joked.

"All six worked in Naples," Natalia reiterated. "Segli was the seventh. The two shared a studio at one point, and possibly were lovers. He fancied himself a rival of Caravaggio's. But they were scarcely in the same league."

"Gentileschi was well known beyond Naples. Certainly Caravaggio was far more famous," Villari said, "— and rightly so." He sighed, exasperated. "Seven 17th century artists have their early paintings stolen from different church buildings where Drina performed. Three French painters last summer. One painting's been sold off. The rest, apparently not. Why would someone be stockpiling works of such modest value, relatively speaking?"

The phone rang and Villari answered, quickly handing it over to Natalia. "It's for you."

It was Cesa Cherubini, her former teacher. She told Natalia she'd gotten word through a French dealer, that an important work of art had found its way to town.

"You said to call if anything interesting turned up. I don't know if it's related, but it's very interesting. I've arranged for a private viewing. Care to join me?"

"Absolutely. And may I bring a friend?" Natalia said, looking at Captain Villari.

"What?" he said, as she hung up.

"My old art teacher," Natalia said. "She's suspicious about a recovered painting."

"And she thinks it's related to what we are pursuing?" Villari inquired.

"Very possibly but don't ask me exactly how just yet."

***

This afternoon, Cesa's glorious hair was gone, cropped and feathered. A queen without her crown, Natalia thought as her former art professor greeted them. Not only that, her high heels and splashy mini had been replaced with a pair of black pantaloons and an oversized grey sweater.

The apartment was spare as well – a grey futon couch and low lacquered table on which a deep purple tulip peered from a ceramic vase. The walls were devoid of art. Natalia saw no evidence of personal memorabilia – photographs, scraps of paper, mess of any kind. A meditative space, she thought – as if her former professor was retreating from the world. Once upon a time not so long ago, Cesa strutted through the world a woman aglow with ideas and a mission. The flamboyant woman who sported rainbow streaks one day and green hair the next was nowhere in evidence.

"Such a tasteful apartment," Natalia said.

"Thank you. I'm in my Japanese phase," Cesa explained. "Simplify, simplify. I'm afraid I've given up coffee as well. Is tea all right?"

"Of course."

"Good."

She prepared their tea with a whisk and poured it into rust colored ceramic bowls. Natalia noticed that her hands were shaking.

"How do you like the tea?"

"Interesting," Villari said. "My daughter is always brewing roots and herbs."

"It's delicious." Natalia said. The truth was she was never a fan of tea, and found this concoction somewhere between dirt and leaf.

"Violetta could never stand the stuff. It was coffee – as strong as it could be made. My partner," Cesa explained to Villari. "We were together for nearly forty years – youth to old age. She passed earlier this year."

"I'm sorry," he said.

"Don't be." A flash of the young Cesa sparked in her eyes. "I'm still very much alive, and I consider myself lucky. Violetta and I enjoyed a full life together. I'm thankful for that." She tipped the bowl against her lips. "Of course back then we had to be careful. Nowadays it's different, thank God. There's something to be said for change."

She finished her tea and set it aside. Her guests had stopped drinking theirs.

"Shall we be off then?" Cesa said "I've never had a police escort to an art gallery before."

Villari drove, using the flashers and siren, and got them there in minutes.

"Cesa and Captain Monte," Annalisa Russo said after she realized Professor Cherubini hadn't arrived alone. "What a pleasant surprise." Her expression shifted slightly but she managed to keep her bright smile intact. "Delighted to see you all. Welcome to the Gallery Russo."

Natalia introduced Villari and explained he worked for the Art Command in Rome.

"Fascinating," Annalisa responded – aqua nails fingering drop earrings – topaz that glinted as she turned her head. "And Professor Cherubini. Your reputation precedes you. We are honored to have you here."

"Reputation?" Cesa said. "Hardly. A couple of articles."

"In the finest journals in Italy," Natalia said. "And there were several books."

Cesa waved off the compliment and clapped her hands together.

"This is very exciting, getting a preview of something so remarkable. When are the public viewings?" she asked.

"They were to start tomorrow," Annalisa said. "But I've been contacted by some investors … so I'm not sure the public will have their peek after all."

"That's too bad," Natalia said. "Surely it deserves to be seen and appreciated."

"Certainly, yes. I was very much looking forward to unveiling it. The press, the favorable publicity. But what can you do?" she shrugged. "It's business. They made quite an offer. The seller would be a fool not to accept."

"That is a shame," Villari said.

Cesa said, "I do hope the seller won't be hasty about accepting. I have several international clients who would be very interested in what you are offering."

"Unfortunately the sellers want minimum exposure of their treasure," Annalisa said. "It's a shame. Personally, I'd love to have it exhibited where everyone can see it. Would you believe I've had several inquiries from museums – one in Amsterdam, two in Tokyo. A Russian collector called from London and offered to pay for bulletproof glass gratis and to put down a guarantee just for the right to make an offer. How they got word I have no idea."

She led them through her office, a minimalist space in which her malachite desk floated above an off white carpet, all it bathed in light from the large plate glass window. A crimson leather settee took up one wall. Above hung a raw canvas slashed with thick red paint.

They passed through an imposing black door manned by an armed guard, and followed him into a dim room, its walls covered in brown velvet. An embroidered Victorian chaise lounge and two matching chairs were arranged in the center, positioned around a spotlighted frame suspended from the ceiling and covered by a panel of green cloth. Annalisa pulled a silky black cord and the covering slid away, leaving visible a small painting.

"Caravaggio's *Mary Magdalen Washing the Feet of Jesus*," Annalisa announced.

"Amazing," Cesa said, stepping closer. "For once, he used a prostitute model aptly. Lovely. Truly exquisite."

"Yes, isn't it?" Annalisa said. "Created right here in Naples during his last days."

"Mmm," Cesa said, taking in the wondrous rendering of the woman kneeling at the feet of the Christ.

The positioning of the main figures seemed right to Natalia, as did the palette and Caravaggio's famous ethereal effect with light and shadow. It pooled around the halo of Jesus and Mary's lovely countenance. The overarching color scheme was Naples' yellow, that having been a favorite pigment of his.

Cesa located the *N.S.* for *Nostro Signore*, meaning "Our Lord," which was inscribed whenever a composition depicted the Savior, then checked to make sure there was no signature, as it was not then the fashion for artists to sign their work. Appropriately, only *Michel Angelo da*

Caravaggio pittore appeared on the wooden plaque affixed to the frame.

"Isn't that Caravaggio himself?" Natalia asked, indicating the figure of Jesus, depicted as a stocky man with a thin beard and unruly hair.

"Mmm. It might well be. He often used himself as a model," Cesa said. "He seemed especially determined to remain in the world. Freud says we can't imagine our death, that we immediately cast ourselves as the observer. Such is the ego." She appeared amused. "I suppose that's even truer for the geniuses among us. We ordinary mortals have to make do with a few kind words from loved ones, and slip away into obscurity."

Villari leaned closer, examining the buxom figure in blue. "I'd say this Mary Magdalen is Fillide Melandroni, his favorite model."

"Exactly right," Annalisa exclaimed, excited. "That's exactly who our experts said."

"Such splendid work," Cesa said, peering closely at the canvas. "Perfect. You hardly ever see one of his pieces this size. Most are so large, of course."

Natalia nodded. "*Seven Works of Mercy* is twelve and a half feet tall and more than eight feet across."

"No doubt he needed to travel light and work small for a while," Cesa continued. "This was after a *Bando Capitale* was imposed."

The assembled were familiar with the death warrant issued by the Vatican after the artist killed a young man in a brawl in Rome. From then on, the artist spent his life more or less on the run.

He'd enjoyed relative peace here in Naples. But his violent nature did not abate. Near the end, he was stabbed at the Osteria Ceviglio, and never fully recovered. He'd collected what works he could, and in the dark of night, boarded a wooden skiff. He was headed to Rome, as the Bando Capitale had finally been lifted. Caravaggio imagined a glorious future awaited him. But it was not to be. He sailed from his beloved Naples, under the brooding eye of Vesuvius – not to his glory, but to his death.

Thus, as it was, many of the latest works had never properly been documented. When Natalia had been a student, Dottore Cherubini posited that the good Sisters of Clare might very well have a masterpiece or two hanging in their convent or possibly resting on a shelf in a cupboard beside a winter's worth of preserved peaches as the nuns in Port Ecole had cared for him as he lay dying.

"Where on earth has this been hiding?" said Villari.

Annalisa perked up. "In St. Petersburg. It was acquired from a Polish dealer during the war."

How? Natalia wondered. Certainly not bought she would bet.

"Such an important work," Cesa said. "I certainly don't mean this as an insult, *Signora* Russo. But why did the Paris dealer contact your new gallery of contemporary art to promote its availability rather than, say, Capodimonte?"

"They wanted to keep a low profile," Annalisa said, "and I think they were slightly worried about its spotty provenance. Excuse me," she looked at her IPAD. "I'll be right back."

The three visitors conferred.

"All seven stolen Italian artists were Caravaggio's contemporaries, all of them his friends," Cesa said. "Odd, no? That these artists may have been heavily influenced by him makes for a nice anecdote, but under the circumstances, the coincidence of Naples and Caravaggio in all their lives is too great not to mean something, don't you think?"

Excitement took Natalia. How could she not have seen what Cesa observed so casually? She and Villari had just skimmed past it like it wasn't there.

Annalisa returned. "Sorry. Another call about our treasure."

"I was curious about your seller. Or is it sellers?" Natalia said.

"I'm sorry – there's nothing much I can tell you. They're offering through a consultant in Geneva. I don't know the consultant's name either."

Seller unknown, buyer unknown, Natalia thought. That was odd. And a gallery in Paris that chooses Naples as the venue to quietly publicize the picture. Odder yet.

Villari turned to Annalisa. "Can you say which continent the offer might have originated from?"

"Asia, but don't quote me."

Cesa addressed a square of the canvas that was brighter than the rest. "You've had a small area cleaned, I see."

"That was a test. I'd have liked to have the whole thing cleaned," Annalisa said. "It's so dingy. I was strongly urged by the bidders not to risk it, however."

"I'm not sure they're right," Cesa said. "A restorer would have done wonders. Though fear of the process lingers. Once upon a time it would have been scrubbed with soap and water ... or worse, ash and lye. Can you imagine? Many great works were undoubtedly destroyed in removing centuries of dirt and soot. Can we see the back?"

Annalisa ushered them behind the suspended frame. "We're going to have it relined," she said. "It's so exciting having it here."

"It must be," Natalia agreed.

Cesa had brought her own small flashlight. The canvas appeared to be made of hemp, correct for the period. The stretchers were heavier than modern ones; the frame elegant, though without elaborate carving. It was painted dark blue, edged in gilt, and ornamented with worn gold fleur d' lys. There was none of the usual seals and inscriptions on the back. Only a lone set of a collector's inventory numbers stamped on and something unintelligible written by hand.

"Pear moldings," Cesa said, remarking on the frame. "Tasteful."

Annalisa said, "The frame isn't original, it was a wreck. We did manage to use some of the original wood, though. Pretty, isn't it? The frame maker was brilliant," she continued. "Look, he even salvaged the worm holes."

"I don't recognize the work," Cesa said. "Who did you use?"

"A young man called Drako. He came highly recommended."

"Who recommended him?" Natalia asked.

"An investor in the gallery. You know him, I believe."

"Leonardo DePretis," Villari interjected, and exchanged glances with Natalia.

Annalisa looked surprised. "Yes."

Cesa put on her reading glasses and leaned close to study the craftsmanship as she continued conversing.

"So, you may cut the offering short because of this Swiss consultant bidding a record sum for his investment group?"

"Yes.

"To think," Natalia said, "Caravaggio once sold his canvases in the street for a few *scudi*. What might this one fetch?"

"I'd guess something in the neighborhood of fifty million euros," Villari said very quietly so she alone could hear.

"Good Lord. Eighty million U.S. dollars?" Natalia whispered back.

"At least."

"You've had it vetted, of course," Cesa said.

"Twice. We couldn't risk a mistake." Annalisa addressed Cesa. "Could I perhaps interest you in writing about the resurrection of the piece, Dottore? Your opinion would be deeply appreciated."

"Hmm. Would it be possible to see the authentications?"

"Of course. Let me get them for you."

Annalisa hurried away. Cesa made a few notes while Natalia snapped pictures of the painting with her phone while looking for signs of *bozzetti,* try-outs where the artist worked out his composition on the canvas with the handle of his brush, correcting and changing as he proceeded. Most copyists would simply follow the outline of the original work, ignoring the traces of the artist's struggle for perfection just beneath the surface. Natalia thought she saw a few.

Natalia leaned close as Villari circled by and said, "You knew DePretis had invested in the gallery?"

"Guessed."

Annalisa reappeared with a file and a large envelope the size of a platter. She placed both on a rolling table and pushed it into more light. Natalia and Villari followed Cesa over and gathered around as she opened the folder, the two Carabinieri peering over her shoulder.

"Let's see," Cesa read, "'Carbon dating of plant fibers that compose the canvas place its age between 1540 and 1650. Microscopic samples taken of paint pigments and resins contain no modern materials. There is chemical evidence of cleaning with turpentine and lavender oil.'"

Cesa glanced over her reading glasses. "Someone beat you to it, *Signora*."

"Yes, by a century or two."

Dottore Cherubini continued reading. "'Forensic imaging failed to differentiate paint layers due to their multiplicity and the presence of a second painting that they overlay.' Ah ha. There's another painting underneath." She looked up from the text and indicated the large envelope. "Is this the X-ray?"

"Yes."

Cesa slid the film out and held it up to the light. Natalia and Villari edged closer.

"There it is," Villari said. "A second painting."

A blur of ghostly lines and levels undercut the topmost layers. This, compounded by white blotches, made it difficult to read. You could make out some religious imagery, but just.

"You see how blocked by the white wisps a good many areas are?" Cesa said.

"You mean where the lead in the pigments is interfering with the X-rays and blurring the under painting?" Natalia said.

"Exactly. All that lead in the paint, especially the white. Caravaggio bought all his pigments from a pharmacist on Via Toledo and always the white with the greatest lead content. There's even speculation that lead poisoning affected his nervous system and contributed to his violent temper and poor health. The poor man died at thirty-eight, as you know."

"What do you think about the attribution of this painting to Caravaggio?" Annalisa asked very directly.

"*Habent sua fata picturae*," Cesa said.

Villari grinned and translated the Latin. "'Paintings have their trials.'"

"Exactly, and this one will too," Cesa said. "The painting is technically excellent, brilliantly done. Nearly flawless. The technique, Caravaggio's best. With all this forensic evidence backing that up, I don't see many experts who would challenge its attribution with any confidence."

Annalisa looked relieved. "Your opinion then is that it's genuine."

Cesa made a helpless gesture. "No one could say with much authority that it's not authentic."

"Wonderful," Annalisa exclaimed. "Will you vouch for its authenticity?"

"I'm so sorry, dear. No. I couldn't."

"Why, if all you say about it is true?"

"There is this one syllogistic fallacy actually, that makes the painting suspect. Let me explain. Caravaggio did make a few small paintings at the beginning of his career: still life canvases, fruits and flowers, that sort of thing. He didn't do any more small works again until the very end of his life when he was hiding out from the Vatican's agents and the relatives of the man he had killed. The paintings he did in Naples during his last months were all religiously themed."

"As is this," Annalisa pointed out anxiously. "What's troubling you then?"

"The model," Cesa said.

"You mean it's not Fillide Melandroni? Does it matter if she's not? I'm confused."

"No, no. It is she, and he always worked from live models."

"But?"

"Fillide Melandroni regrettably never set foot in Naples."

Chapter 18

Natalia and Villari accompanied Cesa home before returning to Casanova. Natalia told Villari she needed a moment away from the station before they met with the colonel. She walked past Castel Capuano and up Via Apostoli. She smelled *panettone* being baked. Businesses were shutting down for the holiday, doorways strung with colored lights. She stopped at the crown of the hill. Clouds scudded the pale sky. She looked out over the rooftops. In thousands of rooms life was going on – children excited about the toys they were to receive – as Natalia had been once upon a time.

There was work to attend to. Justice to be served.

She unfolded a copy of the summary listing all the robberies of canvases similar to the Segli. Things were falling into place, thanks to Cesa.

Villari accompanied her to Colonel Donati's office.

A lieutenant came out.

"Ah," Donati said through the open doorway, "my favorite captains," and ushered them in.

Natalia and Villari took seats by his desk and proceeded to brief him. The murder victim had not witnessed the Segli theft and been silenced, as they initially thought, Villari explained. She was herself the thief who cut it from its frame, only to be killed very professionally later the same day in an outdoor market. The stolen painting was hidden in the sheet music compartment of her violin case, and there was additional forensic evidence that it had held other old paintings of the same vintage. The Segli theft like all the others was intended to appear crude, the work of a novice. That fiction had been repeated ten times: six in Italy, three in France and a seventh in Italy again.

The colonel sat forward and waited for them to continue.

There was no way the victim could have staged ten such robberies by herself, Natalia told him. The research and resources alone needed to locate the art that fit the evident criteria were beyond her. Someone identified and targeted the right pieces and the weakest security systems. Everything pointed to a sophisticated ring of art thieves with a well-developed support system.

"I see," Colonel Donati said. "Yes, quite cunning. But can you tell me why none of the paintings have surfaced? None have been ransomed or fenced that we know of. So what's their brilliant scheme?"

"We don't believe the Italian works were stolen to be ransomed or sold off," Villari told him.

"You think they've been privately disposed of, gone to solitary buyers? Dispersed?"

"No, sir," Villari said.

"You concur, Natalia?"

"Yes, sir. The Italian thefts had an entirely different purpose."

"Which was?"

"They were harvesting the canvases," said Villari, "for their antiquity, for the patina, the paint pigments and oils and resins. All were four centuries old − including the stretchers."

"Why on earth?" the colonel asked.

"To use them as under art," Natalia said, "as very convincing platforms for the forgeries to be painted over them."

"Mother of God," the colonel pressed his hands to his cheeks.

"All of the stolen works were early efforts by young artists – men, except for Gentileschi," Villari added. "All of them in Caravaggio's entourage – including Segli. The thieves wanted indisputable seventeenth century canvases connected to Caravaggio, over which a new Caravaggio seventeenth century masterwork could be imposed and made to pass as genuine."

Natalia explained how the thieves counterfeited old pigments and resins with no modern additives, all chemically correct, and retained the services of a master forger who could flawlessly reproduce Caravaggio's strokes and style.

"Everything was correct," Villari added. "Right down to the stretchers. They even commissioned a wonderfully crafted frame made from antique black market wood allegedly salvaged from original. These people are artisans in their own right, extraordinarily skilled."

"Clever," Donati said.

"Insidiously," Villari agreed. "They even replicated the dirt and *craquelure.*"

"Caravaggio, eh?" Colonel Donati said.

"He's the common denominator in the seven thefts," Villari said. "The artists were all contemporaries and admirers of his, part of his rowdy entourage."

"The thieves had a wide stock of canvases to choose from," Natalia said. "The obvious suggestion was that a canvas had been discarded in frustration by a *caravaggisti*, in the master's studio where they all congregated."

She explained that the artist was known for his generosity – both with food and wine – even life models.

"The only thing Caravaggio wouldn't let them do was paint any of his work – not even a brush stroke."

"No Andy Warhol," Donati said.

"No," Villari chuckled.

Sir," Natalia continued, "the authentication of all this detail was intended to get the fraud past the experts and any forensic examination, to encourage expert consultants and dealers to conclude that the top painting was genuine, just like the painting underneath."

"And the proof?" Colonel Donati asked.

"There's a painting at the Gallery Russo right now," Natalia said. "A Caravaggio – new to the market. We just saw it with Professor Cherubini. Masterful. It might have easily passed as genuine except they made a tiny mistake which the professor caught."

"What nerve," Colonel Donati said. "I must commend you for your fine work, Captains. Will you please have this Caravaggio seized, Captain Villari?"

"Certainly. Though proving it a forgery may be difficult."

"But you said Dottore Cherubini identified the problem."

Natalia explained that proving a forgery was a tricky business – especially nowadays – modern technology notwithstanding. The thieves were keeping pace – using technology for their own advantage. Many experts were fooled.

"Several years ago, Professor Cherubini was called to Milan to authenticate a work," Natalia continued. "It was attributed to Artemisia Gentileschi's father, Ottavio. She suspected forgery. The brush stroke of a particular section did not belong to Gentileschi, she was certain. Meanwhile, the gallery had done its job, used all the latest tools, the photography with the raking light, infra-red, x-radiography. The canvas was correct as to the period, as were the pigments and other materials used. The brush strokes alone weren't enough to prove forgery."

Donati said, "I should inform our French colleagues of this scheme, though I don't see how their robberies are linked to Caravaggio."

"They're not," Natalia said. "Drina stole those three for herself. I believe one has already been sold on by a fence."

The colonel's clerk interrupted. "There's an urgent call for Captain Monte from a Professor Cherubini."

Donati pushed the phone across his desk.

"Cesa?"

"*Signora* Russo wasted no time," she said. "I called the dealer in Paris an hour after we left. The sale had been completed."

Natalia informed her colleagues.

Colonel Donati reached for his phone. "We'll send officers down to Gallery Russo right away to embargo the painting,"

"Too late," Natalia stopped him. "It's probably over the Caspian Sea by now."

"Damn. Talk to the gallery owner," he instructed. "Threaten her with criminal conspiracy, if necessary. She may know something useful about the murder of the gypsy."

Natalia and Villari took off for the gallery. They drove quickly, siren whirling.

They parked in front of the building and rushed inside. The manager was talking to a well-dressed older couple — the man in a tweed suit, the woman swaddled in cashmere.

He left them in front of a thin sheet of pink glass mounted on an onyx pedestal, and hurried to the entrance.

"How can I help you?" he asked in hushed tones.

Captain Villari told him they needed to speak with his boss immediately. The manager informed them *Signora* had left for Zurich an hour ago.

"Business?" Villari asked.

"No," he smiled, "to celebrate our good fortune. A fabulous sale," he confided. "Fifty-three million euros. Now if you'll excuse me …"

Natalia and Villari stepped outside. Natalia shielded her eyes from the harsh sunlight.

"Should we try to have the flight turn back?" she asked.

"Not much use at this point," Villari adjusted his beret. "For one, they're beyond our authority. And for another – what would be the point? As you explained to the colonel – even with Professor Cherubini's report, we would be fighting an uphill battle."

Somewhere, the happy buyers were celebrating their good fortune and awaiting delivery of their masterpiece. Natalia felt defeated. The forgery ring had gotten away with a major score. And there might well be more to come. The desire to own a Caravaggio would overrule many buyers' qualms about the provenance of the work. A losing battle indeed. Losing on all fronts, she conceded.

Across the street from the fancy gallery, pigeons collected on the lip of a broken fountain. A woman cradled her fat infant as a stray dog begged for food. Natalia thought of Caravaggio's dogs. He'd had one in Rome and another here – strays the color of charcoal. He taught them tricks and they went everywhere with him – performing to the delight of the crowds that gathered.

A performer, the great artist – massively talented, true, yet a bit of the con – much like Drina, Natalia realized. It was that – not her gift that had gotten her killed. Who commissioned the murder? What had the twenty-year old done to have her life cut so short?

***

Pierangelo Bertoli's *'Mother Give Me a Hundred Lire Because I Want to go to America'* was playing on Antonietta's antiquated record player.

"Pierangelo Bertoli on the old victrola" Naldo exclaimed, "and my favorite cousin and *Carabiniere!*"

He kissed Natalia's cheeks and showed off his orange crocheted sweater vest, a gift from his mother. Antonietta hauled herself out of a chair and made for the cake.

"I'll take it to the kitchen. You and your cousin can talk about me behind my back."

"She never changes," Naldo said, as he turned the music down. "Except I think she's getting hard of hearing. I try talking to her about it, about hearing aids." He shook his head. "She's so stubborn."

"Proud," Natalia said.

"That too."

A glass front cupboard held her aunt's collection of good dishes and glassware. Once a year they emerged for a thorough cleaning. If Natalia urged Antonietta to use them at any other time, she'd look at her like she was crazy.

Antonietta, like many of her generation, had suffered hardships and deprivations during the last war. Purchases of anything but necessities were few and far between. If someone left a few scraps of lettuce on their plate, Antonietta told them stories of scraping them into a pan and frying them up in olive oil for another meal. Her aunt was frugal and hoarded crackers and packets of sugar, and wore her sweaters until they unraveled. Once, when Natalia bought her a new jar of face powder, she wanted to know if

267

the old jar had gone bad. Natalia tried to persuade her she needn't add water to the pasty crust collected at the bottom, she could buy a new one.

"You mean like the fancy ladies?"

That stubbornness was exasperating but had kept her aunt alive all these years. Natalia prayed it wouldn't flag. The world without Antonietta would be emptier. She was a last link with parents and grandparents, aunts and uncles.

"Sit." Naldo patted the couch beside him. "What's new?"

"Same old," Natalia said. "Busy."

"Before I forget," he dropped his voice, "Luciana wants you to come for dinner soon — no excuses."

"I'd be delighted," Natalia said. "Thank her for me."

Arrangements for Natalia to visit her cousin had to be made surreptitiously. Naldo's wife refused to socialize with her mother-in-law.

"Excellent. I'll tell her it's settled."

"What's settled?" Antonietta reappeared bearing a large platter.

"Nothing," Naldo said. "We're talking is all."

"Look what I got for you – *saguinaccio.*" She put a dish on the Formica table.

Natalia surveyed the platter. A few crackers and several discs of *salami* surrounded the pigs' blood cooked with chocolate and herbs. Never a favorite of Natalia's, it made her queasy just looking at it. An Easter specialty, it was Naldo's fondest childhood dish. The blood and chocolate pooled under the salami as it started to dry and curl up. Once upon a time, her cousin would have dived in.

"Thanks, Ma. I'd better not. Doctor says I've gotta lose some weight." He patted his stomach.

"Why you waste your money going to doctors? What for? You wanna lose weight so you can get sick? When you lived with me your health was perfect. Perfect."

"I was young when I lived here with you, Ma. Now I have to be more careful."

"Your woman, she have you on some kind of diet?"

"Don't start in, Mama. Okay? Remember the heart attack? Look, I gotta go."

"You call this a visit?" Antoinetta threw her arms open and brought her hands to her face, her fingers pinched together. "A mosquito would spend more time."

"Could we not argue this once?" her son begged, hands prayerful. "It's Christmas." He stood up and kissed her head. "Be good, mama. I'll call you tomorrow. Great to see you, Natalia."

"You too."

"Thinks he's a big shot," Antoinetta said, as the door closed behind her son. "Married to that woman. Such a big shot. Look what they got me for Christmas." She held up a box of handkerchiefs. "She's gonna need them before me." Antoinetta paused for a moment and sighed. "You look just like your mother, rest her soul."

***

Claudio intercepted her in her courtyard and embraced her.

"I thought you'd never come home."

"Wait," she said. "There have been developments. Sit a moment, please. We need to talk."

They huddled together on the edge of the front steps, hands deep in their pockets. "That doesn't sound good. What's wrong? You already have a boyfriend?"

"No."

"Don't tell me -- a husband? Former, I hope."

"Nothing like that, no." She laughed at his teasing.

"Thank God." Claudio said. He pulled a hand from her pocket and kissed it.

"I missed you."

He slipped a small envelope into her hand.

"What's this?" Natalia asked.

"The key for my front door. I've informed the doorman you are to be admitted anytime, without question. I cleared some space in the closet. No pressure," he laughed as he leaned over and kissed her.

That's a first, Natalia thought, space in the closet. Why did the timing always have to be so wrong?

"Do you have to go to work tomorrow?" he said.

"I'm afraid I do."

"You have to try some of this in the morning." He took out a jar. "Stewed cherries. A Roma delicacy. I've been saving it for you."

"It looks delicious," she said.

"You're delicious, Captain Monte." Claudio ran his finger along the space between her thumb and her index finger. "We call this the Devil's Saddle. The degree of the angle indicates the will. Yours is very pronounced." He lifted her palm and kissed it.

"Claudio, there's something I want to talk to you about."

"Uh oh. I'm coming on too strong?"

"No. Not that. It's lovely – the key, the cherries – it's about your cousin's death."

He looked troubled. "You found her killer?"

"We're getting closer."

"That's good."

"The thing is, Lenny DePretis' name keeps cropping up. It looks like he was involved with the art thefts ... and possibly her murder."

"No."

"What do you mean – no?"

"Lenny was like an uncle to her."

"I'm confused. You told me at the morgue that he was a client and friend of yours paying his respects."

"He was, but ...."

"Evidence, Claudio. There's a lot of it mounting up that we can't ignore. He's tied to some of it."

"What's mounting up, *cara*, is my desire for you."

Natalia moved up to the step opposite him. She said the art thefts along the route of his cousin's French pilgrimage, and the ones in Italy were too much of a coincidence – Drina had stolen them. But Drina wasn't capable of researching and planning such an operation, finding paintings of exactly the right vintage and value. Drina had worked for a criminal gang – one with contacts and the financial wherewithal to fund it.

"I can't bear to hear this," Claudio stood, agitated. "I need --."

"Wait," Natalia said. "Come here. Sit."

He returned to her side and put his head in his hands. He looked pale. Natalia touched his shoulder trying to comfort him.

"I thought you and I could be something different," he said.

"What do you mean, Claudio?"

"Drina and I – we're filthy gypsies – *zingari*".

He looked terribly upset.

"Listen," Natalia said softly. "I'm sure Drina had her reasons for her choices."

271

"Choices? Is that what you call it? She should have stayed in the community. She'd still be alive if it weren't for me."

"Claudio, please."

"I'm sorry. I feel like hell," he said and quickly left.

Chapter 19

Lenny DePretis rang her bell promptly at eight. Natalia put the last touches on her make-up and slipped into a pair of rarely worn heels. Her black sheath looked passably elegant. The red Czech glass necklace helped fancy it up a bit. Why she was bothering? She wasn't sure except you didn't go the Teatro San Carlo dressed casually. And tonight she'd be in a box.

She arranged a lilac wool wrap over her black cloth coat and proceeded carefully down stairs.

A low slung black BMW with tinted windows was parked in the *piazzetta* across from her building. As she approached, DePretis got out of the car. Not afraid to show his face. A man who was confident that he controlled his surroundings. Natalia glanced around quickly to see if anyone was taking notice.

Smoothly shaved, seriously gelled, he'd dressed for the occasion, a paisley scarf artfully arranged around the collar of his tuxedo. But even a tuxedo failed to smooth away his rough edge. He was like so many of the boys Natalia had grown up with —with their thick limbs and knowing smiles. Dangerous and attractive, there was no gentlemanly façade. Ironically, in many ways she was more comfortable with him than with her current heartthrob.

Claudio Palumbo had come from a background equal to if not worse than DePretis'. It was different from her own, and therefore mysterious. Despite the hardscrabble start, he'd transformed himself into a genteel and cultured man. Not so her date of this evening.

"I'm glad you called," he said, appraising her as he flicked the ignition and the engine purred to life. "You look good. Better than good."

Natalia had dispensed with her vest – she wasn't expecting trouble, and figured a touch of cleavage might encourage Signor DePretis to talk more freely. Leonardo's appeal notwithstanding, her weapon was strapped to her thigh. She wondered if he'd managed one under his snug-fitting suit jacket. There was no tell-tale bulge. No guard and no weapon? The man was cocky.

They pulled out of her alley and turned onto Tribunali. Idling in front of the barber shop, Luciano Panetti looked up from his Blackberry and tried to make out the occupants of the fancy car. No way through the tinted windows, thank God. But Natalia was certain DePretis' license plate was duly noted and the information passed along. There were plenty of people interested in the comings and goings of a prominent Don – not to mention the identity of his companion.

Natalia hadn't been to the opera in a while. She adored the San Carlo. Lovely from the outside, it was even more impressive inside with its luscious red and gold décor and the enormous crystal chandeliers. It was beautiful, with brilliant acoustics. Companies from around the world vied to perform there.

"I thought we'd eat after," DePretis broke into her thoughts. "I made reservations at the Royale."

The Royale was one of the most expensive restaurants in Naples. Housed in a grand *palazzo* not far from Capodimonte, it commanded a view the Bourbons would have envied.

As they pulled up to the entrance of the opera house, a valet materialized. DePretis slipped him a bill and they proceeded inside. Her crystal necklace notwithstanding, she paled beside the elaborate gowns of the other women moving through the lobby toward their seats. There must be millions of *euros* represented in the diamonds dripping from ears and necks alone. Not to mention full length minks and stoles.

Natalia tugged at her unruly curls.

An usher escorted them to a private box overlooking the stage.

"Champagne?" he offered when they'd gotten comfortable.

Not too shabby, Natalia thought as she accepted the offer.

"I hope you like Verdi," he said as he handed her a champagne flute and poured. "To a pleasurable evening," he toasted.

Natalia wondered what his idea of 'pleasurable' included.

The seats were filling quickly. The bells signaled that three minutes remained before the performance started. She took a sip of the bubbly drink as she glanced through the program. *Il Trovatore* — a story of doomed lovers and gypsies. How appropriate.

DePretis leaned over and touched her arm: "I'm glad you're here, Natalia."

The lights dimmed and the curtain rose. For several hours, she lost herself in the lush music and dramatic singing. Only when the monks intoned the finale and the curtain fell did she come back to reality as the audience exploded with applause and bravos. The third curtain call brought on the house lights. She was momentarily sad that they had to leave.

"Hungry?" DePretis asked as he helped her on with her wrap.

"As a matter of fact, I'm starving."

"Good." His arm lingered on her shoulder.

His car was waiting in front of the theater. Another bill changed hands, the valet held the doors, and in minutes they whizzed away from the waterfront.

Natalia had never been to the Royale. It was where many of the 'families' celebrated special events – a graduation, a baby shower, a merger, whether by peaceful means or not. Camouflaged by tall pines and thick magnolia trees, the path was lighted by glass lanterns. A hostess in a tuxedo studded with rhinestones led them to their table.

Candles flickered, voices were hushed. The room was a picture of gentility, Natalia thought.

"So what did you think?" DePretis asked after they were seated and the waiter brought two enormous leather-bound menus. "Terrific, wasn't it?"

"Yes, it was," Natalia agreed.

"Verdi," he said. "I'm reading up on him. Man was prolific."

The city twinkled in the far distance. Beyond, the harbor was dark – the gleam of a freighter the only light. Fairyland, Natalia thought – as if the troubles of the world were far, far away.

"Mind if I order for both of us?" DePretis asked, closing the menu.

"Why not?" She inhaled the jasmine that was arranged in bouquets on every table.

"You like lobster, right?"

"I do."

Lobster Fra Diavolo and *Fettucine Alfredo* — the kind of dishes a boy from her neighborhood would choose to impress a girl.

Natalia smiled.

"What's so funny?" he ripped into a piece of bread.

"Nothing."

"Glad you're not one of those females who don't eat," he said. "My mother always said you couldn't trust someone who didn't appreciate food."

"She alive?" Natalia asked.

"No," he looked sad.

"Sorry."

"I worshipped her," he said.

At the far end of the room, a man played Chopin on a grand piano.

"Nice," DePretis said. "They get some real talent here."

"A young man from Bari," Natalia said. "You've come a long way."

"So has the girl from Trevi Street. How is it she ended up in the military police?"

"A girl has to eat," she said and devoured a wedge of bread.

He laughed. "You are a character, Natalia Monte, and very attractive."

Their first course arrived, delivered by two attentive waiters who wished them a good appetite and disappeared.

DePretis said, "I don't suppose you would consider doing some consulting work for me?"

"We're not really permitted to rent ourselves out for security work."

"I was thinking more along the lines of an art connoisseur."

"Yes, I've heard you're investing in art. This is delicious by the way."

"I'm glad you like it. I assume you know about the galleries I've bought into."

"I do," Natalia nodded. "Milan, Venice, Rome, and of course the one in town."

"I'm thinking about London, and New York. Maybe in the spring."

"Ambitious," Natalia said.

"That's me," he grinned. "I'm trying to re-invent myself — the divorce and all. You reach a certain age and you wonder what your legacy will be. You have kids?"

"No."

"Me either. I have a couple of nieces and nephews. I want to be a good role model — a legitimate businessman, you know what I mean?"

"I do."

"I take an interest in the younger generation."

"Like Claudio Palumbo's late cousin?"

He put down his wine. "May she rest in peace. What about Drina? A fabulous musician. Such a shame."

"It was. The musician was stealing art while on pilgrimages — playing her wonderful music in churches in Italy and France."

DePretis didn't say anything.

"She cut the canvases from their frames, stashed them in her music case, and walked out."

"Poor child. I wish she hadn't done that."

"She was working for you, wasn't she?"

"I'm hoping we'll be friends, Natalia, so I'll spare you the evasions. I'm in the crime business. But only as an investor. I'm not involved in the day to day operations. No, she wasn't working for me. And I didn't order the hit, in case you wondered. Not my thing. Never was. Between us, they were ignorant to kill Tortou."

"You bankrolled the operation?"

"God, you're direct." It seemed to please him. "Yes, just as I trade in stocks of companies I have nothing to do with."

"You invested in the robberies she committed. What was your share of the Caravaggio, Annalisa sold yesterday?

"Eleven million."

"When the Segli was taken from the Brancaccio Chapel in the home church of your confessor, you were there. Quite a coincidence."

"I had no idea. If I had known, I would've tried to talk her out of it."

"Drina steals the painting and soon after is murdered in a collection zone you've controlled since you cut a deal with Bianca Strozzi."

"I told you – her death had nothing to do with me. You trying to ruin my appetite?" He put down his utensils and retrieved his wine.

"These robberies of hers, they're quite a mystery," Natalia continued. "Curious assortment. Seven paintings by so-so and better Neapolitan painters – Three works by minor French *artistes*. Why? Are we going to discover another newly discovered masterpiece in a gallery you've invested in – say in Milan?"

"Are you always so serious?" DePretis signaled to the waiter.

"Occupational hazard."

"You're a Carabiniere. You do your job well. I do mine. I'm not a killer, Natalia. Never have been. I treat people with respect. But I think you already know that."

"Unless they prove unworthy. And then what?"

"Listen, Natalia Monte, *Captain dei Carabinieri*, I don't want anything bad to happen to you. I wouldn't like that, not at all. You need to be cautious. This art syndicate has set up a large, lucrative operation. Really efficient and professional. They're not like me – interfere with them and they kill."

"Is that what Drina did — she got in the way?"

DePretis looked at her. "You know I can't go there. And it wouldn't do any good at this point if I did. She's gone" He took out his wallet. "I like you. Captain. Call if you ever need help. I mean that. I feel lousy about Drina. I feel lousy that I'll never have a real chance with you."

***

Drako sat in the interrogation room, very still and alone. Natalia faced him across the plastic table top.

"Where is everyone else?" Drako said. "Why are you dressed up?"

"I'm off duty," she said. "This is a private chat, Drako."

"I don't have to talk to you."

"I have to warn you. We've gotten answers to a number of questions about Drina's death. We may not need your information and can simply charge you. Do you understand?"

He didn't answer.

"Okay," she pulled her things together and stood.

"I didn't kill her."

"You were there?" Natalia sat down.

Drako nodded.

"How so?"

"She called me – said she needed money."

"Did she explain why?"

"She couldn't talk. People were after her. She had to leave town. I put together everything I had and brought it over."

"Why didn't you tell us this before?"

"I was afraid you wouldn't believe me. We grew up together. I made her first violin."

"She was alive when you got there."

"Yes. I gave her the money. She took the violin from its case. She told me to get away. I stuck it under my jacket and ran."

"She gave you a violin worth way more than a hundred thousand euros in return for less than four thousand in cash?"

"You see. You don't believe me. Forget it."

"No. It's just surprising. You brought her what, a thousand euro?"

"Twelve hundred. She said the violin wasn't any use for her – if she played they'd find her. She was going far away. She'd called her brother to come get her on his bike and take her to another town where they wouldn't be watching the rail station and airport. They'd take ordinary roads, not the highway. I begged her to tell me where she was going. She refused."

"Did she tell you exactly why she was running?"

"She pissed them off."

"The people you worked for?"

"Yeah."

"Go on."

"She stole the painting from the Sant'Angelo church."

"Wasn't that her job?"

"No. Not for herself. She'd been warned — last summer."

"Warned by whom?"

"They called themselves *Consorteria*. They'd commissioned the six heists. Drina did the six. It took several years. After the last one she complained. They were going to cash in big and she'd taken all the risk. Last summer she made three scores for herself in about two months – quiet robberies in small French towns. Sold them on her own."

"Fences?" Natalia said.

"Yeah."

"Did she try to sell the painting she stole that morning?"

"The word was out that no one was to deal with her. They were all too scared she said. They had ratted her out, in fact, and the bosses were onto her and closing in on her fast."

"Why take such a chance?" Natalia asked. "That's what doesn't make sense."

"She wanted a particular violin," Drako said.

"A Stradivarius?"

"Yeah. I knew of one. Hot. No way they could sell it on the usual market – the price was way reduced: half a million."

"Drina made that much from the French thefts?"

"From the first six in Italy, and the three for herself in France, yeah. Almost. That's why she grabbed the Segli. I was going to fix up the Stradivarius – change its identity but not its sound."

"Dangerous game," Natalia said.

"I told her. When she was a kid, her grandmother had Drina pour molten lead into water to see her fate."

"What did she see?" Natalia asked.

"She'd be successful early," Drako replied. "But then she'd burn – flame out like a comet."

"You saw the murder?"

He didn't answer.

Natalia rummaged through her file and pulled out an array of morgue photos: close-ups of six males, their heads supported by concave blocks under their necks. She slid them across to Drako.

"What is this?" he asked.

"Mug shots."

"These guys don't look so good," Drako said.

"These are morgue photos taken at the Medical Examiner's," Natalia explained. "You recognize any of them? You can't hurt any of them," she said, when he remained silent. "They're dead."

"This guy." He pointed to the second photo. "Who is he?"

"Local muscle. No one's going to miss him."

"He grabbed her in the little alleyway behind the stalls. It looked like she fainted. I knew he had done something bad to her."

"What did you do?"

"I ran. I hoped he hadn't noticed me. Nobody came looking so I guessed he hadn't."

"Who is this *Consorteria*?"

"I have no idea. Everything was by phone and motorcycle courier. They never took off their helmets or their shades."

"You have any idea of where any of them are?"

"No. My guess would be France. Maybe Holland."

"Why do you think that?"

"Accents."

"Did Drina come up with the idea of playing sacred music – so she could work the churches – get invited in?"

"I don't know. Yeah, probably. I mean, why not? She played like an angel. Looked like one too."

Chapter 20

Deep within the labyrinthine alleys, explosions concussed the city's ancient walls. Car alarms shrieked, pigeons took off for higher ground. The canyons of buildings boomed with the odd Neapolitan tradition of huge firecrackers set off to celebrate the birth of Christ. Natalia and Mariel linked arms and pushed through the crowds. A flock of Asian nuns in long blue garb swept past them up the cathedral stairs. Inside, red and white poinsettias lined the aisles. The two friends stopped to light candles for their parents and departed loved ones.

They found Lola waiting in front of the confessional, phone out, texting, the screen framed in diamonds. People stared. She was decked out in a blue velvet skirt, slit up one side, black lace stockings and red boots. Her black mink jacket was cropped above the waist and she had on a navy cloche, with matching veil draped over her face.

Natalia scanned the crowd. There were relatives from a dozen notorious families congregating in their customary section of the pews. Where ordinarily they were competitors, three times a year they met up in church and wished each other well. Lola was still at it as her boss's twins paraded by, resplendent in black satin and white mink stoles, large crosses prominent on their ample chests. The girls stopped to pay their respects to Lola, nodded to Natalia, and took their seats. The service wouldn't start for a while yet but coming early was mandatory if you wanted to get a seat.

"Where's your daughter?" Natalia asked Lola.

"She and her beau are hosting a dinner party. Cocktails and a sit-down. Very grown up." Lola put her phone into her bag.

"Will we see her tomorrow?" Mariel asked.

"Certo. Of course. She's spending the morning with her father's mother. Said she'd be home right after."

Lola flicked up her veil. She'd gone for a muted palette — mauve eye shadow and cocoa lips. There was something happening around her eyes again.

A young man exited the confessional and Lola moved in.

"I'll be quick," she said. "Save me a seat."

"Si, *Signora*," Natalia curtsied.

Lola flashed her middle finger and disappeared into the wooden booth, drawing the velvet curtain.

"Em, did you get the caviar?" Natalia asked as they located three places halfway to the altar, and squeezed in.

"Special delivery this afternoon. You?"

Natalia nodded. "Got the bread."

"Good. Lucia will be closed tomorrow."

"Remember when my parents brought us here the first time?" Mariel said. "What were we -- six?"

"I remember," Natalia said. "I pointed at a lady in a gigantic purple hat? Your mother leaned over and whispered that it was impolite to point, so I turned the finger toward myself?"

Suddenly there was a commotion by the confessional. Voices were raised, Lola's among them. Hunched over, wreathed in black, an old woman had leaned behind the curtain and was berating the occupant. She wagged a finger at Lola as she pushed past to get out.

"Did you see that crone?" Lola said as she slammed into their pew. "I'm still making my confession when the old biddy sticks her head in and says, 'They need a special line for the likes of you. I haven't got forever.'"

"She must be close to a hundred," Mariel said. "Take it easy.

"She's a witch is what she is."

People were still pouring into the cathedral, the humble and the grand side by side. On an ordinary evening, the priest's sermon would have echoed in the empty cavern. On Christmas Eve the place was packed. Natalia's aunt, though, wasn't there in her usual spot.

The organ sounded, signaling the beginning of the processional coming down the center aisle toward the altar. The choir surged. Natalia closed her eyes and let the swell of music overtake her.

***

The city was quiet as Natalia headed for her aunt's place. She traipsed across Via Sapienza. The strong smell of garlic and meat still hung in the air.

Across from her aunt's house, a boy was trying out his new scooter – showing off for his mother and aunt.

"Bravo!" one of them called tepidly, before returning to her cigarette and gossip. The women were haggard with brittle hair – tight leather pants, mink vests over low-cut blouses, gold lame heels.

When they saw her, their conversation stopped. Once upon a time – it seemed like a hundred years ago, she'd hung out with them, teased her hair, experimented with white lipstick. Those days had long passed. As far as the Minotti sisters were concerned – Natalia had made her decision. She was no longer one of them.

A plastic wreath hung on Antonietta's door. It was late but Natalia could hear the television yet again running the Pope's blessing of the season delivered that morning. Natalia rang several times. Finally, her aunt responded.

"When are you going to let me make an appointment for you to have your hearing checked?" Natalia said as she hugged her and went to turn the volume down.

"I didn't think I'd see you," her aunt said.

"We missed you at the mass. I came by to check on you. Wish you a Merry Christmas." Natalia handed her a wide silver box tied with a satin ribbon. "It's from the three of us."

"You can take some cake for them."

"Mariel for sure. Not Lola. She's on another health regimen. I'll bring it to Mariel, thanks."

"You partying all night?" Antoinetta said.

"No. Just for a little while with the girls. I go on duty in a couple of hours."

"Christmas Day?" her aunt said in a disapproving tone. "Why?"

Natalia didn't want to say it was because she was single, without much family and not all that good a Catholic. Her cell phone chimed. The caller ID read *Claudio*.

"Excuse me a second, Toni. I have to take this."

He wanted to wish her a Merry Christmas, he said, and see her, to make amends for his behavior.

***

Natalia climbed the steps past the marble portals of the 5th century church. She pulled open the door and surveyed the interior, the terra cotta apse. A sacristan rearranged chrysanthemums at the foot of the altar after late services.

Monks had gathered in the choir stall for their first prayers. They chanted in low voices.

"Mater   purissima,   mater   admirabile,   mater prudentissima ... ora pro nobis."

Mother of purity, mother of admiration, mother of prudence ... hour of our reckoning.

A collection of angels appeared to float from the blue and gold coffered arch above.

Natalia slid into a pew and bowed her head.

In a minute she rose and walked out to the small plaza. She went to the nearest bench and sat, as instructed. She pulled a black shawl from her bag and wrapped it around her.

"You're so deep in thought, *Cara*," Claudio said as he joined her.

"*Sarshin*," she said. "Merry Christmas."

"Your Romani is getting pretty good."

"I'm sorry you missed Midnight Mass."

He opened a tote and took out two glasses and a half bottle.

"Maybe this will make up for it. Merlot for a Christmas picnic," he said. "Let's see if I can get this corkscrew to work."

A woman teetered by on white platform boots, matching mini, a sparkly green hairband perched atop her long black wavy hair. A gust of wind sent a gold leaf skittering.

"Success!" Claudio said, as he pulled out the cork and poured. He raised his glass. "To Spring," he toasted, "when everything will be new again."

The ruby liquid was black in the dark.

"To Spring," she repeated, sipping with him. She wrapped the shawl tighter.

"What a pretty spot," Claudio surveyed the empty plaza. "You know, I've never been here – hard to believe. I've been thinking, maybe it's time to ease up, enjoy life more – get to know our city." He took a sip. "And when it gets a little warmer, I'd love to show you where my grandparents had their farm. It's gorgeous – nothing but wild flowers and fig trees. Hundreds of birds. I'd wake up early, lie in bed and listen to them singing."

"Sounds wonderful," Natalia said.

"It is. There's so much I haven't seen – Venice, Rome... Never been to the Coliseum, I'm embarrassed to say. I've never even stepped foot in the Museo at Capodimonte. You can be my guide." He stroked her cheek.

"I would enjoy that. Very much."

"Terrific. It's settled. *Duvelungo Divvus*, Darling. *Buon Natale.*"

He produced a velvet box. "Open it later."

"Claudio, no," she said. "I don't have anything for you."

"You're my gift. Consider this a bribe in case you have any ideas of leaving me."

Natalia started to tear.

"A fellow gives you a present and you start to cry? Come on, Sweetheart."

Natalia wiped her eyes.

"I'm on duty in a few hours."

"It's a holiday," Claudio handed her a handkerchief. "You can't take the day off? Your case is over, no?"

"I'm the watch commander. It's my turn."

"You are so like Drina, you know? Driven."

A light came on in a building across the way.

"What happened to Drina?" Natalia asked.

"What do you mean?"

"You must have set her up with them. It had to be you."

"I knew it," he said, almost laughing. "I knew you'd figure it out." He put his glass down and pressed his hands to his face.

"Oh, Claudio."

A cat shot past them. Its eyes shined like emeralds before it was swallowed in the dark.

"It was all my fault," Claudio said, finally. "I recruited Drako and Drina both."

Natalia didn't speak.

"You have to understand," Claudio pleaded, "I had no say in what happened to her, no choice after what she did."

"We always have a choice, Claudio."

"Maybe. I'd covered for her once – persuaded them she was young and inexperienced, and they should excuse her, and they actually did. It was a miracle. Four months go by and she does it again. Snatches the Segli, a picture she knew they were lined up on. Why, damn it? Why did she do it?"

Natalia let him talk.

"She had enough for a nice apartment – a real bed. I told her to enjoy her talent and her life. Her violin was good enough. She didn't need another fancier one. I couldn't believe she did it again. I pleaded with them. They said it was no longer my concern."

He shook a little, from the cold or nerves.

A bomb went off, shaking windows. Natalia jammed her hand in the special side flap in her shoulder bag and gripped the automatic. Another gigantic firecracker.

A man passing the church made the sign of the cross and hurried away, head bent against the chill.

"Why did you get involved in the first place?" Natalia said. "Weren't you doing well enough?"

"Not really. My office, the apartment, the car – everything cost – her mother, her brother, Drina. Keeping up appearances – you know? I did okay for a while, until the novelty of a gypsy lawyer wore off. Lenny DePretis put in a word for me with this cartel, figured they might need legal help at some point, and I had my great idea."

He closed his coat and turned up the lapels.

"Are you cold?" she said.

He nodded.

"Let's go. You'll be warmer moving."

They stood, leaving behind the glasses and bottle. Natalia took his hand.

"Monday," Claudio said as they turned up Vico Pace, "she called my office – said she was running, leaving immediately, perhaps forever. She knew of a caravan on the road in Romania. If she could get there they'd never find her. I begged her to tell me where she was. She cursed at something and hung up."

A *motorino* gusted by. They walked pressed against each other. A lone customer nursed a coffee at an outdoor table set down between large concrete planters, their bushes covered in burlap. Painted black on the wall in big letters, *'IERI'* – yesterday.

Another omen, Natalia thought. They were everywhere tonight. Yesterday, she mused, which could not be brought back nor be undone.

"*Aspetta,*" Claudio said quietly. "Wait."

They paused by the massive column where the old man sold his eggs. He'd been there for as long as anyone could remember, his product neatly stacked. Never missed a day. The empty cardboard nests sat waiting for his return.

Natalia followed Claudio below the arches. He cupped his hands around her face.

"I'm going to miss you," he said, and pulled her close.

"And I you." She stroked his hair.

"I'm scared."

"I know."

"Jail, my God. I'll lose my license for sure. And I'll lose you."

In an hour or two, a few feet from where they stood, Salvatore and Marcella would arrange potatoes and argue. Tonio would pass by on his way to Mass – face flushed, navy muffler knotted around his neck. The dwarf would offer Natalia a blessing.

But before that, she would snap handcuffs around her lover's wrists. She and Claudio would arrive at Casanova, cross the green tiles, pass the wooden chairs. No one would pay them the least attention. On the second floor, she'd take his confession, and remand him to a cell to await the prosecutor.

But for a moment longer they held one another in the shadows of Tribunali.